LAWS *for* CLAWS

TJ WITHERS

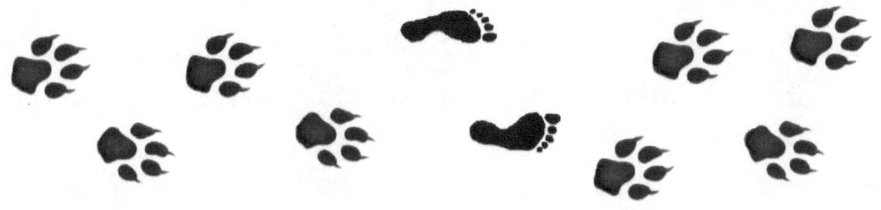

Laws for Claws

a novel

TJ Withers

Book 1 of the *Fur in Uniform* series

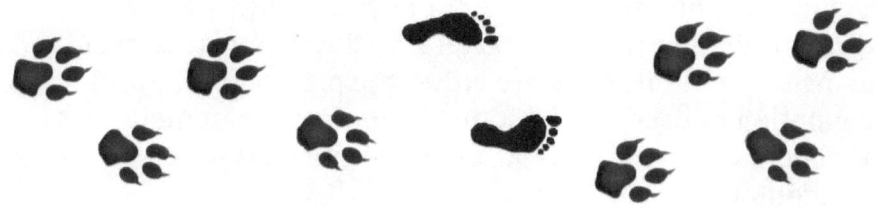

First published 2023 by TJ Withers.

Paperback edition produced by TJ Withers in Google Docs.

https://tjwithers.com

Cover design by TJ Withers in Canva and KDP Cover Creator.

Internal design by TJ Withers in Google Docs and Paint 3D.

Typeset in 12/14/18/20 pt Cambria by TJ Withers.

ISBN 978-0-6451467-5-2 (paperback)

ISBN 978-0-6451467-6-9 (ePUB)

ISBN 978-0-6451467-7-6 (Kindle)

Disclaimer: This novel is a work of fiction. Unless otherwise indicated, all the names, characters, businesses, places, events and incidents in this book are either the product of the author's imagination or used in a fictitious manner. Any resemblance to actual persons, living or dead, or actual events is purely coincidental.

to all the shes, theys, and gays
untaming their wild

Content warnings: This novel contains some fantasy/paranormal violence and themes related to violence against women, trans women, and non-binary people, reflecting the urban setting of this story. I do not condone violence by anyone. Please skip past any pages you need to, and enjoy the rest of the story.

PART ONE
then

1

Addie

We all knew the bastard had done it, but I didn't have enough evidence to prove it was intentional. Instead of being put away for life for murder, or even 15 years for manslaughter, the perp was going to walk.

And it was all Officer Lee Hauata's fault.

I'd had the perp in my sights! Yet another loser, an abusive boyfriend who'd killed his partner when she finally got the courage to leave, and I'd had everything I needed to put them away for good… Except that the lead police officer involved in the case had let a fire at the scene burn up a lot of the evidence.

Thankfully, his tracker dog had still been able to track the guy down and drag him to court. But without enough admissible evidence, I couldn't prove the crime was murder, not an accidental death, and the perp had walked.

The second the judge announced the sentence and left the courtroom, I slammed my binder shut, packed up my things, and stormed out.

After a few hours spent trying to work through a red haze of frustration at the office, I gave up and headed out. With just my phone and a card in my pocket, I strode into the streets, determined to find something to eat and calm the hell down.

One Subway and Diet Coke later, I was still pissed.

Somehow, I found myself standing outside the precinct police station. I stomped inside in my clickety-clackety court shoes – all the way to the pit, where the detectives worked. It was an open-plan office, so noisy that it gave me a headache.

My eyes lasered in on the one I wanted: a man about my age, with that broad, islander build and muscles for days, golden-brown skin, and big, dark eyes.

His beautiful partner, a German Shepherd, was lying down next to his desk. Her ears pricked forward as I approached.

'Officer Hauata!' I snapped.

He looked up, eyes narrowing in on me. 'It's Constable Hauata, actually, counsellor…'

He'd forgotten my name. *Unbelievable.* 'Counsellor Adrienne O'Connor, *Constable*, and you lost us that sentencing today.'

'Not my fault. There was too much conflicting evidence at the scene.'

Conflicting because you let it get all burned up. Out loud, I snapped, 'Seems like your dog is better trained than you are.' And she was a truly gorgeous dog, even I could admit that. Fur sleek as anything, with a face that would melt the hardest heart. Unless you were a criminal, in which case, her mouth held way too many sharp teeth to be beautiful.

She stood when I mentioned her, alert, ready for anything. Far too intelligent, German Shepherds. It made them brilliant police dogs, and wonderful family guard dogs, but give them a second alone to themselves, and they would burn the world down out of boredom.

The constable smiled slowly, like a predator eyeing prey. 'Not "my dog". My partner, Gal.' He touched the dog's head and pointed at me. 'Whaddaya think, girl? Friend or foe?'

Gal stood and sniffed at my hand while I tried to calm myself down. Slow breathing, no eye contact, no teeth bared. I didn't need her thinking I was here to attack her handler – even if I did intend to give him a stern talking to. She looked back at Hauata, then gave a little wag of her tail and sat.

'Friend,' I said firmly, adjusting my glasses. I didn't know why his dog thought I was friendly, but I wasn't about to admit that. 'I'm a *friend* who wants to talk to you about how today's murder case got messed up.'

'What's going on over here?' A big voice cut over the top of both of us, and I pulled back, shutting up.

The man who approached us was about 40, with a salt-and-pepper beard and the confident stride of someone who had seen just about everything and knew how to handle it. I eyed the three stripes on his shoulders – this was the precinct sergeant.

'Sergeant, your Constable here just lost me a case.'

The sergeant glanced at Hauata. 'That right?'

Hauata shrugged. 'Not quite. Still got 'em recorded on the DV watch list.'

'Because we didn't have the *evidence* for murder or manslaughter, thanks to you,' I said.

The sergeant gave me a piercing look, then nodded at the Constable. 'Lee, I'll take this from here. Counsellor, if you'll follow me, let's talk about this in my office. Less noisy.'

I tried not to let my shoulders sag. *Be strong, Adrienne.* I could tell already that the sergeant wasn't going to do anything about it, but I had to stand my ground. It was frustrating not to have any power or influence – not to be able to do anything about failures like this – but I was a recognised specialist. I had a right to at least have them listen to my point of view. Otherwise, I'd just have this same trouble again, on the next case Hauata was assigned to.

And this was only my first year with the Office of the Director of Public Prosecutions (the DPP), after an unsatisfying long-term relationship with the corporate law firms. If I wanted to impress, I needed to get a few wins on the board, put a few bad eggs behind bars.

Of course, I genuinely believed there were so many people out there who ended up in the criminal justice system for no reason – because they were in debt and desperate; because they'd been drunk or high and done something stupid; because they were addicted; because they were homeless; because they didn't think they had any other options.

But there were also a frightening number of people – too many to count – who intentionally hurt others and got away with it. People who didn't deserve to be let free, because they would only hurt more people with their freedom.

The perp today had been one of those. If a man thought he had the right to beat a woman to death because she dared to walk away from him, then as far as I was concerned, he'd forfeited his own right to be free. That kind of human was a threat to everyone around them.

So I strode after the sergeant through the pit to their office. He opened the door for me and waved me in. As I walked past him, I caught a tantalising waft of scent – no heavy cologne, just a hint of woodsmoke and rain over his own masculine musk. I was hyper aware of my arm brushing his as I squeezed past him into the office.

'I'm Sergeant Scott Davids,' said the sergeant, shutting the door behind us and taking one of the many seats in the office. He held out a hand for me to shake, and didn't sit down at his desk right away. No immediate power play – *interesting*. 'And you are?'

I shook his hand, and his grip was warm, firm but not crushing. It sent a bolt of heat right to my lady bits. I leaned back against one of the shelves for a moment while I remembered my own name. 'Adrienne O'Connor, attorney for the prosecution.'

He blinked, and seemed to reassess me. 'O'Connor, as in…'

I resisted the urge to roll my eyes. 'As in Inspector Rex O'Connor. Yes.'

My dad was a legend no matter which police station I walked into. At least his name bought me some street cred I wouldn't have otherwise, as a woman in a male-dominated industry. He was an Inspector, one rank above Sergeant, and one rank below the big brass – the Captains and Commissioners.

Sergeant Davids must have sensed my discomfort, because he moved on instantly. 'So, Counsellor, what seems to be the trouble?'

'Inadmissible evidence,' I explained. 'Now that abuser is back out there on the streets already, probably picking his next victim as we speak. He'll hurt more women for sure, because we couldn't get him convicted.'

'Any chance of an appeal?' Davids asked.

'Not without new evidence.'

'Ah, I see.' Davids rolled his neck from side to side, and muttered, 'Kid gives me a migraine.'

'Excuse me?' I raised my eyebrows.

He raised his hands in apology and made a rueful face. 'Sorry, not you. Lee – Constable Hauata – is young. Sometimes, he can be a bit reckless.'

I noticed.

'I'm working with him on that tendency.'

My shoulders sagged a little. I mean, that was better than nothing, but it wasn't the outcome I'd hoped for. I wanted Hauata off any important cases I might end up working.

Again, he must have noticed, because he said, 'I mean it – I'll keep an eye on him. I promise. It'd be helpful if you gave Lee a break on this one.'

'Why, is he on probation or something?' I asked bitterly.

'He was in that big drug bust down in the valley. Helped get everyone out alive … except the ringleader.'

'Well, shit.' Everyone knew that story – a drug mob had recently kidnapped and tortured three cops until they were discovered, mostly-dead and traumatised, in an abandoned warehouse. I'd heard that their ringleader, the mob boss, had been killed in the rescue. But more than just killed – he'd been ripped limb from limb.

Some people were calling it yet another unjust killing of a civilian by a cop, but others were calling it an eye for an eye, a just killing of a serial murderer. It was a situation fraught with anger on all sides.

'Yup. A lot of the higher-ups would have preferred he left the ringleader alive to be tried. Only just got sign-off to send Lee back into the field last week.'

I bit my lip, and caught his eyes flick down to my mouth. I realised he was waiting for a response, so I scrambled for something appropriate. 'I guess that's good to know.'

'So look, here's what I can do in this case.' Davids moved around to his desk and began typing a note on his computer. 'I'll organise a stakeout of that guy. I'll free up a resource somewhere, make sure we can watch him for the week. At the very least, we'll keep people safe from him for a week. If we're lucky, we'll catch him acting up again. Whether it's assault or something else, we'll have him then.' He looked back at me, his gaze piercing. 'That's the best we can do in the short term.'

I nodded, surprised and encouraged. 'Yeah, that's great, actually.'

'Wonderful.' He moved to open the door for me again. 'I'll email over the details this afternoon. And Adrienne—'

I stopped halfway through the door, acutely aware of his chest a few inches from mine. 'Yes?'

'Call me anytime you need something, okay? In this line of work, it pays to work together closely.'

Oh, goodness. He probably didn't mean anything personal by that, but somehow, my whole body heard that as an invitation. I could feel a blush heating my cheeks, but I tried to ignore it. I absolutely could not have a crush on this guy. Kind or not, helpful or not, I had to work with him and his officers.

I adjusted my glasses again, even though I didn't need to. 'Of course,' I said.

On my way out, I passed Hauata – Lee – walking his dog out of the office on a leash, and gave them both a quick nod of silent, steely acknowledgement.

Lee grinned, canines flashing. 'See ya, Counsellor.' And then the cheeky thing shot me a wink! Unfortunately, that wink bypassed my brain and went straight to my core, a fluttering flash of desire.

What is it about this precinct? Down, girl!

I got the hell outta there, as fast as I could.

By the time I got back to my office, there was an email waiting for me.

Adrienne,

It was a pleasure encountering you.

Please find attached a summary of our discussion this afternoon.

I look forward to working with you again. Don't hesitate to get in touch if you need anything.

Regards,

Sgt. Scott Davids

I fanned myself and stared at the email. Something about his phrasing pulled on my romantic heartstrings, which seemed to be incurable, unfortunately. Just like the touch of his hand against mine had made other parts of me tremble.

It's just work, I told myself. *It's just work.*

2

Scott

Word was there was a feral on the streets – a lone wolf, not allowed to be in any pack because they had gone crazy and attacked a human. So I asked Lee to help me make sure the borders of our territory were clear later that night. And I texted some of the stronger fighters in our pack, told them what to keep an eye out for. I didn't want to worry the others until we knew more.

The rest of the day was eventful for us in Crimes Against People, as usual. Assaults at the major bars. A missing child that was being passed to us as a suspected abduction. A knifing in the underground walkways at Central station.

I was finally on a sergeant's income now, and glad to have it. It meant I could afford to buy a house sooner, maybe in the next year or so. I even hoped I might make it to captain one day, if everything went smoothly in my career.

I already had a reputation as the 'dad' of the precinct. I was the one everyone went to for a beer after work if they needed advice, help moving house, or even if they just needed a hug after working on a violent case.

But I wasn't about to get bullied by anyone who thought my kindness was a weakness. I made sure I still did enough of the dirty work that both coworkers and criminals remembered I could still take down a perp on foot. And I was also still working out most days, keeping up enough muscle so everyone showed me some respect.

And in the evenings, after drinks with my work mates, I took the train home to my pack. Being a lyko – a lycanthrope or werewolf – meant even though I lived alone, there were always people close by if I needed them, or if they needed me. There were always a bunch of kids playing outside our block of units.

In the wild, true wolves lived in family units of two adults and their shared children, until the kids were old enough to leave the family and make their own. Lykos like me needed family more than anyone, but the family we were born into didn't always stick around after we'd turned. So we valued the family we found or made for ourselves, and we took care of each other.

Like all the lykos in all the packs I knew, I was well and truly in the working class. But I was luckier than most. First, because I'd been able to hold onto my self-control more than others, so I'd held down a job for a lot longer than many others could. And I'd managed to keep a rental without damaging anything during unexpected transformations. Then once I got a permanent full-time job on the force, I was able to use personal leave or annual leave if I had to disappear at full moon.

Of course, being surrounded by people almost 24/7 didn't completely erase loneliness. If there was one thing that could have improved my already-great life, it would be a life partner. Someone to do all this with me.

Someone to take care of me the way I took care of everyone else.

Someone who'd let me take care of them.

I shifted in my train seat, wishing I'd done more than just email that pretty lawyer. I could tell immediately we were both sexually attracted to each other, and I'd liked her attitude, her spunk. She hadn't been shy about coming in person to deal with Lee. And that fire in her eyes, to match her fiery hair…

I liked the way she moved – easily, comfortably, even in fancy lawyer clothes – a great sign of confidence in herself.

And in spite of that confidence, I loved the way she'd restrained her fire when I explained to her about Lee. The way she bit her lip – I wanted to bite that lip myself. I wanted to see what it took to get her to stop holding back and just let everything go.

I was struck.

It was more than just sexual, though. She was an amazing prosecutor. My team had as much professional respect for her as I did; she was the only lawyer any of them wanted to work with now. There was a lot to respect about Adrienne O'Connor.

But there were definitely some potential problems with asking her out.

She was young, for starters. We had a 10-year age gap. From her Instagram profile, I knew she'd just turned 31; I was 41. She must have made a career change, to start police prosecuting later than her 20s. I wondered what the story was there.

Then there was the simple fact that we worked together. If we acted on our feelings and then broke up, work could get awkward for a while, and I didn't want that. I loved my job, and now that I'd made sergeant, I didn't want to do anything that could possibly mess up a good thing.

And last but certainly not least: she wasn't pack.

It was always hard, carrying on relationships outside the shifter packs that populated our city. I had to keep my pack safe, which meant keeping my secrets and theirs, not telling a potential romantic interest what was really going on. They could never know why once a month, I would disappear for a day or two at the full moon, so I always had to give a lame 'I feel sick' or 'I'm going out of town' excuse. While we could shift at will normally, none of us got a choice at the full moon – that transformation was always required.

No, it was better to stick with looking for a woman from the packs around our area. *We'll be better as friends. Coworkers.*

Running the borders that night with Lee, slipping in and out of wolf form to sniff out any trace of the feral, I kept reminding myself of that. I needed to focus on the search, not on a pretty coworker.

We tracked the feral all around the perimeter of our territory, but the scent was faint. They were clearly avoiding coming too close, just tiptoeing in and out of pack borders.

But a feral could be deadly. They lived to kill humans, and their insanity gave them a strength that could kill their fellow werewolves. We could run the feral off, but it just meant more innocents would die until another pack found them.

No.

Our choices were to capture it and try to cure the wretched beast ... or kill it.

One way or another, we had to find it, and soon.

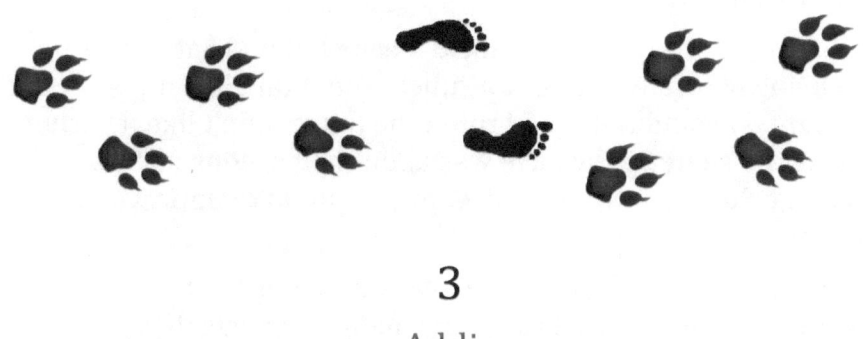

3

Addie

The next time I saw Scott was in the courtroom. He was there to give evidence on a couple of big cases, so he'd probably be around for the full day. He was a dominating presence – big, strong, and when he gave you his attention, you felt it. I could see how the witnesses and defendants all reacted to him. Even the judge wasn't immune to his confident air of leadership.

'Busy day?' Scott asked me lightly from behind the barrier between the bench and the stands for onlookers.

'Always,' I said with a smile.

When we broke for lunch, I approached him at the bench, trying to sound professional, easy, undemanding. 'Hey Sergeant Davids, can I ask you for some feedback?'

He nodded. 'Of course. I was just going to go grab a kebab down the street. Walk with me?'

Butterflies immediately fluttered in my belly at the invitation. I accepted, trying not to sound too eager. I pulled on my wide-brimmed sunhat, because a sensible redhead never leaves the house without sunscreen and a hat.

He smiled. 'Cute hat.'

On the street, as we walked, I asked him, 'That last sentencing before we broke for lunch. You didn't like my argument – I could tell. And I think the judge didn't like it, either, because the sentence he gave was about half as long as I was expecting. So I was wondering what I could do to improve for next time.'

He considered it. 'Your analysis was fine. Your use of precedents is very good. I think the main thing was that you're scatter-gunning. Your argument just can't be that long; you don't have that amount of time in court to cover everything. So you should be focusing on just the key pieces of evidence and analysing those a little deeper.'

I sighed; I had cut out so many precedents and pieces of evidence to fit the brief *this* time; how could I cut back any more and still have enough proof? 'Any chance you could give me an example of where I could've cut some of it?'

He stopped outside the kebab shop and gestured us into the shade. 'Let me think. There was that big chunk you quoted from the Magistrate's transcript – I wouldn't have included that. I probably would have focussed more on the motivation of the accused.' He raised his hands. 'But keep in mind, I'm not a lawyer. No law degree here. The partners at the DPP can give you solid advice if you're worried.'

I nodded. I felt calmer now, determined to do better next time with the tips he'd given me.

'I'm going to order a kebab, you want one?' he asked.

'Yeah, I'm gonna get a vegetarian one,' I said.

He smiled, and before I could stop him, he had ordered and paid for our two kebabs.

'Oh, thank you,' I said, beginning to feel flustered again. I already had a crush on this guy, and now he was paying for me, something I could've read a hundred different ways. Kind, or controlling? Chivalrous, or misogynistic?

We sat together on the steps down to the ferry terminal, watching the river while we talked. By the end of lunch, we were both talking more easily, even joking with each other.

I caught his gaze lingering on me. I smiled, trying not to blush. I got the feeling he was attracted to me, not just by the way his eyes drifted to my lips, but also from the way he leaned in towards me, and the fact he didn't check his phone once while we were talking.

I felt the force of his full attention. There was definitely more to him than any other men I'd ever met before. I was attracted both to him and to the connection I felt around him. I kept touching my face, checking there was no kebab left there.

Someone approached us, waving at Scott. I assumed they were coming to him for help because he was in his copper's uniform, but Scott smiled and stood, so they must be a friend.

They were shorter than Scott, and covered in wiry muscles, with long, straight hair and Asian facial features. They had an overall androgynous look, so I couldn't tell their gender, and I knew better than to make assumptions until told otherwise.

'Hey, good to see you!' they said as they pulled Scott in for a hug.

Scott hugged everyone, and it was one of the things I liked about him most. He would give anyone who needed it some physical affection, not holding back from anyone. I'd even seen him hug a victim's mother once, after she broke down crying during a sentencing. It took a lot of kindness for others, and a lot of confidence in your own strength, to embrace others without fear.

I wished I was that strong.

'Kenny, this is Counsellor Adrienne O'Connor, from the DPP. Adrienne, this is Kenny Nguyen, one of my mates from the estate where I live.'

I held out my hand, and Kenny grinned and shook it enthusiastically. Their grip was like jamming my hand in the car door.

My mouth fell open, and I tried not to yelp. I yanked my hand back, heart racing. *What the heck? That's a dick move.*

Their face fell. 'Oh, sorry.' They looked up at Scott, then back at me. 'Too hard?'

Scott took my hand and checked it over, handling me gently. 'You okay, Adrienne?'

I stepped back, tugging my hand to my chest, ignoring the way my breath caught at Scott's touch. I watched them both warily as I said, 'Yeah, that hurt, actually.' I'd never been one to pretend or say 'it's fine' when it wasn't, and I was curious to see what their reaction would be.

'Sorry about that,' said Scott. 'I've been training Kenny in weight-lifting, and they don't know their own strength yet.'

'Well, you better be careful,' I said, raising my eyebrows. I wasn't about to let them get away with it.

I also felt annoyed because when I'd first met the sergeant, he'd apologised for Lee, and now he was apologising for Kenny. This better not be a trend. I didn't want to have a crush on someone if all the people around them were dangerous.

'Definitely, I'll be more careful next time,' Kenny said, with an apology in their voice. Again, they looked at Scott for approval, then at me.

Scott gave Kenny a bit of a nod of reassurance. 'You coming to the building meeting tonight?' he asked them.

They smiled. 'I'll bring the steak.'

I checked my phone while they talked. Nothing urgent – just a message from my bestie, Charlie, saying I owed her a drink. I'd been pretty busy lately – as always – and I felt bad for not being there for her. Plus, I missed her. She always made me laugh, made me smile, no matter what was going on.

so true, sorry, I texted back. *next Saturday? about 6pm? happy with wherever you want to go.*

I looked up to see Kenny was heading off.

Scott said, 'See you later, then.'

'Cheers,' said Kenny. They looked at me, and it almost looked like there was pity in their eyes. 'Good to meet you.'

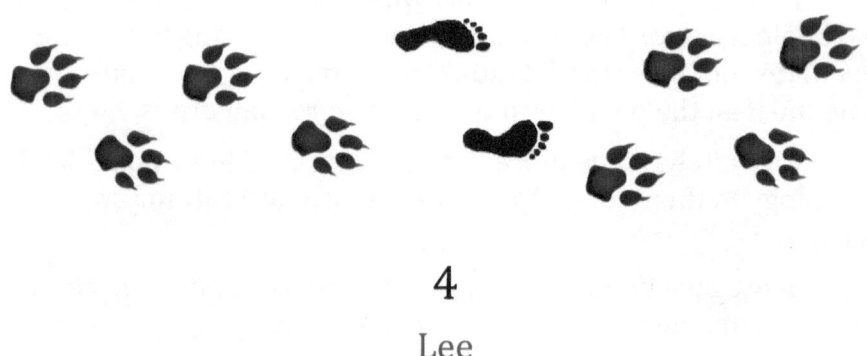

4

Lee

The DPP's office was just on the next block down from the precinct station. An easy walk, even in the hot sun, and I was able to leash Gal in the shade next to her portable water bowl.

Gal seemed content to wait outside for me, and I knew I wouldn't take long, anyway. I liked telling people she was named after Galileo, or after the planet 697 Galilea, or even after the region in northern Israel called Galilee, but it wasn't really true. Gal was just my girl, my gal, and that was all there was to it.

Normally, I could be pretty impulsive, but I actually planned out this encounter. In fact, once I'd printed out the case file, I thought about it for *at least* 30 seconds before I popped on Galilee's leash and headed out.

Inside, it was easy to find the pretty lawyer's cubicle. She must be a junior, if she didn't have an office of her own yet. Although I'd heard a lot places were just hot-desking now. No more corner offices – everyone just fighting each other to find a desk for the day, or working from home. I couldn't relate; most of my job had to be done in person, either in the precinct or in the field.

Either way, a desk job would be death by boredom to me. Better to be outside any day. Even in the heat of summer, running around and taking a nap on the grass under a tree was nicer than sitting behind a desk in the air-con.

'Hey, you,' I greeted her.

She froze when she recognised my voice. Then she turned in her seat, putting on a strained smile. 'Officer Hauata, hello.'

Pretty much exactly the reaction I was expecting from her. I couldn't hold it in – I doubled over laughing. Other people craned their necks around to see what was so funny. She was staring at me, too, so I dragged another chair into her cubicle and straddled it, so people would stop looking and get back to work.

Trying to be quiet, I said, 'You should have seen your face! What did you think I'm here to do?'

She shrugged and replied bluntly, 'I'm thinking you're going to tell me to keep away from your cases, because I embarrassed you in front of your boss.'

'Embarrassed?' I grinned. 'Nah, it was hilarious. I'm not easily embarrassed.'

'Why, do you get in trouble a lot, *Lee?*' Her mouth quirked up in a half-smile, and I knew she was teasing, making up for calling me 'Officer Hauata'.

I raised my hands as if to protest my innocence. 'Hey, well, I mean, define "a lot". There was that one time, but just the one! And maybe some other times, too.'

'Oh really?'

'Yeah, well. My bad.'

'Shocking.' She sat back, crossing her legs. The motion tugged the skirt of her dress over her knee, revealing the top of her thigh-high pantihose, and a flash of milky thigh. 'So, what *are* you here for?'

Suddenly my mouth was very dry. I waved the big file in my hand, and handed it to her. I had to clear my throat before I spoke. I tried hard to keep my eyes off those delicious, thick thighs, but I don't think I succeeded. 'Info. For a case. The image files were too big to email over, and the ODPP doesn't want us using the restricted file transfer programs unless it's for something serious.' I rolled my eyes at the idea of red tape.

I didn't tell her the other reason – the real reason. *I wanted to see you again.*

She opened the file, scanning the details quickly. She pushed her glasses up her nose, an adorable motion that I don't think she was aware of.

I caught myself gazing at her as she took in the details of the case. She held things as if they were precious – even now, when she was only holding her pen and the sheaf of papers and photos.

Her wavy, fiery curls draped over her shoulders and chest like a rich, silky scarf, outlining the swell of pink flesh from collarbone to breast. She bit her full, lower lip for a moment, and something about the indent below her lip made my pulse race.

Dude! I pulled myself up short. *Cool it. Scott's into her, she's into Scott, and we all work together. Keep it clean, dude. Let Scott have her; he's a good guy; he still believes in love… They could have it real good together.*

I'd often thought monogamy was an outdated concept, but when it came to Scott, I figured he deserved whatever he wanted, and I knew he was a monogamous guy. I owed him everything. I owed him my life. I didn't want to do anything that might threaten his happiness. So, if I was going to suggest ethical non-monogamy to anyone, it wasn't going to be the person Scott had his eye on.

Even if I thought being in some kind of throuple-type situation with Scott would be incredible.

She asked me a few questions about the case, setting the scene for herself, and I tried to keep my mind on the case enough to give the right answers.

'Okay,' she said finally, setting the file on the desk. 'I can use this. Thank you.'

'Yeah, no worries.' I tapped my fingers on her cubicle partition, trying to think of something to gain me an extra few seconds with this gorgeous woman, whose brain was as sexy as her body. 'Got fun plans for the weekend?'

'Apart from this, you mean?' She pointed at the file and laughed. 'I'm going to see an orchestra perform Taylor Swift songs. Candlelight Concerts, it's called – it's a whole series.'

I liked her answer. She didn't seem embarrassed about sounding like a nerd for going to see an orchestra, or about outing herself as a Swift fan. I grinned. 'A fellow Swiftie?'

'You bet!'

'Favourite song?'

'I do love "I Did Something Bad",' she mused, 'but don't tell my boss!'

I laughed, and she laughed with me. It was a beautiful sound, a throaty chuckle that sounded like it came from a person bigger than she was, and I was struck dumb for a moment.

Then she asked, 'How 'bout you?'

I cleared my throat. 'I could never pick just one Taytay song. Maybe "Trouble". Or maybe "Lover".'

She raised her eyebrows, surprised.

Fuck, did I just tell a hot girl that my favourite song is a cheesy ballad about true love and leaving the Christmas lights up? I tried to move on as fast as I could. 'So that sounds like fun. Got a hot date for the occasion?'

She bit her lip again and looked away, but she couldn't hide the blush that started in her cheeks. 'Yeah, no, I'm just going with my sister, actually. Girl's night out.'

'Well have fun!' I had to stop this being weird. *Time to go.* 'Okay, see ya, A-team.' I winked and left, trying to ignore the part of me that was howling to return to her, claim her. Talk with her more – hug her – kiss her – *something.*

Later that night, while Gal was eating a well-earned dinner and I was microwaving a veggie lasagne, my phone pinged with a notification.

Adrienne89 has tagged you in a Spotify playlist. Want to listen?

Instantly, I was back in high school again, in the days when people traded CD mix tapes with each other to share their favourite songs. *She made me a whole playlist?* Okay, now I definitely wanted to listen.

I hit play, and it buzzed into my ear pods. It was eclectic, to say the least. Mostly Taylor Swift because of our conversation, but also some BTS, Billie Eilish, and even The Rolling Stones.

I smiled.

Yeah, she likes me.

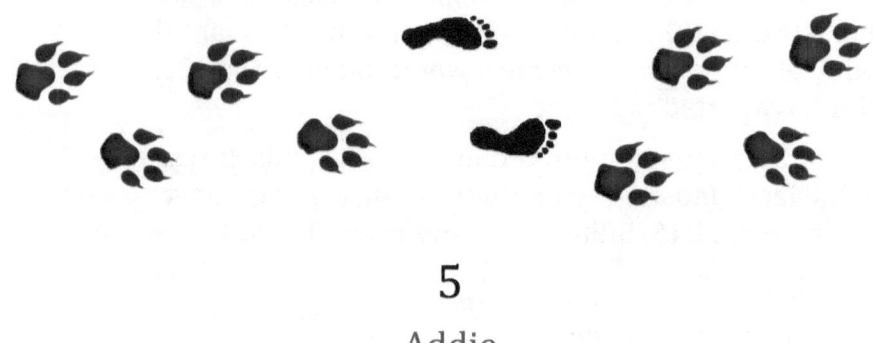

5

Addie

We all worked together well for a few months. If I'm being brutally honest, and I usually am, I was obsessed with them.

Both of them, unfortunately.

I couldn't stop thinking about them, analysing what they said and did, waiting to see them again.

And it was physical, as well as mental – I had an animal magnetism with both of them that I couldn't explain. With Scott, it made sense. I was hot for him – so what? A girl could dream.

Whenever Scott had a day in court, we were constantly trading glances. A wry smile when a defendant said something stupid or self-contradictory, or when the judge made a cranky remark. I liked watching how he managed witnesses – he was a natural leader.

I lived for the moment after I made a good argument or an insightful comment, when I would catch his eyes on me, a smile playing at the corner of his mouth, sometimes even half-nodding in agreement. I thrived on his praise, spoken and unspoken. I loved to provoke that impish sparkle in his eyes, the one that said, 'I can't say it, but you're a clever, cheeky thing!'

But I was terrified that my words, my look, my manner might give me away. I *knew* Scott must have guessed I had a crush on him, but he didn't say anything.

I felt a little thrill in my gut every time I spotted him in the precinct. I smiled; he smiled; and I dropped my eyes. I could tell he was curious about my reaction, and I knew I was probably blushing a bit each time, which was just embarrassing.

Scott had a number of different faces. There was his court face: decisive and fixed, moving from one foot to another, addressing the judge, then the court, then the barristers. When he was listening, his eyes were keen and involved, his jaw sometimes clenched as if he wished he could counter or question every comment.

And his amused face appeared often, when talking with his fellow cops around the precinct. Everyone wanted to talk to Scott. I loved the way the lines of his eyes softened or sharpened when he spoke and laughed with different people. His deep chuckle was my new favourite sound.

Then there was a face I had seen only twice in the weeks I'd known him. It was a face so open and unguarded that all his previous confidence and charisma seemed an act, a mask. For less than a second, when he looked at me, he looked surprised, as if finding himself without an answer to a question I hadn't asked.

His undone face fascinated me. It was the one face I couldn't forget, couldn't erase from my mind's eye.

And I don't know how, but I seemed to run into Lee a lot more than I expected to. More than I wanted to, honestly. I felt like I couldn't get away from him. He showed up everywhere, whether he and Gal were on crowd control at a protest, sniffing for drugs on the streets, or just training the newer canine squad members.

And somehow, he always caught my attention. Like I said, there was an animal magnetism there; he was hot, and he knew it. But the guy still rubbed me the wrong way.

He didn't do anything more than occasionally tease me, calling me any name that started with 'A' except for my real name. We'd exchange a bit of banter, maybe flirty, maybe just cranky. He spent as much time deliberately trying to irritate me as he did making me laugh. So there was no reason for me to think about him so much…

I studied the two of them whenever I could. Not that I had a lot of spare time to do it. It made the moments I did see them all the more captivating. I felt like a photographer keeping an eye on rare jungle panthers or something, angling for the perfect photo.

Then Lee had to do a difficult job and disappeared for a week. He and Gal were assigned to track down the murderer of a young person, something that would have made anyone sick with fury or heavy with grief. When Lee came back, he was different. He spent more time at the bar after work, drinking with his workmates. He took every shift he and Gal got offered. And he was more hyperactive than I'd seen him before – and for someone who never seemed to stop moving, that was saying something!

Not that I cared.

Obviously.

One Friday night, I gave in to peer pressure and went out for a drink with the other junior associates at the DPP. It was a tough job, and we were all in our first year of it, struggling through the culture shock of seeing the dirty underbelly of our city. Constantly in court or trying to prove ourselves through long hours at the office.

I wanted a drink to relax, and I was sure I could keep myself to just one this time. Just one drink. Just one night.

I tried to pace myself on one daiquiri, but then someone bought me another, and I didn't want to be rude. And when I got to the last sip of that one, I was already thinking about another. Or a round of shots. Or a whisky on the rocks.

I wandered over and leaned on the bar, trying to remind myself to get a water or lemonade instead. *If you're gonna fall off the wagon, you better get right back on again afterwards.* That's what Dad always used to say, when he was in the process of getting sober.

Someone tapped my left shoulder. I turned, but saw no one.

At my right shoulder, Lee crowed, 'Rookie error! Back to primary school for you, Addie Bear.'

I rolled my eyes at him. 'At least I'll be in good company, since you'll be there, too, learning how to read.'

He laughed.

I rubbed my eyes, tired all of a sudden.

'You look like you've had enough,' he said.

'Oh, what do you know.' I scowled up at him.

He put a hand on my bicep. 'Nah, I can smell it. Reckon you're done for the night, babe.'

'I'm not your "babe"!' I ripped my arm out of his hand. It made me stumble backwards, but I caught myself. My friends looked over from a few feet away, checking if I was okay. I sent them a little wave, like, *I'm fine, don't worry.*

Lee narrowed his eyes at me, then bared his teeth in that wicked grin of his. 'I'll race you for it.'

'What?' Was this guy crazy?

'The bridge is right there. I'll race you to the first pillar. If you win, then clearly you are still in safe shape, and I'll buy you your next one myself. If I win, I'm putting you in a cab.'

'Uber's cheaper,' I said, automatically taking the chance to needle him. Truth was, I'm competitive as hell, so I couldn't help myself; he didn't need to twist my arm to get me to race him. I already knew it would be fun.

He leaned back, looking smug. 'Yeah, whatever. You in?'

I looked down at my feet – I was in court shoes with a small heel, but if I took them off, I could run damn fast. I'd played club soccer in uni, and I'd always been one of our team's best forwards. 'Sure. And *when* I win, you'll buy us shooters, and I'll drink you under the table.'

'All right, race!' cheered one of the junior associates. 'Everyone outside!'

I heard the group of them follow us through the crowd, laughing and joking around as we made our way outside. The cool breeze hit me and cleared my head a little. Maybe I was a little buzzed. *Quite* buzzed, actually. I've always been a lightweight, and two standard drinks was definitely enough for one night, especially when I'd deliberately stayed sober for months now.

I wondered if I could even run in a straight line right now. *Oh well, too late to back out now. Can't give him the satisfaction.*

I took off my shoes, handed them to one of my coworkers, and ran for it.

'Hey, I didn't say "go"!' Lee yelled after me, and I heard him pounding the pavement behind me until we hit the grass.

The pillar of the bridge rose up before us, lit up with the golden glow of sconces along the bricks. Lee thudded up beside me, not even breathing hard.

Of course the asshole works out, I thought. *He's a cop!*

He was fast – too fast. In fact, he was going to beat me. So I did the only logical thing I could do to win.

I gave him a little push.

It barely nudged him aside, but he made a surprised noise, then grinned with untamed delight.

He gave me a little push back, which sent me sprawling. Everything spun, and the dark sky tumbled under me, then over me again, until I crashed into the grass so hard I actually bounced. I rolled another few feet, then stopped, flat on my back.

All the wind was knocked out of me.

'Fuck,' I gasped, but the word barely escaped.

Everything hurt.

And everything was blurry. My glasses had flown off my face, probably somewhere in the grass.

People were yelling, but my head kept spinning for a moment, so I wasn't sure what they were saying.

Lee raced over. 'Shitshitshitshitshit. Are you okay?' He crouched over me, filling my field of vision. His eyes were wide and he seemed genuinely concerned. Damn, he even looked hot when he was worried – so annoying.

'My glasses,' I choked out.

There was a moment as he scuffled around in the grass, and then he handed me my glasses.

I slipped them on, and suddenly I could see him a lot better. Even though I couldn't breathe right now, something about having his big arms on either side of my head… My body reacted as if we were doing other horizontal activities. Even if I wasn't winded, that would have made me breathless for a whole other reason.

'Ant Man? Talk to me!'

I rolled over onto my side, coughing to try and pull some air in. Eventually, the pressure eased, and I bent my knee up to look at it. I'd mostly landed on my wrists and left hip, which were torn and bleeding, but my knee had taken a worse scrape when I bounced. It stung like a mother.

'Ah, fuck it,' I whispered, looking at the bloody mess there. *That's gonna scar. And everybody saw…* 'I'm never going to live this down.'

'Shit, you lawyers are so fragile.' He stood and waved his hands around. 'So much blood. Should I call an ambulance?'

I frowned, sitting up slowly and painfully. 'Just a first aid kit for now, thanks. And a shot of something.'

'Oh, no!'

'For the pain,' I protested. 'It's a perfectly reasonable request!'

'I'm not falling for that! If you're well enough to drink, you're well enough to go home.' He gestured to one of my coworkers, Paul. 'Hey. Go get the first aid kit from the bar.'

Paul scrambled to his feet and ran for the building. I scowled after him, not sure whether he was driven by wanting to help my situation or just because he wanted to escape Lee's stern face. It was terrifying.

I was embarrassed to be injured in a childish race, and I could feel a blush spreading over me already. Knowing that I was blushing only made me even more frustrated. This was all Lee's fault, for suggesting this stupid race.

'I'm getting an Uber,' I muttered. 'What a shitty night.'

'Not my fault you've got a drinking problem.'

I gestured to my leg. 'But it *is* your fault I'm bleeding!'

He raised his hands and stood, backing up. 'You pushed me!'

I mock-hissed at him and looked away. *Typical man. Arrogant, annoying, hyperactive, hypocritical...*

When I looked back, he was gone. I scanned the area in irritation, then confusion, but there was just my other coworkers, who were starting to approach, asking if I was okay.

That loser had actually left me here!

If I never saw Lee Hauata again, it would be too soon.

'Don't you have any normal friends?' I asked Scott over the phone while I checked my bandages the next day. I was making myself toast for breakfast – well, brunch, I guess. I wasn't really hungover, just in pain, both physical and emotional.

'Not really, why?'

'Lee got me busted up last night. Why's he such a dick?'

'Hmm.' The noise of his hum – such a deep, growly noise – sank through me, shivering through every nerve ending. 'Okay, what's he done now?'

I sighed, not wanting to tell the story. 'He embarrassed me in front of my coworkers, and then I got injured, and he just ran away! It was nothing.'

'Injured?' Scott's hard, demanding tone made me want to sit bolt upright. 'What happened? Are you all right? No, you know what, I'm coming over.'

Oh, wow. 'Um, if you want to? I'm mostly fine, I'm just going to have a quiet day to recover.'

'Humour me, Adrienne. For my peace of mind, I'd like to see for myself.'

I was *not* ready to have him in my space, especially when things were a bit messy, because I hadn't done any cleaning this morning after my late night. There were dishes in the sink, and lingerie drying on the shower rail. I pressed my lips together, trying not to worry about it. He would just have to deal with it, and so would I.

But when he arrived, his presence was more than I had bargained for. He was bigger, and more muscled than I remembered, and just somehow *more*. It was like he filled my whole apartment.

He checked my wounds, fully in competent first-responder mode, and said briskly, 'Looks like you're healing fine, and no concussion. So, you said he ran away after it happened. I'll talk to him.'

I shook my head vehemently.

'You don't want me to talk to him?'

'Nooo, it's – you know, whatever. I'm just *very* annoyed at him.'

'Hmm. I mean, if there was blood, and it looks like there would've been plenty?' He raised his eyebrows, and I nodded. 'Then it's better for everyone that Lee got out of there as soon as he could. He's not the best with blood.'

'What, like he would've fainted or something? He's in the police!'

Scott huffed, almost a laugh. 'Something like that.'

'But why? Seriously, what's his deal?'

He frowned and went silent for a long time, changing my bandages with tender hands. Then his expression softened, and he met my eyes. 'Guy's had a rough life, Adrienne. I wouldn't ever say someone can use their background as an excuse to get out of anything. But it's different with Lee. If he hurt you, I can almost guarantee he's more torn up about it than you are. Maybe one day, he'll tell you his story, but that's his business.'

It sounded like if I wanted to be with Scott, I had to find a way to not just tolerate Lee, but to be friends with him. And I really, really wanted to be with Scott.

Scott started looking around, probably noting the general disarray. 'Shall I do the vacuuming while I'm here?'

'You calling my place messy?' I bristled.

He chuckled. 'Well, not exactly. But doing chores with a bung knee is never fun. Believe me, I've tried it.'

'I bet. I've seen how you cops are always getting beat up on the job. Climbing over fences to catch a runner.'

'Or climbing into a stormwater drain to rescue a kid's toy, yeah.'

I liked that he said that. I liked that he didn't try to match a macho cliche. It was refreshing. Relaxing, even.

'Where's your vacuum, then?' he asked.

I pointed at the pantry cupboard. 'Hanging inside the door.'

And then I watched, definitely drooling a bit, as this hunk of a man took out my vacuum, powered up, and began cleaning my apartment for me.

So. Hot.

This wasn't about a man doing the bare minimum. We weren't in a relationship, and if we were, I would have expected him to do half the household chores – cooking, cleaning, laundry. And half the mental load, too – planning activities, communicating, making grocery lists, that kind of thing. That would be the bare minimum I wanted from an equal, a true partner.

Instead, this was a man who wasn't obligated to do anything, and he was helping me out just because he could. In fact, I would've appreciated it even if he was only doing this to try and get into my pants... *Down, girl!*

He looked up at one point and caught me staring. Ogling him, maybe. He smiled slowly, then just kept on going.

I sat there on the couch, stunned.

When he'd finished, he emptied the vacuum into the kitchen bin. I swallowed as he walked back towards me. He knelt on one knee in front of me, and my heart began pounding.

I reached out and touched his bicep. 'Thank you so much, Scott. That was ... ummm ... yeah, thanks.' *Why am I so awkward?*

He smiled, a twinkle in his eye, and stroked my calf below the big bandages on my injured knee. 'You're welcome,' he said simply. 'You need anything else, you call me. Even if you just want help changing the bandages.'

My skin tingled under his big hand. I wondered if everything about him was big... Suddenly the room felt *very* warm.

He stood and walked over to empty the bin, pulling out the whole bag of trash.

'I'll take this down to the garbage skip. Call me,' he said firmly, almost an order, and nodded goodbye.

I just stared at the closed door after he left, feeling all twirly inside.

Later, when I finally got up off the couch, I saw he'd even put a new bin liner in the bin. *Is he even real?*

With everyone wanting their cases closed before Christmas, work was crazy busy. The end-of-year awards dinner for the state police and prosecution departments came up faster than I'd expected.

I was elated, gliding down the city streets in my best cocktail dress and heels, makeup done, hair half-up in fancy braids. I knew I looked nothing like I did at work, and I enjoyed that feeling. I felt special. Beautiful, even.

The awards dinner was being held in a great hall I'd been to before, but I'd never seen it like this. It was covered in swathes of deep purple and blue cloth, with dim lighting so that everything looked magical, and lights projected little snowflake images onto the roof. Giant lanterns shaped like snowflakes hung from the roof, emitting an ethereal glow.

There was an open bar at the back of the room, with an array of bottles glittering in the cool lighting.

I spotted Scott waiting at the bar before he saw me. He was wearing a grey suit with a gold-striped tie, looking strangely more formal than he did in the dark uniform he wore to court. These colours showed off the silver in his 5 o'clock shadow and in his mercurial eyes.

Those eyes were hypnotic.

I smiled as he looked up. I walked over, aware of his eyes following my figure as I approached. *Oh, yeah. I definitely want to sit at his table, not at my boss's table.* I dropped my bag on the bar stool next to him and did an impromptu twirl before him.

'How do I look?' I asked, keeping my tone light.

'Gorgeous,' he said, and I smiled. He ordered champagnes for us both and gestured to one of the tables at the edge of the room. 'Closer to the door,' he said dryly.

Lee joined us at our table, running late, as always. 'Admiral.' He touched the back of my seat as he slid into the one next to me. 'What did I miss?'

I glanced up at him and gave him a cool smile. Polite, even though I was still mad at him for the bridge incident. 'Just some pre-drinks.'

'Well, fuck.' He looked forlorn. 'I better catch up.' He grabbed my drink and downed it in one gulp.

'Hey!' I elbowed him in the ribs. *How does he have muscles in his ribs?*

He winked at me. 'You didn't really want it, trust me.'

I couldn't help but laugh in spite of myself. What a total *guy* he was. Immature with a capital 'I' as in *I don't know whether I want to slap him or fuck him…*

A few of my friends among the junior associates in the ODPP joined us, and some of the brass stopped by to talk with Scott.

One of them slapped Lee on the back. 'Hey, mate, you made it after all! Thought you were gonna miss it. Stuck on island time again?'

Lee tensed, but Scott caught his eye. Lee smiled lazily and reclined in his seat. 'Can't be caught working too hard.'

I didn't like that Lee felt like he had to be easy-going when people were making a racial slur that implied he was lazy. If it had been one of my fellow lawyers, I would have told them straight up not to be a dick. But since it was one of the police brass, I would only get in trouble if I said anything.

But even though I didn't really like Lee, casual racism like that made me see red.

'Was that supposed to be a joke?' I asked the man, casting a glance over his jacket. His dress uniform had a couple of medals attached to it. *Better be careful, O'Connor. Don't run your mouth.*

He laughed. 'Haha. See ya later, lads.'

And then he walked off with the other brass, and I was left steaming, imagining every way I could have changed the conversation. Scott brushed my arm with his hand, and I tried to pull myself back to the present. I tried to copy Scott and shake it off, say nothing, even if I hated it.

When I looked up, Lee caught my eye. His eyes showed surprise and curiosity. I looked down again. *You don't even like the guy*, I reminded myself.

There were the usual rounds of speeches – great work everyone for your work at the precinct, out in the field, and in the courtroom this year, blah blah blah – interspersed with a few funny moments where the higher-ups poked fun at each other. I was only too glad when the wait staff began delivering dinner to the tables.

I focused on avoiding starting another drink and avoiding thinking about how big of a crush I had on Scott, and how I was

still annoyed at Lee about the other night … and feeling embarrassed for trying to stick up for him and failing.

I started getting up and gathering my purse, figuring I would go down the hallway and get a breath of fresh air, when I heard them start introducing the individual awards at last. I sat back down with a sigh.

When they got to the award for best junior prosecutor, they started listing the winner's achievements… Some of which sounded like cases I'd worked on, actually…

And then I heard them say my name. 'Adrienne O'Connor.'

Everyone was clapping and my table started cheering, shouting my name. Scott stood and tugged at my elbow until I got up as well, then gave me a gentle push towards the stage.

'Go on, Adrienne. Up you go.'

In a daze, I took the framed certificate they handed me, shook the Commissioner's hand and smiled. I don't know how I made it down the steps on the other side.

The presenter moved on, but even once I made it back to my seat, my table kept on congratulating me.

Embarrassed by the attention, I slid the award under my purse and leaned over to Scott. 'I need a drink after that.'

'Oh, no, you don't!' Lee laughed.

I scowled at him. 'Why, you gonna race me again?'

He raised his eyebrows and gave me a look, like, *Oh, you mad at me?*

I rolled my eyes.

When they stopped the speeches for dessert, one of the male prosecutors, Paul, stopped on his way to the dessert bar. 'O'Connor, congratulations.' He leaned in close, his hand on the back of my chair, his eyes on every part of my body but my face. 'And I gotta say, pretty sexy tonight, too.'

'Oh… Thanks, but no thanks,' I said. I was careful not to smile. I could feel myself cringing away from him, uncomfortable.

But this guy just couldn't take a hint, either at the office or here, in plain view of everyone. He leaned down next to my chair and said, 'You got plans for an afterparty?'

I shook my head mutely, wondering if I would have to stand up and walk away. There wasn't anything terrible about Paul's words, or even his tone of voice. There was just a feeling in my gut, a vibe that I knew without a shadow of a doubt meant this guy was trouble. He was a predator, and I refused to be prey.

Scott had been engaged in another conversation, but now I felt him lean around me to interrupt. 'Excuse me, I need the counsellor for a moment. Adrienne?'

Paul backed up immediately. 'Of course. See you around, O'Connor.'

I breathed a small sigh of relief and shaded my face with one hand, feeling exposed. I rested my hand lightly on Scott's forearm for a moment. 'Thanks.' Scott's gesture had been protective without being obvious, and I didn't hate it. And it wasn't jealousy that I saw in his posture, either. He projected strength, and I knew without asking that he could and would protect me from anyone who was bothering me.

He nodded solemnly. 'Any time.'

I felt muscles move in his forearm. *Man, do they build these cops out of pure muscle?* I took my hand away and tried to think of something else to talk about.

6

Scott

After the last speeches wrapped up, I had a bunch of brass to talk to. When I finally made it back to my friends, they were all at the bar with another of our beat cop buddies, Vicki.

Addie was talking, waving her hands more animatedly now that she'd relaxed again. 'Now tell me, how is it that I can win an award like this—' She patted her little clutch-handbag-type thing, where she had rolled up her award and tucked it away. '—but I still can't get a *simple*, teeny tiny proposal approved to change the procedural rules for DV cases?'

'Rigged,' joked Lee.

I leaned on the bar, as close to Addie's elbow as I dared, and said, 'Maybe this gives you the leverage you need. Worth asking again.'

Personally, I hoped she got it. I knew she wanted so badly to get known DV perpetrators into mandated programs for DBT counselling, anger management, and relationship communication. She'd even talked about wanting to introduce more measures for instances where DV was suspected – the times when cops were called but no charges were pressed. And for the murderous ones? We both wanted to see them behind bars.

Vicki was complaining about being single for the holidays. 'My family has all these expectations that you'll be married and pregnant by 25, right, and I'm well past that now! And you have to show up for every "family celebration" known to man. These holidays just make me think great, that's one more Christmas showing up on my own to the family Christmas event. And then there's New Year's Eve. Then Chinese New Year's. Before you know it, it's Valentine's Day. Then my birthday. I mean, seriously?' She flicked her black bob out of her face. 'Kill me now.'

I sympathised. 'It's hard for a lot of people, this time of year.'

'Yeah, but it's worse if you're single,' she protested. 'What if I die alone? We've all seen what happens to them – it's days, sometimes weeks, before anyone notices the smell. I don't even have cats to eat me when I'm gone.'

'Come on, Vicki, you got nothing to worry about,' said Lee. 'You're sexy as hell. You've got a good job. You could have any guy at this bar.'

Addie raised her eyebrows. 'If any of them are brave enough to ask!'

Vicki nodded enthusiastically. 'Right, right!'

'You can't ask them?' I asked, keeping my tone light, teasing. I didn't really *want* Addie going out asking any other guys. Unless she was thinking of asking me. *In which case...*

Addie stared up into my eyes, and I could see a blush begin to stain her cheeks. Her skin looked so soft. I wanted to lean forward and kiss those pink cheeks. 'If I found one I really wanted to ask, maybe. But look, I don't know about you, Vicki, but I'm shy. And a woman wants to feel pursued, desired.' Addie waved her free hand for emphasis. 'If some guy can't even be bothered to ask you for a drink, what are you supposed to think?'

I chuckled. 'Believe me, it would take a lot of courage to ask someone like you out. When you find the guy who's willing to take that chance, it'll be worth waiting for.'

Addie searched my face, as if looking for any hint of sarcasm, but I was sincere, although I was amused. It seemed like whatever she saw in my face comforted her.

I hoped I hadn't promised something with my eyes that my lyko-sergeant reality couldn't cash. But honestly, when it came to love, I didn't want to be left out, either. I didn't know many people who'd want to be alone forever, and most of those who did were extreme introverts, or on the asexual spectrum, or had undergone too much heartbreak and trauma to try again.

Later, tipsy on one glass of rose-pink champagne, Addie asked me, 'So, how does an intelligent, funny, good-looking man like you end up single?'

So she *was* into me! My mouth twitched with amusement. How seriously should I take this not-quite-drunken question? She probably didn't want my full dating history, so I said, 'Well, I've dated. But I never found anyone I thought would make it for the long haul.'

She wrapped a strand of hair around her finger. 'Their loss.' Then she bit her lip, and my dick stirred. *Damn*, she was hot.

But I also remembered what Lee had told me when I called to ream him out for leaving Addie alone to wait for the Uber.

He'd said, 'She was bleeding, man, what was I supposed to do?'

'You work around blood all the time, why'd you crap out?'

'I didn't crap out! My wolf wanted to get all up in it, to mark her or something.'

'To *mark* her?' That was weird. Normally only happened between two lykos. And only when they were deeply, seriously in love.

'I don't know, man. It just seemed safer for her and everyone else for me to leave.'

But that was a while ago now. I wondered if he remembered, and if his wolf still wanted to claim her as his. I wondered if I would let him. I didn't want to step on Lee's toes here, not unless I had to.

Not unless she picked me.

My phone lit up, and I sighed when I read the screen. More brass. *This better be important.* 'Be right back.' I headed outside, wanting to hesitate, to ignore the call. Regretting every step I had to take away from her and that bar.

7

Addie

I went to the bathroom, and when I came out again, Scott was still in the hallway, shifting his weight as he listened to whoever was on the other end of his phone call. I waved and smiled, slowing down. I contemplated leaving him to it and just walking back to the party, but I wanted to talk to him.

I couldn't *believe* I'd just come right out and asked him why he was single, the question I'd been wondering ever since I met him. I was so embarrassed, and I wasn't drunk enough to be okay with being embarrassed, since I cared more about his answer.

As I was about to pass him, he ended the call. So I slowed my steps and tucked my purse under one arm.

'Hey,' he greeted me, smiling as he put his phone away.

I tried to think of something interesting to say, some reason to approach him. 'Great party, isn't it?' *Smooth, O'Connor, so smooth.* I winced.

'Always is,' he said, 'when you're around great people.'

I ran a hand through my hair. 'You always know just what to say.'

'I wish.' His gaze turned rueful. '*Some* lawyers make me forget how to talk in proper sentences at all.'

I faked looking around the hallway, wide-eyed. 'Who, me?'

He laughed.

'Well, don't worry, there won't be any interrogations tonight,' I said with a shrug. 'You look great, all scrubbed up.' I put my fingers on my mouth, as if I could pull those words back inside. *I didn't mean to say that.*

But his eyes lowered, dragging down my body, then back up again. 'So do you.'

It didn't feel *at all* the way it had earlier tonight when Paul had tried it on with me. Heat began to prickle all over my neck and chest, a light blush. *Oh, hell.* Of the many faults with being this pale and red-headed, not being able to hide it when I blushed was definitely the worst.

All of a sudden, I felt vulnerable, and not in a physical way. I wanted his attention, craved his attention, and now that I had it, I was nervous. Tipsy enough to feel free to talk to him, but not confident enough to feel like I knew what to say or do next. I wrapped my arms around my elbows, as if I could guard my heart inside my chest.

'I'm glad you came,' he said.

'Really?'

'Of course, are you kidding? First time I haven't fallen asleep at an awards dinner. I was having fun.'

I nodded slowly and reached out to touch the side of his arm. 'Well, yeah, it has been fun. I'm glad you came, too.'

As I lowered my arm, he caught it in his hand.

My breath caught.

He held my hand close, and stroked one side of my wrist gently.

I didn't pull my hand away – didn't want to. My core clenched deep within me, with a thrill I couldn't deny. I swallowed, hard.

'So how's it going?' he asked.

My mouth started rambling with barely any connection to my brain. 'Oh yeah, a bit tired, ready to go home soon, I think. I mean, it's been a big week, so. Well, I mean, they're all big weeks this year. Big, long, stressful…'

'Ah, yeah, sounds about right. You okay?' He opened his arms easily. 'Need a hug?'

I smiled. *Classic Scott.* Without hesitation, I stepped forward, right into the circle of his arms. My hands slid around his middle under his jacket, finding muscles around his ribs and back. I was holding my purse in one hand, trying not to bang it against any of his ribs. He was so big my arms didn't reach the whole way around him.

He wrapped me up, bringing my whole body against his. I felt his cheek lower to rest against the top of my head.

A tiny part of my brain whispered, *Danger! Don't get any more attached than you already are!* But he felt big and warm and so, so right.

When I inhaled, his scent flooded my senses, layered with a sweet cologne for once. I smiled softly, feeling light-headed.

I was hyper aware of everywhere we touched – breasts, belly, thighs, even my heels nudging up against his dress boots. Every part of his body lined up against mine.

Having him welcome me into the safety of his embrace was comforting and thrilling, both at once, and I felt confused. Would I ever be brave enough to tell this guy I liked him, not just as a friend, but as something more?

'You know what's funny?' he asked after a while.

'Tell me.'

'I've never found anything I like as much as running, or hiking, or hanging out with friends. But this – tonight, just hanging out with you – I like it.'

'You're fun to hang out with, too,' I said, smiling into his chest. His heat was seeping into me through his shirt. My voice shook, just a little – had he heard that, too?

At some point, I realised our hug had probably been going on for way too long – definitely way longer than normal people would hug in public. I eased back an inch, starting to slide my arms out, not wanting to let go, but also not wanting him to think I was the most awkward, needy person on the planet for giving him the longest hug ever.

But when I met his eyes, I froze.

His grey eyes were smoky, like he was seeing more than just a friend standing in front of him. Like he knew exactly what I wanted to do, which was way more than just hugging. He looked like he wanted that, too.

Without conscious thought, my gaze dropped to his mouth. It was a firm line that slanted into a smile as easily as it asked pointed questions, barked out orders on the street, or told a joke in the office. Now his mouth tilted at the corners, the merest suggestion of a smile.

I was captivated by the silver stubble that scraped over the lower half of his face. I wondered what that stubble would feel like brushing over my cheek, my neck … my breasts.

Oh geez, what if he can tell what I'm thinking? My eyes darted back up to meet his. I couldn't read what he was thinking behind those dark brows, so I tried to move back another inch, to break the embrace.

But his hands stopped me. He wasn't holding me tightly, but the way he was holding me made it clear he didn't want me to go. His brows lowered and he lifted one hand, wonderingly, to brush my chin.

My lips parted, wanting more of his touch on my skin.

Does he want me?

If I knew anything about Scott, it was that he wouldn't do anything without my consent. Did he know how much I wanted to kiss him right now? That was what helped me decide: I wanted him to know that I wanted this. I wanted him.

So I tilted my head up and closed the gap between us again. I brought my lips to the corner of his mouth, brushing his cheek with a feather-light kiss. I held my head carefully, so I didn't bump my glasses on his face.

He inhaled sharply, and moved his head so he could kiss my mouth. One hand pulled me against him, crushing all my softness into his hard muscles. His other hand slid up my back, my neck, to cup the back of my head, deepening our kiss.

My hands slid down his back, aching to cup that hard ass I'd been eyeing in that suit. But my purse was still in one hand, and I didn't want to put it down…

That thought broke my trance. We were in a hallway, and I was about to drop my purse so that I could grab the ass of a guy I worked with.

What am I doing?

I broke our kiss.

An inch of air whispered between us.

He stared at me for a moment, his gaze still intense and hungry, but stopped. I don't know what expression I was making, but his brows lowered in a worried frown.

I ripped myself out of his arms and fled. My shoes tip-tapped down the hall as fast as I could, right past the auditorium, to the outside doors.

It took forever, took an hour, or maybe just a few seconds.

Cool, fresh air blasted my face when I made it out.

He had kept pace with me; his cologne wafted back to me. Or maybe I was just smelling the scent of him imprinted in my clothes, my skin.

'Adrienne, wait up.'

I turned.

8

Scott

Following Adrienne went against my better judgement – because it was pretty clear she didn't want to talk right now. It was a total sucker punch that she seemed to regret our kiss. And confusing as hell, because I *knew* when we were in that moment, she'd been into it. So I wanted to talk, and this might be my only chance.

When she turned around, I said, 'Adrienne, I have to apologise.'

She blinked. 'Oh?'

I held my hand out, gesturing for us to walk together. It was only a few metres down to the boardwalk along the river. Moonlight and stars shimmering on the water mirrored the jewels in her ears. I was surprised when she walked towards me.

I felt like I was really going to have to put my heart on my sleeve, and it was an uncomfortable sensation, one I wasn't used to. I stared at our feet on the boardwalk, then rubbed the back of my neck as I admitted, 'I'm sorry about what just happened, in there.'

'It's all right,' she said, clearly an automatic reaction.

'No, I'm serious. I didn't mean to wind up kissing you like that, and based on your reaction, it might not have been what you wanted, and if that's the case, I'm deeply sorry. Consent is so important to me, but I realised we didn't talk about it beforehand, and I'm kicking myself about it. It sucks, because we've had a good working relationship until now. And I respect you so much, and I would never want to do something you didn't want—'

'Hey, no. It wasn't like that.' She swallowed. 'I … I liked it. I wanted it.'

I smiled, pleased but not surprised. 'You did?'

'I mean, I kind of started it.' She began to blush again, an adorable smattering of pink lighting up underneath her freckles, and she began to trip over her words, talking faster. It was endearing as hell. And under it all, the scent of her arousal was growing again, making other parts of me stand up and pay attention.

She said, 'I mean, that would be really fun to do again sometime! But it seemed to me like something that maybe you or I might regret later, so I don't want to make it any more awkward for both of us than it is already.'

I stopped, and leaned down to try and make her meet my eyes. 'So … you ran away. I get it. But you think it would be fun to make out again sometime?'

She licked her lips – fuck, those lips were killing me – and said, 'Right, yeah, definitely, but I'm worried…'

'Yes?' I wanted to be connected to her in that moment, to reassure her, so I caught her hand in mine. I rubbed my thumb over her palm in a light massage, and her breathing turned shallow.

'Scott, we work together. And I don't want to make it weird.' Her voice was a whisper by the end, as if she could hide in silence. 'You know cops and lawyers are a disaster combination.'

I was scenting her arousal even more strongly now. Despite her words and the way she was holding back, she wanted to get closer to me again. And I wanted that more than anything. An urge was growing in me to take her, right here and now, behind a tree off the boardwalk. Anything to claim her as mine.

'Well, we're both sensible people,' I said. I kept my voice as quiet as hers. 'It's not against the code of conduct or anything. And we both wanted to do it again. So the question is...' I took a half-step forward, then gave a slight tug on her hand, a clear invitation. 'Do you still want to?'

'Hey, there you are!'

Adrienne jumped, pulling out of my hands.

I restrained a groan and closed my eyes. *Can't catch a break.* I really should've heard Lee approaching. Not a good sign, that I'd let someone sneak up on us.

'Geez, Lee!' Adrienne's voice caught.

'You two just disappeared there.'

And then the arousal I was sensing from Adrienne, her intoxicating scent washing over and around me, doubled. *Interesting.* Either she had a bit of an exhibitionist kink, or she was attracted to Lee, too.

I clenched my jaw and met Lee's eyes, pushing my frustration down. 'We just needed some fresh air,' I said.

He raised his eyebrows, sensing I wasn't happy. But he lifted his hands in surrender and said, 'Well, great. Ready to go back in? They're about to close the bar.'

I resigned myself to losing the moment with Adrienne, and followed as she hurried away after Lee.

9

Addie

I spent a full two days reliving that moment, remembering Scott's lips on mine, his breath brushing my neck. Over and over, I felt his touch again, my belly producing wave after wave of horny butterflies.

After that, I tried to avoid Scott and Lee at work for a few weeks. It wasn't as hard as I thought it might be. I spent extra time at the office and less time at the station. And it seemed to me like Scott was spending less time at the courtroom and more time in and out of the station, running investigations. We were like ships in the night.

It made me sad. I wished stuff wasn't weird between Scott and me – I wished I hadn't kissed him, or that I hadn't run away after I kissed him.

'It's a new bar, almost no one knows about it yet,' said Charlie. 'But it's sooo good, and they've got a rooftop garden. Trust me.'

I groaned. 'You know those two words never end well for me.'

Charlotte Rose Akello, my best friend in the whole world, was a thrill-seeker. I was not. Most of our adventures started with her saying, 'Trust me, it'll be great!' and ended with me falling in a creek, or dropping my camera halfway down a zipline, or getting lost in the backstreets of the city.

This time, our adventure was The Nocturnals, a pub in the valley. As we wandered in, I spotted Kenny, Scott's friend from the other day. They were behind the bar, mixing a mojito. Sparkling in one of their ears was an earring shaped like a ninja star.

I smiled as we approached, even though I remembered how they'd nearly crushed my hand when we met. *That was an accident,* I reminded myself. 'Hi Kenny! You work here?'

'Adrienne, hi! Yeah, every day,' they said, and smiled. 'This is my family's place.'

'How do you two know each other?' Charlie asked.

'We met in the city, a few weeks ago,' I said. 'Kenny lives in the same estate as Scott.'

'Any recommendations?' Charlie asked, leaning forward on the bar, turning on her insta-flirt magic.

'Well, a margarita is always nice,' said Kenny. 'And it's always amazing in the rooftop garden at this time of night.'

They weren't wrong. Fairy lights twinkled above rows and rows of blooming shrubs, trees, flowering plants on trellises, and even a small vegetable garden in raised planter boxes.

And everywhere that wasn't varnished wood boards was grass – real grass. Stools and tables were scattered around the space with just enough room to walk between them and the plants. I wondered how they kept it growing, so thick and lush, when people must be stepping on the greenery all the time.

There were a bunch of young men up there, playing a card game and drinking at one of the tables. I sighed inwardly. In my experience, drunk, young guys in a bar were a bad combination; they always ended up breaking something, or fighting in the bar, and then wound up spending time *behind* bars for it.

When Charlie and I walked in, a couple of the guys lifted their heads and flared their nostrils, then turned to look right at us.

I accidentally bumped one of them with my bag as we passed, grazing the top of his carefully-sculpted faux-mohawk hair. 'Oh, sorry.'

Fohawk leaped to his feet. He peeled back his lips over his teeth, and growled at me. Actually *growled*, like an animal.

That seemed to set off a chain reaction. Two of the other guys stood up so fast they knocked their chairs over, with their fists balled up, ready to go.

Before I could move, Kenny reappeared beside us, a hand on Fohawk's arm. 'Hey, dudes, chill.'

'I don't *do* chill,' said Fohawk, the one I'd bumped. He was clearly some kind of ringleader here. His face looked real familiar to me, but I couldn't place him. His face and neck were marked with a line of prison tattoos.

'Hey Kenny, what the fuck,' said one of Fohawk's followers. 'Letting normies in now? This is supposed to be our place.'

'"Normies"?' I murmured sideways to Charlie.

'They're friends,' said Kenny. 'My place, my friends. And who's this dickwad?' They jerked their head at Fohawk.

Fohawk clenched his hands into fists at his sides. 'Name's Grendel.'

Kenny snorted. 'Well, Grendel, this is my bar.' They sniffed loudly. 'And you don't smell like my pack. So don't make trouble, or I'll kick you out so fast it'll make your head spin.'

It was dawning on me that if I recognised a random, angry man with prison tats, that was 99% because I'd seen his face in court, either in the witness stand or the defendant's box. Either way, it meant Charlie and I were *not* safe here. I raised my hands and said, 'It's okay, we'll go.'

Grendel took a big step forward, right into my personal bubble. 'Damn straight, you will.'

'Hey!' Kenny barked at him.

The other two guys stood up as well, and everyone seemed frozen in place for a moment, nostrils flaring in anger. The tension was thick in the air, like breathing in soup.

'What the fuuuck?' Charlie muttered, echoing my thoughts.

Grendel leaned in.

I froze, suddenly unable to back up. Something purely animal had gripped me, like a rabbit trembling before a sabre-toothed tiger. All I wanted to do was flee, and I couldn't.

He took a big, long sniff of my hair, and his eyes darkened as he backed up. 'Hmm, interesting. I smell wolf all over your clothes, but you're not one, are you, Red? You're just a weak, vulnerable human. Actually, now I think about it, I remember that red hair. Yeah, from a courtroom.'

Oh, shit. I gulped.

He took a step back, nodding to himself, a wicked grin spreading over his face. '*You're* the one who sent me to jail.'

Kenny turned their head slightly to me and whispered, 'You need to go. Quickly. And call Scott. Or Lee.'

I frowned. But what was Kenny supposed to do? I'd brought trouble to their place of business. 'Okay, well … see ya later, Kenny.'

Something about this had me very worried – Kenny, a full-grown adult, backing down to a random drunk and a bunch of their own friends? This made no sense. Was I leaving Kenny in danger? Should I be calling triple zero?

I took a beat, then looked each of the guys in the eye as I said, firmly, 'You know, if I put this guy in jail, it was for a good reason. And if you hang out with him, he'll land you in jail, too.'

Charlie backed me up with, 'That's right, she's a *lawyer.* You better calm the farm. She'll put your ass away for *life.*'

Then everything got real weird.

Grendel jumped into the air, and changed shape in mid-air. Where a young man had been a second ago, there was a big, *big,* brown dog.

No, not a dog.

A wolf.

It – he – leaped towards me. I threw myself backwards, my arms up in front of me.

It crashed into my forearms, tackling me to my knees against one of the plant trellises. Its paws raked my arm as I screamed and tried to shove it away.

Then something ripped the big wolf off of me. I saw a smaller, grey wolf bite them by the back of the neck and pull hard.

The big wolf twisted and bit the grey one's leg. The grey wolf yelped in pain.

Charlie grabbed my hand and hauled me to my feet. I couldn't see Kenny anymore, so Charlie and I fled from the rooftop and booked it down the stairs. My heart was beating so fast and hard, I felt like I was going to trip on every step.

Once we were downstairs, I could still hear snarling and human shouts up on the roof, and the scuffles of fighting. There were like three other people down here now, and another bartender was behind the bar, but nobody was looking at all concerned by the noise.

Then I heard the crunch of a chair breaking upstairs.

'Okay, that's it, I'm calling the cops.' I started digging in my bag for my phone.

'We gotta get outta here! Call them from outside!' Charlie dragged me to the entrance.

Scott. Call Scott first. Outside, I whipped my phone out and scrolled to Scott's name.

He answered on the first ring. 'Hello, Adrienne.' He sounded like he was smiling.

Later, it would warm my heart to think that he was happy to hear from me. Right now, I hurried to say, 'Scott, there's some people beating each other to shit and we need you here, now, or they're gonna hurt Kenny.'

'Okay Adrienne, where are you?'

'The Nocturnals, in the valley. Kenny's place.' I hugged myself. 'It's really messed up, these guys are like growling at each other and screaming and throwing things around, and two of them must have had dogs or something, and Kenny said to call you or Lee.' I absolutely refused to say out loud that someone had literally turned into a wolf right in front of me. 'I don't know why, I don't know what's going on, I'm *freaking* out.'

'Okay, Lee is just around the corner, so he'll get there first. And I'm on my way. I'll be there in ten minutes,' he said firmly.

Everything in me relaxed. Scott was coming.

Charlie gave me a hug, and I could feel her heartbeat thumping hard and fast against my chest.

I squeezed her back, shaking.

'That was so fucking weird,' she said. 'Let's get out of here.'

'I want to wait for Scott and Lee.'

'That's crazy! What if those guys come back down here? They'll see us!'

I shook my head stubbornly. Bits of me were starting to shake as the adrenaline let-down hit. And my arm was hurting now, so bad that I couldn't believe I hadn't noticed it before. I checked the rips in my denim jacket – each one was about 10 centimetres long, going over my shoulder and down my bicep.

Charlie pulled my jacket sleeve aside, across my bare shoulder. 'Oh shit, Addie, you're bleeding.'

I winced. She was right; there were long, wide cuts in my skin, blood streaming down my arm. My clothes were doing nothing to stop the bleeding; my top was sleeveless, and my jacket was ruined.

'Shit, no wonder it hurts,' I gasped. 'What about you? Are you okay?'

Charlie shook her head. 'They didn't touch me. But screw waiting for the cops! We need to get you to a hospital.'

'And tell them what?' I wondered out loud, pulling my jacket back up again. 'A big *dog* scratched me?'

Lee raced up then, with Gal running hard beside him. He was in uniform, his police hat in his hand as he ran. His buzz cut shone in the city lights, looking cool as hell. Normally not the first person I'd want to see, ever, but tonight I was so glad to see his face that I almost started crying.

'Addie, you okay?' he called as soon as he was within earshot.

Gal sniffed around me, whining.

I nodded. 'They're fighting up on the roof!'

'I'm on it.' He and Gal bounded inside together, and I snuck a peek after them. Inside, Lee changed mid-step, his form shifting. He hit the stairs as a big, black wolf, bigger than Gal. Gal didn't flinch, just leaped through the door into the garden alongside Lee.

Lee.

A wolf.

I shuddered, overcome by shock and confusion and I don't even know what else. My mind was still processing frantically, like a terrified hamster running for its life on its wheel.

Wolves. No – not wolves. Werewolves.

Just then, a police car screeched to a stop beside the curb on the no-standing line. It was one of the big ones, like a Toyota Land Cruiser or something. Scott stepped out, and I let out a big sigh of relief. He came straight for me, pulling me into his arms.

I nearly broke down crying with relief. I breathed in deeply, drawing in a lungful of Scott-scent and gathering my strength again, with his arms around me. He was still in uniform, even though I knew his shift normally ended at 5pm.

'Lee's inside, with Gal,' I told him.

Scott nodded. 'Okay, I'll go check they're on top of it. I'll be back in a minute.' Then he froze, his nostrils flaring. 'Adrienne, are you wounded?' His voice became hard with urgency.

I nodded, shaking.

'Who hurt you?' He ran his hands over me, and I whined as he squeezed against the wounds on my arm. He peered at it for a moment, then put one hand on my cheek, holding me still. 'Adrienne, this is important, did any of them bite you?'

'N-no. No bites, just scratches.'

Scott let out a big breath. 'Thank fuck.' It was the first time I'd heard him swear, so I knew it must be serious. He pulled a roll of bandages out of his uniform pocket and handed them to Charlie. 'Okay, that's good. Just start wrapping it up, apply pressure to the wounds. I'll go get everyone out of here, and I'll be right back.'

He went inside, and I heard some shouting. Then everything went silent.

Scott came back out and said, 'They're gone. Come on inside to the bar, and we'll get you cleaned up properly.'

Charlie just stared at him. 'Are you sure? Shouldn't we take her to a *hospital?*'

'Yes, but you want to get the wounds clean as soon as possible, to prevent scarring,' said Scott. 'I'll clean this up for you, then take you to the hospital myself. I'm a first responder, so I should go with her either way.'

Kenny and Lee came down the stairs, both 100% back in human form. Gal followed them, panting on their heels but looking unfazed.

Charlie and I sat ourselves on a couple of bar stools, and I leaned hard against the counter. Kenny wordlessly slid behind the bar and lifted out a first aid kit. They shot me and Charlie an apologetic look as they handed me the red box.

Charlie refused to meet their eyes.

Kenny looked pained. They grabbed a broom and went back upstairs, probably to clean up the destruction made by those crazy guys – wolves – whatever.

Lee leaned into Scott's side and turned away from me so I couldn't read his lips, but I still heard what he murmured under his breath: 'Ferals.'

I slid my jacket off carefully, hissing in pain as the denim scraped past the slices in my flesh. As Scott began washing my wounds with saline, I breathed in deep through my nose and just looked from Scott to Lee, then back again. 'So don't take this the wrong way, but ... what the fuck is this? Are you all werewolves, or something?'

'Yep.' Lee popped the 'p', and downed a shot of what looked like whisky.

I could tell he wasn't joking around like usual. And I knew he wouldn't lie to me. So this must be for real.

Scott sat back, holding my and Charlie's attention. 'They're in a different pack to us. Kenny's in our pack, otherwise they would've been able to get the others to calm down. Seems like the guy who started it was a feral wolf.'

'Feral. Packs.' I stared between him and Lee. 'Like, actual werewolves. Will someone please give me a coherent explanation. Now!' I snapped.

'Seconded!' said Charlie.

'Well, normally our two packs are totally fine,' said Scott. 'We each stick to our territories, apart from this bar, because it's one of the only spaces in the city that's lykos-only. It's not noticeable by humans, so normally, only lykos can find it.'

'Right, they said something about "normies",' said Charlie. I wondered if she was buying any of this. 'So how did I find out about it, then? I mean, it's not in Google, but my friend at work recommended this place to me, and I've never seen *her* wearing a fur coat!'

Lee shrugged. 'Some idiot must have brought a human friend here and broken the barrier somehow.'

'It should have been a non-event anyway,' said Scott coolly. 'Normally, humans and pack get along okay. It was that feral.'

I was mad. And it wasn't just the pain and the adrenaline let-down. I'd just realised Scott had introduced me to two other werewolves – Lee *and* Kenny – before I even knew Scott was a werewolf. He'd drawn me into his world without giving me the information I needed to decide if I even wanted that.

And if I'd known … maybe I would have stayed away. I mean, I guess that was unlikely, given that I was so drawn to him. But still.

Finally done with the saline wash, Scott began applying antiseptic cream.

It really hurt. I took deep breaths and tried not to swear.

He murmured, 'I'm impressed that you stood up to the pack. Kenny said you didn't even seem afraid.'

'Well, I'm freaking out now! ' I protested. 'Geez. First, Kenny tries to break my hand. Then Lee nearly breaks my leg cheating in a race that *he* started. Now some random drunk turns into a wolf and slices me to bits. I'm starting to think you're all just bad news.'

Scott looked sad at that.

Lee looked away, his jaw tensing.

Well, whatever. Be pissed. It's your fault any of this is happening to me. Except it wasn't all their fault, if what Grendel had said was true.

'I remember that red hair,' he'd said.

Charlie asked, 'So if humans and werewolves normally get along, why did that guy, that feral, attack Addie?'

'Drunk?' Scott grunted, a question for Kenny.

Kenny shook their head. 'He just had a Pepsi.'

I shifted my arm and propped my head up on my uninjured hand, starting to feel tired and lightheaded as the pain increased. 'It was more than that. That guy – the feral – he called himself Grendel. He said I put him in jail. He must've been a defendant in a case I worked. But I didn't recognise his face, or that name.'

To my surprise, it was Lee who replied. 'We'll take care of him. Make sure he doesn't bother you again.'

'And I'll tell you anything you want to know about our kind,' Scott added. 'If you promise not to tell anyone.' He gave Charlie a meaningful look. 'Both of you.'

'I'm not promising *anything* until I know what the hell is going on,' I said.

'Let's get you home. We can talk on the way.' Scott nodded to Lee. 'You take Charlie home; I'll take Adrienne home.'

Lee looked like he might disagree, but then he nodded and gestured for Charlie to follow him.

Charlie raised an eyebrow at me. 'A stranger taking me home? No thanks. At least in an Uber, I've never seen someone grow a tail.' She gave me a quick hug and whispered in my ear, 'Hun, are you okay? This whole night has been messed up, and these guys are weird as fuck.'

I nodded. 'It's okay.' For some reason, I still trusted Scott and Lee.

'Okay, then.' Charlie finger-waved goodbye and scurried outside.

Lee shrugged, and whistled for Gal. She'd been having a drink at the doggie water bowl, but she came straight to him, and they strode out together into the night.

'Later, Addie,' Lee said easily. As if this was just a normal Friday night.

I supposed it must be, for a cop.

Scott's police car – the Land Cruiser – was just as huge on the inside, and it made me do a bit of a double-take, because it was spotlessly clean. What's in a guy's car says a lot about him, and this said he was a clean freak. And the radio didn't turn on when he started the car, which made me wonder if he normally drove in silence. I'd actually expected him to drive a normal car, not a police cruiser, since he was a sergeant, so I would've thought most of his job was behind a desk, not driving around on shift.

I was starting to realise that, as much as I had a huge crush on this guy, I knew almost nothing about him.

My glasses fogged up for a minute when the air came on. I took them off in frustration, and fought the urge to bite my nails from the stress and pain. Instead, I clenched my nails into my palm and started talking just to distract myself. 'So I bet neither of you will ever need glasses, huh?'

'Probably not,' he said calmly, his eyes locked on the road as he drove.

'Law school ruined my eyesight, I'm pretty sure,' I said. 'Too much reading tiny print in textbooks and then researching stuff on backlit computer screens.'

'You should sue,' he said, then laughed to himself.

I turned my whole body to stare at him. *Sir Serious told a joke?* I let myself laugh with him, relieving some of the tension in my body.

He glanced at me with a smile, and kept driving.

'What a crazy night,' I murmured.

His jaw tightened, but he didn't say anything.

'No, look, I get it,' I continued.' I sent this random dude, this "feral", to prison. It probably ruined his life. When people come out of prison, what do they have? Less than nothing. They've usually got debts, and then they have no access to their money in jail so they can't pay them off, so the debt gets bigger and bigger with interest and fees. And then it's hard for them to get a job.' I sighed.

'You don't need to be resigned to being attacked,' said Scott.

It meant a lot to me that he said that – and I agreed.

At the hospital, he parked in one of the normal parking spots, not the spots reserved for emergency vehicles, and opened my door for me. When he helped me climb down out of the Land Rover, I caught my breath. There was an undeniable connection there, a spark.

Scott told the triage nurse I'd been bitten by a dog. They praised Scott's first aid technique, gave me a tetanus booster shot, and told me to come back for antibiotics if it started looking infected at all. It didn't even need stitches, thank goodness.

When we were finally back in his car, I wriggled down in my seat, getting comfortable. 'So. You were going to tell me about ferals?'

His voice grew grim. 'Yes. Werewolf saliva has some healing properties, so lykos sometimes lick humans they care about. But a bite will infect a human, turning them into a werewolf. And if a lyko *eats* any human flesh, it sends them feral. That becomes all they want to eat. Most ferals are caught by pack patrols because we find them eating a victim or digging up recently-buried corpses in the cemetery. There are legends that say there might be a way to cure ferals, but I've never seen one with enough willpower to try the cure.'

Who cares about a cure for ferals? I just wanted to know why this was happening. Part of me wanted to tell him to piss off, honestly. This all sounded dangerous, and impossible, and it seemed like something no tiny human like me should be involved in.

But a bigger part of me – the part that always said yes to Charlie's latest adventure – wanted to know more. And all of me, even the part that was mad at Scott, wanted to spend more time with him.

When we made it to my place, I said, 'I still have so many questions. Do you want to come in? Answer some more of them for me?'

He looked up at the steps up into my apartment building, and I could see him considering it. He rubbed his hand over my good arm, and I trembled, my skin lighting up from the warmth coming off him. Eventually, he said, 'No, I can answer all your questions tomorrow.'

I almost whined with disappointment. 'I'm not going to be able to sleep after what just happened. Why not come in and talk with me now?'

He lifted his hand and brushed my cheek. 'Because you're injured. And right now, I'd like to strip these clothes off you, so I can run my hands over every inch of your body and check for any more injuries. But it's not a good time.'

My mouth dropped open. When my brain cleared enough to talk, my voice was husky with longing. 'Well, when is a good time?'

'I'll come by tomorrow,' he said. 'I'm so sorry I wasn't there to stop you getting injured. I hope you'll give me another chance.' He kissed my cheek, then ran his nose from where my neck met shoulder, up to my ear, breathing in deeply, as if he was memorising my scent.

I didn't move, struck with desire and confusion, wanting only to pull him against me. I should have just wanted to get away, after everything he'd told me. And especially since I was still mad he hadn't told me until it was too late. He was a werewolf.

I've kissed a werewolf.

Dangerous.

But I only wanted to get closer.

I didn't sleep well, unable to stop thinking about the fact that not one but both of the people I had a crush on were werewolves.

Actual, real life werewolves.

Finally, I gave up on sleep and went to the couch. I opened my laptop and Googled 'werewolf packs'. I had to start somewhere, and all they'd told me so far was that werewolf packs existed, and so did feral werewolves.

I skipped over most of the information from the 1800s onwards – all of that had been covered already in movies, TV shows, books, and comic books.

The older lore and legend about werewolves was confusing. Nobody agreed on what caused lycanthropy to make a human turn into a werewolf – a bite, a scratch, a disease, a curse by a witch or sorcerer, or a genetic condition specific to one tribe or clan…

But not everybody viewed it as a curse.

In Turkish folklore, the wolf was their people's totem animal, so their shamans made it a goal to become able to voluntarily transform into the *Kurtadam* – the wolf man. Their people took great care to pay respect to any wolf, in case it was a shaman in their true form.

In Scandinavia in the 9th century, the *kveldulf* – the evening wolf – was a state that some berserkers could go into. They were named after Bjalfason, a berserker who was immortalised in generations upon generations of Icelandic sagas.

In Greek mythology, Lycaon was a king who tricked Zeus into eating the roasted flesh of Lycaon's own son, to see whether the all-knowing Zeus could tell. To punish Lycaon's evil, Zeus transformed Lycaon into a cursed wolf, the *lykos*.

And it wasn't just wolves, either.

In Ethiopia, blacksmiths in stories sometimes became were-hyenas called *bouda*.

In India, they had were-tigers called *chenaku* or *cindaku*.

In Mesoamerica, they revered shamans called *nagual* who could shapeshift, with some turning into were-jaguars or harpy eagles.

Some shifters were reviled for being human-killers, sheep-killers, and the like. Others were worshipped as immortal demi-gods.

Most of the pop culture about werewolves showed them being poor, living in shabby houses. Their places had torn-up curtains from unexpected transformations, peeling walls they didn't have money to re-paint, and leaking plumbing.

The one thing I knew was incorrect, based on my experience so far with my furry men, was that lykos didn't need to get naked to transform. Their clothes shifted with them, as if they were part of their aspect. So they didn't need to spend all their time running around shirtless and shoeless, like they did in *Twilight*.

I took my glasses off and rubbed my eyes wearily, then kept reading.

I fell asleep on the couch sometime after midnight, and dreamed of Lee transforming in front of me, back and forth. He became a wolf, then a man – an exhausted man, panting on his hands and knees – and back to a wolf again, over and over.

About 8.00 on Saturday morning, Scott knocked on my apartment door, as he'd promised. That made me happy – I'm a morning

person, and I'd made it pretty clear last night that I wanted answers asap.

'Come on in,' I said. 'I'm making a cup of coffee, can I get you one?'

'First, let me check your wound,' he ordered.

I sighed and hopped up onto the kitchen bench. As he lifted up the bandages to add some more antiseptic cream, I asked him, 'So you can turn into wolves whenever you want?'

'Yes. Except at full moon. That's the one time each month that you *have* to turn; your wolf side doesn't give you a choice about it. I've known two people who had enough control that they could avoid turning, but that's it. And it's not pretty. Not smooth, like you've seen so far. It can be painful at full moon, especially if you're not expecting it or you try to fight the change.'

'How did you become…' I nearly chickened out and said 'like this', but instead, I forced myself to say the word. 'Werewolves?'

'A bite from a lyko can turn someone. Whether they're in their wolf or human form. Nothing else. That's why you don't need to worry about this scratch.' He gestured to my arm, now freshly re-bandaged.

'That's right, I forgot you told me that last night.'

'You were in pain.'

I waved him to sit while I moved to put the kettle on. 'So, someone bit you, then?' From what Scott and Lee had said, a feral would have happily bitten him on purpose.

'Yes, when I was in my twenties. The pack I'm in now found me, the first time I turned. It's like that, usually. We can sense when one of our own kind is near, and the scents of fear and rage are so strong with a first turning, it's fairly easy to sniff out. Then when our old leader passed away, I stepped up.'

'Sergeant *and* alpha...' Something inside me quivered, and I looked down, pretending to focus on getting out two coffee mugs. I'd read enough smutty books to know that meant something. 'Is it true what they say about alphas? Does everyone have to do what you want?'

He hesitated. 'Sometimes. I don't usually try to control others. That's not a real wolf thing; they only do that distinct alpha/beta thing in captivity. But there is a certain authority that you get from being the main leader of any group, and as long as the pack is happy with you as a leader, there is something a bit magical to it. There's a bond where I can feel how the members of my pack are doing and sense where they are, something more than just empathy. So you could say I'm a democratic leader, unless there's some important reason I need to make people listen, but even then, it's their choice what they do. Or of course, there are those cases where someone *wants* to be ... dominated.'

That made me sneak a peek at him, and he caught me looking. He smiled, slow and knowing.

Oh, girl, you are getting way in over your head here. I blushed and hurried to ask another question. 'And you're strong?'

'Very strong. Very fast. Very quick at healing.'

'Jumping tall buildings in a single bound, sort of thing?' I joked.

But Scott nodded. 'Sometimes.'

I blanched, thinking of how differently last night could have ended. Maybe that feral Grendel would have flat out *ended* me, if Scott and Lee hadn't been there. 'Sounds like no one could survive ... if a werewolf wanted them dead.'

His tone turned grim. 'If you're ever in trouble again and I'm not there, you should use my name. Or Lee's. All the packs in this state know us.'

'Why do they all know you?'

'I'm the leader of a big pack, and Lee is my right-hand man. People come to me with a lot of problems, and they know Lee is different, but they also know he's strong, so sometimes they go to him for stuff they don't want to bother me with.'

'So people do respect you, even if the alpha thing is more of a myth. What about if someone's already in wolf form – will they still pay attention if I give them your name?'

'Nooot necessarily. It's harder for wolves to reason. If they're already in wolf form, then you should try to trick them back into human form; that's your best form of defence. When we return to our human forms, we become weak for a minute or so. It's debilitating. Makes us slow – slow-moving and slow-thinking. Although—' He held up a finger. 'The more often someone changes form, the stronger and tougher they get in both forms.'

'What about silver bullets?' I asked.

'Definitely a problem,' he said. 'Even wearing silver can cause an allergic reaction for most of our pack. And the hospitals use silver as a natural antibacterial agent in a lot of medical equipment like needles, stethoscopes, even breathing tubes. That would be a big problem for us. So most of us just get our childhood vaccinations and then try to stay away from doctors and hospitals. It's usually pretty easy, because we heal faster than normal humans. And thankfully, most of the other ways we use silver in the modern world are less tactile – it's in things like car engines, electronics, solar power – where the silver is hidden inside the thing, so you aren't touching it directly. But back in the day, people used to use silver for everything. They'd put drops of silver nitrate in newborn babies' eyes to prevent infection. They'd wrap battlefield wounds in silver foil until they could get to the field hospital; they even used silver sutures for major internal surgeries.'

'And these ferals. You said the pack usually just kills them?'

'Yes. They're rare, so it's not usually a problem. But sometimes, if there's not a strong enough pack in the area, or if the feral is good at hiding, they can create chaos. There was a feral in Lozère, in France, who killed about 300 people in three years. That was back in the 1760s: the Beast of Gévaudan. These days, my pack does regular patrols, so we pick up any ferals as soon as they arrive. Exterminate them before they do any harm.'

'I thought you said there was a cure?'

'No, I said there were legends of a cure. In Ancient Greece, there were a couple of cults who sacrificed wolves to Zeus. They said if a feral werewolf could hold themselves back from tasting human flesh for the next nine years, they would return to human form. But I've never seen a feral who had any control over their actions. Once they turn feral, their hunger to eat is what drives them.'

I sat back and blew all my air out in a slow, shaky stream.

'You look overwhelmed.' Scott's eyes were calm, but concerned.

I stared at the scratches on my arms. 'If I hadn't seen what I did last night, I would say you're crazy. None of this can be real. But now…'

He cupped my elbow in his hand. 'I'm so sorry they marked you. I've spoken with the other lykos who were there. That kind of behaviour is not on, no matter how young they are – no feral should be able to get other people to fight for them like that.' His gaze grew warm. 'You did the right thing, Adrienne. If you ever need anything, I want you to call me, no matter the time of day or night.' He leaned back, and stretched, giving a giant yawn. 'But for now, I need to head home. Lee and I were up patrolling all night, sniffing around.'

He'd been up all night, keeping me safe? A swirl of surprise and happiness washed through me.

'Thank you.' Then I remembered this was all Scott's fault for not telling me, so I added, 'I'm still mad at you.'

'I know.'

He kissed me on the forehead.

And then he left.

I took a few days off work and thanked the saints for sick leave. When I made it to Saturday, my phone rang about 6.00 in the morning. I nearly didn't pick up, because for the love of all things holy, it was the *weekend*.

But I checked the caller ID, just in case it was work, or my little sister, Eloise – Elle.

-Lee Hauata-

I blinked. *Why is* he *calling me?* I could only assume either Scott had ordered him to check in on me, or Lee was worried that I would tell someone about both of them being wolfy. (Not that anyone would believe me.)

I hit the answer button and reached over to find my glasses on the bedside table. 'Ello.' My voice was a croak.

'Hey, Addie.' There was an easy smile in their voice. 'Gal wants to take you for a walk.'

'It's a Sunday. It's too early. And I'm probably going to have to work this arvo. *And* on top of all that, I got attacked by a werewolf because *you* guys didn't tell me werewolves were real. I'm going back to bed, dude.'

'Nah, trust me, it'll be fun.' He paused, and I tried hard to hear what he wasn't saying. Something in his voice sounded almost like pleading. He must really want to play nice for me – or for Scott's sake. 'Mild exercise will be good for your arm, and your knee – which I know, I know, I still have to make that up to you. So. Whaddaya say?'

'Umm, sure. But like, I'm not awake yet.'

He chuckled. 'Well, put on pants, Adam Ant. I'll be there in fifteen.'

He hung up, and I groaned, then shuffled into the bathroom to get ready for the day.

Lee picked me up in a beat-up ute instead of his usual motorbike. Gal stuck her head out of the window and panted at me in a doggy smile as I approached.

'Hey girl.' I smiled and scratched her behind the ears.

She *whuffed* and licked my hand, then dug her nose in the backpack I had over one shoulder. I wrestled it away from her while Lee laughed, then opened the door. He pulled Gal over to his side of the cabin so I could jump into the passenger seat.

'What've you got in there, coke?' he asked.

I rolled my eyes at him and roughed up Gal's ears the way she liked. 'I've got a sandwich, and an apple, and *mayyyyybe* one little treat for the beautiful Gal. So anyway, you still haven't told me where we're going for our walk.' I narrowed my eyes. 'You know I've got Google Maps sharing my location with about five people, so everyone will know where you've dumped the body.'

He just laughed and pulled out into traffic. 'It's a hike, actually, so we're going out of town a bit.'

I groaned. 'Hiking? You said "walk", I thought we'd be at the dog park. That's misleading, officer.'

He drove me and Gal to a walking trail not many people knew about, a little hidden pocket of national forest within just an hour's drive of the city. I was slipping my ponytail through my hat when I heard a low chuckling behind me.

I looked up to see Lee shaking his head.

'What?' I frowned.

He gestured at my hat. It was my Grade 5 Scouts camp hat, featuring a cartoon tiger cub about to pounce. I made a face and laughed with him, then brushed past him to the trail entry.

'Coming?' I teased.

Barely 50 metres into the leafy trees, the temperature dropped five degrees, countering the rising heat outside. Surrounded by the green scrub, I felt my nerves rolling off my shoulders. I caught Lee's eye as he walked alongside me, and we shared a smile.

As we walked, he pointed out things we could eat if we had to.

'Is this stuff your folk taught you?' I asked.

'Nah, they're Samoan, so they taught me how to open a coconut, but not much about Aussie bush stuff. But I did one of those cultural trips with school, to visit a First Nations community up north. They took us camping overnight and showed us lots of stuff like that: bush tucker, making a lean-to out of palm branches, that kind of stuff. And at night, around the campfire, they'd tell us stories about the massacres of Aboriginal and Torres Strait Islander people. There's some real horrific shit the colonists did.'

'Crazy, isn't it?'

Gal found some hidey-holes that were probably animal dens in winter. But it wasn't that cold yet, so I reassured myself they were probably only full of the usual deadly snakes and spiders.

'I know if you do get bitten, you should lie down, so the poison can't spread as quickly through your blood,' I said.

'Yeah, most people who get bitten just panic and run around, so the poison gets to their heart faster,' he said. 'Depends on the snake, but they usually end up really sick, or really dead.

We wouldn't have as many accidents if more people knew what to do.'

After a while, we didn't need to talk. I let the sounds of the mountain filter in through my bones – the rough, natural whispers of leaves on bark; boots crunching on dry leaf litter; birds squeaking out of time with my heartbeat.

Lee's silence was confident, comfortable. It hung in the air between us, broken only by our breathing, dotted with my footfalls. He and Gal padded much more quietly than I did; even his shoes seemed to mould to fit the uneven surface. His shadow breezed over the rocky, leafy trail while I struggled up and over each rise and rock.

We didn't see anyone else on our way up.

I still wasn't sure why I was even here, but I said, 'It's beautiful out here.'

'Yeah, right? It's like, the rest of the day, I'm … a bit hyper, like crazy restless. You know, I've got actual, diagnosed ADHD, so it is what it is.'

'Wow, no kidding?' I laughed.

He rolled his eyes at me, and I wondered if I'd hurt his feelings, implying that his ADHD symptoms were easy to spot. 'But here…' He spread his arms wide and breathed in deeply. 'It's so easy.'

'Yeah, it is pretty peaceful out here.' I took a breath and started to apologise for the poor joke. 'Sorry, I didn't mean to—'

'No, no.' He took my hand and tucked it into the crook of his arm. 'I know, I'm a nut job.'

My breathing sped up, feeling my hand against his warm, hard chest. I shoved him off and laughed. 'So, do your ADHD meds affect your werewolfiness?'

He cracked up laughing. '"Werewolfiness"! Fuck that's funny!'

We laughed for a while, going single file around a boulder.

Then he said, 'Yeah, nah, it does help. The meds. The short-acting one messes with my metabolism a bit, so I'll probably never be as big as some of the other shifters can get.'

My eyes widened. Like many men with Pacific Islander heritage, Lee was already *huge*. Scott had more height than Lee, but they were definitely matched for strength, and Lee's muscles were as bulky as his frame. I couldn't imagine him being any bigger.

'But the long-acting one I'm on is really helpful for focus, and you need to focus to make a smooth transition from human to wolf and back again. So yeah, it's great. I only take the short-acting one if I have to now, like when they had those meds shortages last year.'

Leaves swum in the breeze over our heads, showing a myriad of different shapes and colours – leaves like drops of hot wax; leaves like downy feathers; leaves like dull spoons. Plant seeds kissed my legs. Webs of tangled vines choked their way up the tallest trees.

We walked for an hour, stretching ever upward, the path so unclear sometimes that I couldn't see how Lee was finding the way, what inner compass he was using. But I wasn't worried he would get us lost.

Even though he normally annoyed me, I was actually loving every moment. It made me remember how much I loved being out in nature, with the trees and the bird songs, the sound of the breeze rustling leaves all around me.

When we got to a big tree trunk that crossed the path, I slowed. The knee I'd injured at the bridge race still wasn't 100% yet, and it wouldn't let me forget it. I hesitated, groaning.

Gal hopped over the fallen tree without pause, but Lee held out a hand. 'I've got you.'

'Thanks.'

I thought he was going to just help me step up, but he leaned over and slid his hands around my waist and physically lifted me up onto the tree. His fingers brushed under my shirt as it rode up, and I tried to ignore the flutter in my belly at the feel of his big, strong hands on my body. We were so close that his breath hit the skin on my neck, and I shivered. His eyes met mine, and my chest started to rise and fall quicker. His gaze dropped to my lips, and the air crackled with thick tension.

I bit my lip and looked down. *What is wrong with me? Wanting to kiss Lee when I've been flirting with Scott for weeks?*

'There ya go.' He helped me step down the other side.

Adrenaline and a whole bunch of hormones were still pumping through me when he let go. To break the tension, I joked, 'Is this your superpower? Cardio?'

He burst out laughing, and Gal turned to look back at us.

I was confused for a moment, then realised what I'd said, and I started laughing, too. I couldn't believe I'd forgotten for a moment that he actually had a real superpower of sorts. Superpower … curse … whichever.

'Kind of is,' he said. 'I reckon I could run forever without getting tired. Did a marathon last year, actually.'

'Oh, good on you!'

'Yeah, it was for some charity, homeless teens and all that. Scott made a big deal out of it, so I had to make sure I didn't place in the top three, or it would be "suspicious".' He rolled his eyes.

'Would you have won, if you'd really let loose?' I asked.

'Bet. Hands down, no contest.'

I pretended to focus on my feet so my expression wasn't so visible. *We couldn't be more different if we tried. No wonder he normally gets on my nerves.*

'And what's your superpower?' he asked me.

I made a face. 'Not applicable. Don't have one.'

By the time we were approaching the summit, I'd worked up a good sweat. I began to hear a rushing sound, and soon the path led to the start of a waterfall.

At the top, we didn't stop at the tourist lookout – instead, we walked around to the far side of the waterfall. We stood on the rocks to the side, watching the water tumble to the cliff edge and throw itself into the air. At the bottom, a black pool of water punctuated the rich, green forest.

Mountains sprawled in every direction, like a fortress of green spread out before us. It was like the border with a different world.

The climb had taken it out of me, and I needed to sit down for a rest. I put my rain jacket down on the rocks, and sat in the shade, so I could take my hat off. The breeze tickled over my scalp, and I sighed in relief.

Lee joined me, and Gal spent her time splashing in the very edge of the stream that led to the waterfall, then running back to shake water on us.

Eventually, Lee began talking. 'I'm sorry I ditched on you, that night when we did that stupid race to the bridge. I shoulda stuck around to patch you up.' His jaw tensed.

'Why didn't you?' I tried to keep my tone light, not judging.

'Because it was my fault,' he said. 'I've got a bit of a thing about…' He shrugged.

I made a noise. 'Well, yeah, you pushed me. But it wasn't all your fault. Even if it hurts me to admit it. So … you've got a bit of a thing about what, exactly?'

He was silent for a long time before he said, 'Hurting someone. When I first turned – transformed into a lyko – I didn't have anyone around to help me understand what was happening. Normally, if you get bit, other lykos can smell it from miles away. It's this strange mix of human and wolf genes all blending together. So they'll help you find a pack. But I was alone when I got bit, and then I blacked out. I woke up and I just thought I was sick or drugged or something, I was wandering around, all lost and dizzy. When I finally made it home that night, I was so angry about the bite and I was scared I was going crazy, and I was sweating with this mad fever. I don't even really know what I did, just that my mum and brother were trying to talk to me about something – probably school, I wasn't great at school – and I lost it. I lashed out, and in that moment, I turned again, and it was so painful, I had no idea what I was doing. I was angry, I was in pain… I slashed them both with my claws. Could've killed them. They freaked out. I freaked out. And I ran. Didn't come home for a week. Scott's the only reason I ever did. He was a beat cop back then, and he found me on the streets. He could tell just by smelling me what was going on, so he knew I wasn't high or anything. He checked on my family in the hospital, told them some story, I don't know if they believed it. My mum, and my brother, they've both got scars from where I ripped into them. But because of whatever Scott told them, my mum let me keep living there till graduation, and Scott visited us all the time. He helped me learn about controlling the wolf side, the transformations. I owe him everything.'

'Wow. Wow.' I didn't know what to say.

'You're the only one I've told that, except for Scott, and our pack healer,' he said gruffly, rubbing a hand over the back of his head. 'Didn't even say that when the shrink was prodding at me, after the drug bust.'

That was huge. He'd shown me a glimpse through his hard shell to his one big regret, that he'd hurt the ones he loved most. And, I realised, his biggest fear as well: that it could happen again, if he got close to people again. I put my hand on his arm, admiring the rock-hard muscles under my slender fingers. 'Thanks for trusting me.'

He looked at me with those dark, soulful eyes, and my insides melted.

Oh, girl. You've got it bad. Try to remember how annoying he normally is. I slid my hand away.

'Thanks for trusting *me*,' he said. 'Especially after I ran off on you.'

I shot him another sidelong glance. 'Why did you ask me to come here with you?'

'I mean, Scott said he'd kick my ass if I didn't apologise eventually,' he said.

'Well, yeah,' I scoffed. 'But you could've sent me a text or something. You called me, brought me out here. Made me exercise my busted knee. Why?'

He took his time about answering. 'You're kind of … calming. I enjoy it.'

I couldn't deny he seemed genuine. So I gave Lee what I could – my presence.

After about half an hour of chilling, Lee and Gal both tilted their heads and sniffed a few times, smelling something I couldn't. 'Gonna rain soon. Let's get the hell outta here.'

'Afraid of a little rain?' I teased.

He grumbled something unintelligible in response.

I poked him with a finger in his ribs. 'Sorry, what was that?'

He grabbed the finger, then my whole hand, and hauled me to my feet. 'Being out in the rain sucks. Hey, it's not just me, Gal will tell you. It's a furry thing.'

I laughed. 'I already know being in the rain sucks.' I pointed to my glasses. 'These don't come with windscreen wipers, you know.'

'So let's hurry the fuck up, then.'

On the way back down the mountain, the path was more challenging on my injured knee. I hadn't noticed how steep the drop-off was on the way up, but coming down, the leaf litter and narrow path was giving me extra hints of 'I might fall to my death' kind of adrenaline.

Lee made it look easy as he padded down, but dirt and rocks kept scrabbling around under my shoes. I started resting one hand against the cliff wall as we went, just in case.

Now and then, Lee turned back to me and held out his hand. I didn't take the hand he offered again, trying to keep my distance. But he still waited as I took each step on the tricky bits.

'You didn't tell me I might die on this "walk"', I gasped once.

Lee winked. 'I won't let you fall, Ace.'

After that, he called me randomly a few times, about work stuff. It was never a long phone call, but it was enough that I wondered about it. We weren't friends, exactly. He just called me when he needed to talk, and the rest of the time, he could take me or leave me.

But we weren't total enemies anymore, either.

I met Charlie and Elle at Eat Street on Sunday night, since Elle had managed to find a babysitter. We went straight to our favourite food truck, the Sexy Mexy Burrito Van. We'd been regulars for so long that we knew Mateo, who ran it, very well. He told us Mateo was the Spanish equivalent of Matthew, so we should call him Matty.

He wasn't actually Mexican, but he was Colombian, so he passed – for anyone who didn't ask, anyway. Charlie had asked what his ethnic background was, of course, because she always asked every awkward question. It was part of what I liked about her; it meant I never felt bad asking her anything in return.

'Did you have a good time on your hike?' Charlie asked, her voice teasing.

'Yeah, we didn't kill each other,' I said.

'So you had fun, then?'

I shrugged, feeling defensive for no reason. 'Whatever, I guess.'

Elle's eyes narrowed. 'Hmmm, sure.'

'He knows a lot about the bush and survival skills and all that. And he's less annoying than he used to be.'

'Such high praise,' Charlie laughed.

It was a busy night, so we had a bit of a wait, but eventually we ordered, and kept chatting while our burritos toasted.

'Life's weird, right?' I said eventually. 'Like, it's not just me, always stumbling along, trying to figure it out?'

Charlie laughed. 'Of course life's weird, it's not just you.'

'But what do you mean, stumbling along? You've got a great life,' said Elle gently.

'For sure, I know, yeah. But like…' I bit my lip. 'Forget about the hike with Lee for a second. The truth is, I'm kind of focused on someone else right now.'

'Ooooh!' Charlie clapped her hands together.

'Yeah, there's definitely "ooooh!" stuff about it, but there's also "oh nooo" stuff.' I made a face, then collected our burritos with a 'thank you' for Matty. 'It's Scott.'

She put both hands on the table. 'Scott *Davids?*'

'Yeah, you met him at The Nocturnals the other night.'

'Your hero, the *hotty* who chased off the feral werewolf?'

I choked. 'I mean, technically, he's a werewolf, too.'

'Well, *daaaaamn*. He looked good.'

'That's your first thought? Cos my first thought was that I might actually be insane, for liking an actual fairytale monster.'

'Well, no, he was the one saving you from the monsters. Him and Lee.'

'Well, yeah.'

'Although.' She tilted her head. 'Scott Davids. Never trust a man with a first name for a last name.'

I laughed. 'Oh, like that's a red flag, and "werewolf" isn't?'

'Are you convincing me or am I convincing you?'

'No, no, I mean, he's so sexy, and he's funny.' I raised my eyebrows. 'And he likes coffee.'

'Sounds perfect for you. Did you get black beans on your burrito?'

I spoke through my mouthful. 'Uh, no, but it's all good.'

Charlie shook her head and yelled into the food truck window, 'Hey, Matty, you forgot the beans!'

'But it's just … I'm just … confused. Like, I know how it goes with lawyers and cops. And he's not the only person I'm attracted to – it's not like it's a full-on "he's the one" kind of feeling. So, I mean, am I crazy for even considering this?'

Charlie saw that Matty had walked away for a moment, and rolled her eyes. 'Ah, fuck it.' She grabbed the door and climbed up into the food truck. 'Go ahead, I'm still listening. You were going crazy.'

'You know as a lawyer, I *have* to tell you that you're trespassing right now.'

'Yeah, yeah.' Charlie scooped out some beans and plopped them into her burrito, then closed it up again.

Elle rolled her eyes. We both knew you couldn't stop Charlie doing something she wanted to do.

I sighed. 'I just want to do the right thing. Even without the "going furry" thing, cops and lawyers is just – ugh. There's just so many problems.' I ticked them off on my fingers. 'First, you're both seeing the worst of humanity, so you both think like, "well everyone lies", so you can't trust each other. Next, you're both cynical about the world so you think romance is dead. Then there's the fact that you're both working 24/7, so there's almost no time for conversation or sex or just to *see* each other. But…' I shrugged. 'I like him.'

Charlie laughed. 'Yeah, you do. You want some?' She waved the bean scoop at me.

I handed over my burrito. 'Okay, so let's say I date him. When we break up, it's like we don't just both get our hearts broken – it sucks even worse, because we still have to work with each other. Unless one of us transfers out of the precinct. Which I don't want to do.'

'I hear that,' said Elle.

'I mean, I work with him and his officers every single day! There's no way to keep him out of my life. And what if someone notices?'

'Well, you know it's not banned for cops and lawyers to date, right?'

'I know, that's what he said.'

Charlie leaned against the counter. 'I mean, it's almost a perk of the job – you're taking care of each other, you're *taking care of* each other…'

'Maybe I'm being too serious, right?'

Charlie laughed and handed me back my burrito, with beans added. 'Dude, always. Fucking law school, man. You used to be fun.'

I made a face.

'Sorry, I'm not sure I see what the problem is. Just walk away and find a teacher or something.'

'Yeah, maybe I should loosen up a bit. Plus it'd be great to – you know. Give my vibrator a break.'

'Addieeeeee!' Elle squealed.

Charlie cheered, 'Oh, 100%, fuck yeah. Get you some! Get those endorphins, and all the other fun, sexy hormones!'

Matty stormed back into the truck and yelled at Charlie, 'Get out of my van!'

Charlie raised her hands, still clutching her burrito, and backed out of the van. 'Talk about needing to relax, Mattyyyyy. Okay, okay, I'm going. You forgot the beans though, dude.'

She was right. I had my degree, a great career, a hot bod… And now I was going to complain about meeting a great guy? I picked at my nail. 'There's just one last thing, if you're not sick of talking about this yet.'

Charlie took a big bite and spoke through it. 'Iss fine. Wha'?'

'Do you think you can be attracted to multiple people at once? Or if you can … *should* you?'

'Well, for sure you can. And I mean, poly isn't that rare anymore.'

I must have had a blank look on my face, because she clarified.

'Polyamory. Is that what you mean?'

'No, no … I mean … I mean, *maybe.*' I waved a hand in distress. 'But like, how do you know … if someone would be open to that?'

Charlie laughed. 'You ask!' She licked sauce off a finger. 'Why, who else—? Oh, my sweet baby child.' She grabbed my arm. 'Is it Lee?'

Elle stared at me. 'I thought we were just joking before!'

I blushed and turned away for a moment, biting my lip. I could feel a blush creeping over me, like an avalanche roaring down a mountain. I couldn't help it. After our DNM, the tingle of his body close to mine had been working a magic spell on me. I found myself daydreaming about him on the commute to work, imagining his muscled arms around my waist, his face buried in my hair, his breath heating my neck, his lips brushing the skin behind my ear, his thick thigh between my own...

'Oh, go on,' Charlie teased. 'No come-back?'

'I don't have anything to say to that,' I said. 'It's just ridiculous.'

'Just admit it, Addie! You're hot for him, in all of his black sheep, bad boy on the block, glistening muscles, uniformed glory.'

I groaned. 'But I can't be. I *just* told you about Scott, didn't I?'

'As long as you're careful.'

I frowned. 'Why, what do you mean?'

'Didn't you say he was one of the first responders when you two got attacked at that bar?' I'd given Elle the CliffsNotes version of that story, without the wolves.

Charlie said, 'Yeah, he was there.'

I bit my lip, looking away from the phone and their faces. 'Yeah.'

'Being involved in traumatic events like that can make you feel closer than you would otherwise,' Elle said slowly. 'Makes it easy to confuse your feelings.'

'You saying I'm confused?' My tone sharpened.

'Nah, nah, just that this is a new ... friendship, so like, take it easy.'

'I *am* taking it easy. Look, I don't expect jack of Lee, we're barely even friends, it's fine.'

'You just gotta keep your eyes open for red flags, that's all I'm saying,' Elle said.

'Oh, you see red flags everywhere,' I scoffed, then realised what I'd said to my sister. My DV-survivor sister. I groaned. 'Ah, fuck. Sorry Elle, that was unfair.'

Her face was pinched with pain. 'No, it's true. I do see red flags everywhere. But only because I didn't see any red flags back then, and I should have!'

'Not your fault, hun,' said Charlie. 'You've got a right to be careful.'

Right, but she doesn't need to tell me *to be careful*, I thought. I wondered if I'd put Elle in an awkward position, like maybe this was actually an unwise situation and she was right to warn me... Or if she'd put herself in that awkward position, feeling like she 'had' to say something.

Lee was just a guy. He seemed comfortable with me, and if I could help him open up and process what he'd gone through, I'm pretty sure that was a good thing.

Even if it meant I couldn't stop thinking about him.

And Scott.

Charlie raised her eyebrows sceptically. 'Well, whatever these two have done, sounds like they've *both* gotten under your skin. You better figure out what they're open to, and fast.'

'Ohmigod, I can't even.'

She shrugged and kept eating her burrito. Through another mouthful, she prodded Elle. 'Wha' 'bout you?'

'Huh? What about me?' Elle finished her burrito daintily, and wiped her fingers on her jeans.

'You ever think about getting back on the dating apps?' Charlie asked.

Elle made an exaggerated sad face. 'Kind of hard to get a babysitter for the kids, so I'll probably give it a while longer. So sad. But you two ladies have fun, and I live vicariously through you.'

'Oh no,' we both reacted.

'Well, that's single mum life.' Elle's lips pressed together, like if she said anything more, she'd cry, so we didn't push.

10

Scott

People were scenting the feral everywhere now. They'd gone beyond just hanging around the edge of town, and I didn't know why.

What were they here for? This whole city was very clearly marked as pack territory. Every inch of this place should have stood out as a neon warning sign to a lone, crazy wolf: STAY OUT.

So why weren't they leaving?

I snagged Lee at the end of my shift. 'You and Gal got some time tonight?'

Lee nodded. 'You wanna go for a run, bro?'

We followed the scent downtown, into the valley. The scent hovered for a few hours around a community health clinic, went in, and then came back out again. We went in, Lee bringing Gal in with us.

The inside of the clinic was brightly-lit by strips of fluorescent office lights, and although the walls showed some marks of age, everything smelled clean. Like hospital-grade antiseptic. Gal wrinkled her nose, and I had to make an effort not to wrinkle my nose as well. It probably didn't smell that strong to humans.

Lee wandered over to the big wall of brochures about various diseases and treatments. I didn't bother looking; it was all just the usual, like preventing heart disease, managing diabetes, preventing or planning pregnancy…

'Hey bro.' Lee elbowed me and pointed to one. 'Look at this, and then look at my face. Do you reckon I've got a skin cancer here?'

'No idea, but it's pretty common. You know you need to wear sunscreen every day for it to work.'

The receptionist said something on the intercom phone, then hung up. The doctor came out and waved for us to join them in the first exam room. He was an older man with brown skin – thinner, balding, and smiling cautiously. He walked in holding a chart.

'Doctor, thanks for meeting with us,' I said. Always a good idea to start off by thanking someone, because it makes them feel like they're already helping you – so they must *want* to help you. Then they'll help you out more, so they can avoid the uncomfortable feeling of *not* helping when they clearly *wanted* to help. It was a basic behavioural science tip I'd picked up in a psychology unit I'd taken with the police academy, and it made it easier to get answers from almost anyone.

'No trouble officers, no trouble. Are you here about my report I gave to the station this morning?'

'I haven't been given a copy of the report, but it could be related,' I said.

'In that case, what can I help you with? You need a medical certificate? You want to subpoena a report?' He eyed Lee with a look of clinical interest. 'Or maybe you want to talk about supplements? You look like you work out, but maybe like you don't eat enough vegetables, you know what I'm saying? Because there's always room to improve, even for the fittest people, you know.'

'I knew it!' said Lee. 'Look at my face, here. It's fucking cancer, isn't it, doc?'

The doctor leaned closer to take a quick look, and shook his head. 'It is most definitely not skin cancer. If I had to guess, I'd say it looks like barbecue sauce.'

I stifled a laugh as Lee licked his thumb and started rubbing his chin where the sauce was. We'd eaten burgers for lunch.

'We're looking for a suspect who visited this clinic very recently,' I said.

'Looks like it was earlier this morning,' added Lee. 'Maybe eight or nine o'clock.'

'Well, of course.' He swivelled in his chair and opened some case notes on his computer. He looked up for a second, then shrugged. 'I'm fairly sure the person I reported is the one you're asking about, so I'll tell you about this one first. 8.10am, I treated a man – a 50-year-old, cis, white male, some pre-existing medical history that he declined to disclose. He had some knife wounds that I disinfected and bandaged.'

Knife wounds, or claw marks? Could be Grendel. I flashed Lee a look, and he nodded.

'This guy, I mean, he was a mess. He had a lot going on, both medically and in other ways. He was on anti-psychotic medication that he admitted he was not taking regularly as prescribed. He was actively taking recreational drugs – look, he took one while he was in the waiting room to see me. He said he hadn't slept in days at that point, and he was after some Temazepam, which as you know is an addictive medication, Schedule 8, and it doesn't interact well with recreational drugs, so I said you can have the Temaz if you give me the drugs – only so that I could confiscate the drugs, of course! Here, I'll print you off the case notes I wrote, so you have his name and description… But he didn't want to give me the drugs. Finally I was like, well, apart from the Temazepam, what are you here for? And that's when he seemed to become very agitated, you know, he said I provided an assessment of him for his trial when he was sent to prison, which I don't remember but honestly I do a lot of assessments, it's good money. So that's what I said to him, and he started swearing his head off about how going to prison had ruined his life, and he wanted to know the name of the lawyer who had requested the assessment, and I said I don't know, I don't have any notes on file for him, but it might be public record if he wants to ask for a copy of his court records down at the Magistrate's Office?'

That sounded a lot like what the feral, Grendel, had said to Addie and Charlie at the bar.

The doctor continued, 'Then he attacked me! He started snarling and he hit me with his fingernails, like not a slap, I mean he was trying to cut me with his nails. Looked like he'd been growing out his fingernails and filing them to points. He was acting so angry, and he was just towering over me to intimidate me… I mean, it was weird, and very scary. I really thought he was going to kill me. So I looked it up online and gave him the name. Maybe I should have given him a fake name, I probably should have, but I couldn't think straight. I was scared, what can I say? What if he realised I gave him a fake name and he came back to the clinic to finish me off, you know?'

I said, 'Yeah, absolutely, that does sound scary.' I looked down at the case notes he'd handed me. *Konrad Grendel.* That was the name Kenny had given us. It had to be the same guy.

Lee asked him, 'Did any of his claws or teeth mark you?'

'Yes, he got me with his fingernails all along my collarbone, you see?' He slipped out of his white doctor's coat for a moment and pulled his polo shirt aside.

Under a big surgical dressing, he had four deep cuts, with dark red, angry edges, as if they were already infected after just a few hours. The slashes had ragged edges, like the claws hadn't been taken care of in a long time. They looked nothing like the clean lines that anyone in my pack would have made in a quick fight to settle an argument.

They looked just like the slashes on Addie's arm.

The doctor continued, 'And then he actually bit me! He got me on my elbow while I was trying to push him away, defending myself. Crazy, I tell you.'

I froze, but tried to hide it. A lyko deliberately scratching a human was never okay, since the scar would be permanent. But a *bite* could turn someone.

The doctor turned his arm and unwrapped some pressure bandages from around his elbow. There were two half-moons of puncture marks. Each of the tooth marks were lined with yellow and black; the lycanthropy disease had probably already taken hold of his entire bloodstream.

Lee exhaled in a long, low whistle. 'Damn.' He caught my eye and raised his eyebrows, as if to say, *Do we tell him?*

'Doc, because he bit you, we need to have a talk about the disease he might have passed to you.'

'Oh, no, I already went and got a tetanus shot and a rabies shot from the ER this morning. You don't want to mess around with that kind of thing; I've been assaulted before as a doctor, and crazy people can transfer so many things!'

I nodded slowly. 'Yes, well, you might want to sit down for this.'

As I explained about werewolves and how the disease of lycanthropy could have been transmitted to the doc, his face fell. He was visibly distressed, his eyebrows crunching down, his forehead sweating, his hands shaking. One of his knees started jumping up and down.

'I know this must be a bit of a shock,' I said, keeping my voice low and calm. Emotions were always heightened and almost impossible to control in the first few weeks as someone turned for the first time. If we were going to keep this guy from going furry right now and destroying the clinic, it all depended on what we did in the next five minutes.

The doc licked his lips, his fingers clenching into a fist. 'Yes, a shock. Yes, yes, it's shocking. I don't know why, but I believe you, which doesn't make sense. This doesn't make any sense. If I hadn't seen that guy get so... He...' The doc gulped.

Gal started growling, a low rumble from deep in her throat.

'I don't feel good,' the doc gasped. Then his face changed into a snarling mask. He jumped to his feet and gripped the back of his chair. Both hands were now covered in bushy fur that ended in long, dark claws.

'Hey, you're okay, you're just having a panic attack, doc,' said Lee loudly. 'You're gonna be okay, you just need to calm down and you'll turn human again. Here, sing a song with me, it'll help you slow down your breathing. What's a song someone your age would know? Oh, I know! *You can't always get what you want...*'

The doc just stared at Lee, but he stopped pacing, and gripped the back of the chair again with his clawed fingers, panting hard.

'*No, you can't always get what you want... But I've tried, and I've tried...*'

I hum along, since I don't know all the words to this one. This is Lee's strength. He knows what turns people furry and what brings them back better than anyone else I know in our pack or any other. If he would've let me, I'd have assigned him to working with humans on the meth beats more often. But he only wanted to work in the canine squad, so that's where he stayed.

So if Lee thought singing The Rolling Stones could get this doc to calm down, I trusted his intuition and his judgement. There were some other things we could try if this didn't work ... giving the doc a hand and arm massage was probably out of the question, but we could try counting out loud. Even getting him to stomp his feet to a beat could help take his focus off the panic.

The doc was still shaking, but his claws retracted into his hands. The fur moulted off, falling in clumps onto the floor. That wouldn't happen every time; it was just this first turning that looked so strange.

'What the hell,' the doc growled, his voicebox still gravelly and inhuman.

'It's all good, just take a deep breath and sing it with me. You know the words, right? *I went down to the demonstration…*'

The doc tried, '*To get our fair share of abuse.* Oh no, oh gods. *Singing, we're gonna vent our frustration—*' His voice sounded almost human now. He took another deep breath and cleared his throat as they both stumbled their way back to the chorus.

Lee finished the last line with a flourish: '*But if you try sometimes, you get what you need.*'

The doc laughed at him, and straightened slowly. He looked almost normal now. Only the veins popping out of his forehead and neck gave away what had almost happened. He blinked a few times, staring at the broken office chair, then ran his hands over his face. 'That was…'

'All good, that was just your first try turning into a wolf,' said Lee, patting him on the shoulder. 'Next time, it won't hurt. Next time, you can decide whether or not you want it to happen.'

I got the doc to give me his phone number, and I texted him the details of when and where we had upcoming pack meetings, including a meeting for new lykos who needed training. That way, he'd be able to meet others in his position and learn more than we could teach him here, when he was supposed to be working.

I put my hand on the doc's arm and pushed some of my scent over him, trying to calm him down. He'd had one of the most stressful days of his life, and this was just the beginning. I needed him to keep his cool until I could have our pack healer, Radhika, meet with him. She would be able to clean up his paranormal wounds faster than modern medicine could, and as a health professional herself, she would be able to relate to him better than I could. She could be a soft entry point for him to join our pack.

Once he looked calm and had agreed to come to a meeting and find out more about what had happened to him, I said, 'Now that you have our phone numbers, if you feel yourself freaking out again, you can call one of us, and we can talk you down.'

'Thank you, I will,' the doc said, wiping sweat from his brow with his sleeve. He took a moment to straighten his white coat, then seemed to remember something. 'Before you go, one last thing. I only noticed this after I gave my report at the station. He must have dropped it as he was leaving. Might be evidence.'

Leaning hard on the desk, he opened a drawer and held out a necklace.

I sniffed, trying not to be obvious about checking for silver. But it smelled and looked like white gold, so I lifted it with one hand. I was right; it didn't burn me like silver would. It was a Celtic symbol called the Dara Knot: an interwoven, never-ending circle.

And I recognised it. I met Lee's eyes, knowing he would, too.

'That's Addie's,' muttered Lee, turning to hide his reaction from the doctor. I could almost *feel* him grinding his teeth. 'Why'd he bother taking it?'

'Must have picked it up at the bar the other night,' I replied. 'He could be using it to track her scent easier. Not good.'

The doctor just stared up at us, exhausted from his first almost-transformation. He was paler now, and covered in sweat. I hoped he could take the rest of the day off, with sick leave. He wasn't in a great place to be seeing the rest of his patients for the day.

The receptionist knocked on the door, pushing it open at the same time, and the doctor jumped.

'The doctor's been telling us about the assault this morning,' I said simply. 'Please go and get him a glass of water.'

'Oh, of course!' They scurried away.

After making sure the doctor had recovered a bit and getting him to agree to take sick leave for the rest of the day, we left the clinic.

'Dude,' said Lee, his tone tense. Gal sniffed at his hand, trying to calm him down. 'It's sounding like this fucker, this Konrad Grendel, is after Addie, specifically.'

I nodded. 'From now on, we don't let her out of range. We'll take turns checking she's safe.'

'Shotgun first shift,' said Lee.

I smiled, so he'd know I didn't mind him claiming time with her. I didn't have any right to hold onto her, I knew that. But *man*, I wished I did.

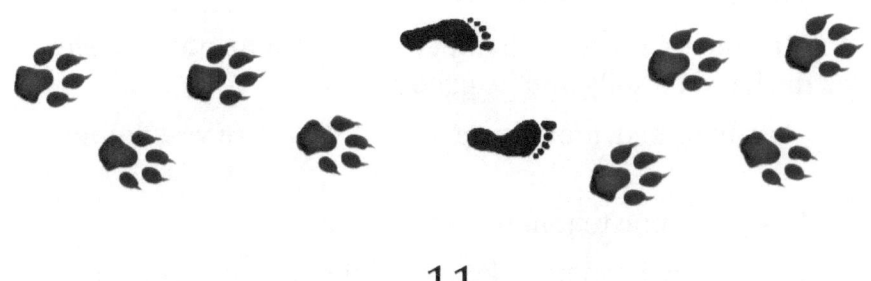

11

Addie

I was on my sunset run when I heard the footsteps of someone else running on the pavement behind me. It's one of those sounds every woman fears, even if they know self-defence, even if they carry pepper spray. I checked the reflection on the inside of my glasses.

Yep, there was a person following me, matching my pace a little too perfectly. And the panting of a big dog with them.

I took my earbuds out and jogged steadily until I got to the corner. Then I threw a quick check over my shoulder as I turned, making it casual, like I was just checking if any cars were coming.

'Hey, Addie!'

What the heck? I slowed down and turned fully to see them, jogging on the spot for a moment. I recognised the guy as he loped up beside me, even though he was in a dark hoodie. I stopped. 'Lee?'

'Hey, Angel Face. How ya doing?' He pushed his sunnies up on top of his buzzed head – no hat, as usual. Gal padded up beside us, panting happily, always happy to be with him.

I bent to give her a pat. 'Who's a good girl?'

She looked up at her handler, and when he nodded, she licked my hand happily and wagged her tail.

I straightened, looking up at Lee. 'What are you doing here?'

'We just came to join in on your run!'

I shook my head in disbelief. 'Without an invitation? That's hella creepy!'

I started jogging again.

He kept the speed up, running alongside me easily. 'It's not creepy. I just sniffed out your route and ran until I caught up to you... Ah yeah, okay, maybe a bit creepy.' He shrugged. 'Whoops.'

'And why exactly did you stalk me on my run?'

'Friends run together! Plus, I got you something.'

'You what now?' *So now we're friends? When did that happen?*

He pulled something out of his hoodie pocket and held it out in front of me. I slowed to a stop, curious, and took it. Gal gave a little *whuff* of frustration, as if asking why we kept stopping and starting.

'Your favourite,' he said.

He was right – it was a 3-pack of lemon squares from Michel's Patisserie. A little smushed from being tucked in his pocket, but they still looked delicious. 'Hmmmm,' I said, tossing up whether or not to forgive him for being creepy. I looked up and caught him staring at me.

He grinned, and gave an exaggerated wink.

It made me laugh.

This crazy werewolf. What the heck was he doing, taking me on random hikes and bringing me baked goods? And now he was stalking me and interrupting my run! I frowned, confused, but I don't think I fully convinced myself to be all that annoyed at him.

I looked for a good way to hold the lemon squares, and settled for one-handing the box while I picked up my feet again. Over my shoulder, I called, 'Come on, stalker, we're running.'

We didn't talk much on our run, since I was focusing on breathing, and not dropping the lemon squares, and not tripping in front of the hot guy and his dog. I also wanted to make sure I was home before the sun was completely down; I always avoided having to run in the dark.

He and Gal joined me right up to the front steps of my building.

As we slowed on my street, Lee said, 'Hey, what's with the vibe with you and Scott these days? You guys are acting weird.'

I looked down. I didn't know how to talk to a guy friend about another man at the best of times. 'Really? Seems like normal to me. I guess I don't see him much. I mean, he's not in court much, and I haven't had to come down to the precinct to meet many witnesses recently.'

When I looked up, Lee was watching me silently, his eyes creasing at the edges. I couldn't tell what he was thinking, but he smiled. 'Right, yeah.'

We stopped on the front steps, and I was sweating a lot more than he was. *Cardio superpower.*

He asked, 'You got much on tonight?'

I was answering when Gal suddenly nudged Lee's hand and barked, loud. She whined, then took a step back and started growling.

'Ah, shit,' Lee said. 'I left it too late. Full moon's rising.'

I looked up at the sky, then backed up a step, through the front door. 'So you're turning furry?'

'Yup! Time blindness – it's an ADHD thing.' He slammed the front door shut between us, making me jump. Then he skipped backwards down the building's steps. 'My bad. I'll see you in the morning, Addie. Lock all your doors and windows! Come on Gal, we gotta go!'

Man, it was weird hanging out with a werewolf.

But at least he'd called me his friend.

12

Scott

I thought about it for days. Agonised over whether I was doing something wrong by wanting to ask Addie out when she needed my protection from Grendel. But she already knew about me. And she knew I was pack, so I wasn't betraying my pack by letting her into my life.

Finally, I just decided to act. It was my turn to keep an eye on her, anyway, since Lee had watched her a few days in a row. So without stopping to think about it too much, I drove to her apartment and parked outside. I took an extra second to put on some of the natural deodorant I always kept in the car – I've done enough long shifts to know it always pays to have some extra deodorant around. And showing up spontaneously didn't mean I wanted to smell like I'd been running around all day, even though I had.

Before I reached her floor, the smell of sugar and butter cooking assaulted my senses, and my mouth started watering. Her big wooden door was open, leaving the screen door shut, probably to let some of the heat out of the kitchen.

I knocked on the screen.

She smiled when she saw it was me, and opened the door easily. 'Come on in. I'm just baking cookies.'

I nodded. 'Smells amazing.' I took a deeper breath as I followed her in, letting my nostrils taste the scent of her underneath the strong, sweet smell of the cookies. She was dressed in running shorts and a singlet, and I tried not to stare.

'Yeah, I decided to bake some Christmas cookies to give as gifts. Being a newbie at the DPP doesn't exactly make me the big bucks, you know.' She laughed awkwardly. 'And Elle and her kids are sick, so I'm going to drop some off at their place later, too. Normally, making Christmas cookies is a family activity for us, but with them being sick...' She narrowed her eyes at me a little, clearly sizing me up.

'Hey, I'm happy to help!' I offered.

'Great.' She clapped her hands. 'I hope you're ready for some manual labour, because my stand mixer is broken, so we're baking by hand today.'

I pulled up a sleeve and flexed my bicep theatrically. 'I think we'll be fine.'

'Get over yourself.' She laughed and tossed a chocolate chip at me.

The chocolate chip bounced off my pecs and landed on the counter, and I stared at it for a moment. This girl had energy! I gave her a look that made it very clear she was in trouble.

She started flushing bright pink.

I stared her down for a moment, scenting arousal coming from her. *Daaaaamn.* I could get hot just from that reaction. I leaned forward and put one hand on the counter.

Clearing her throat, she held out a measuring cup. 'Go on, then. One cup of peanut butter, please.'

I chuckled, deep and low, a sound that bypassed my brain and came straight from my dick. 'Well, if you're going to beg... I hope you've got sprinkles.'

'What?'

'For decorating, once these are done.'

'Oh!' She fussed around with cupcake papers. 'Of course, yeah.' She went silent again, the space between us practically thrumming with tension.

Okay, I had to break the silence. I couldn't take it anymore. 'Hey, Addie. About you and me. Things feel a bit awkward right now, so I wanted to clear the air.' I swallowed. 'You want me to back off?'

'What?' She looked startled. 'No!'

'It's just, you haven't really said much since we kissed at the party, and then there was the whole "I'm a monster" type revelation...'

'No, I – I do want you,' she breathed.

I breathed a sigh of relief and took her hand in mine. 'Okay, great. So this awkwardness between us, is it just the lyko thing? Because I know I'm not exactly normal.'

She laughed. 'You can say that again!'

'Ouch.' I pretended to wince.

'I mean that I'm having a hard time understanding the whole wolf thing because I've just *never* believed in anything like that. So it's hard to even think about if I want to start … dating … on top of that.'

I sighed deeply, stroking the back of her hand with my fingertips. I could see some of the nervous tension melting out of her as I held her hand. 'I wish I could go back in time, stop you going to that bar and getting attacked by a feral. I would go back and find a way to introduce you to my world with your consent. So that if you were still attracted to me, you could have understood what you were getting into. Make your own decision.'

She nodded.

I took it as encouragement, and kept going. 'I'm sorry I got you into this position, but I'm going to try to make it up to you. From the moment I met you, berating Lee without any sign of being intimidated, I wanted to get to know you better. I wanted to be near you, go about things the right way, take you on a date. And then at the awards dinner, I acted without thinking.'

'We both did.'

'And we haven't really spoken about it since…'

She pulled her hands away, looking embarrassed. She pushed her glasses up off her head so she could cover her face with her hands for a moment. 'I know.' She slid her glasses back on and snuck a glance at me, then ducked her head again, not quite managing to meet my eyes.

Okay, so there was something else going on. I'd talked about the lyko thing. I'd let her know how I felt. What more was there I could say? I wasn't used to having to persuade someone it was worth going out with me. 'I know I'm a few years older than you—'

She lifted her head abruptly, and a few stray curls bounced around her face. 'What? No, you're not old!' She looked surprised I'd gone there.

'Okay, well, thanks.' I waited.

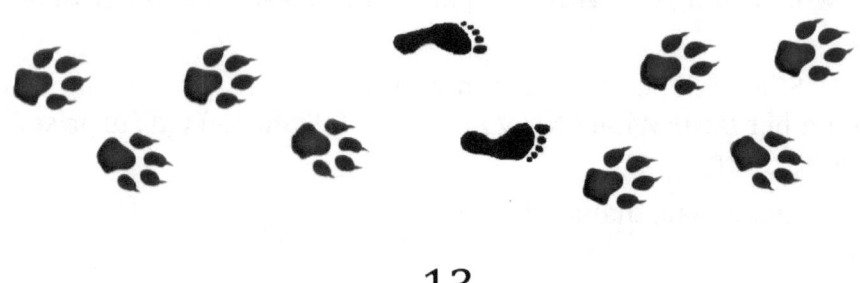

13

Addie

I couldn't ignore that invitation. I couldn't look away from his mouth, that mouth that had haunted every waking and dreaming thoughts for weeks. I took a tiny step, closing the gap between us. 'Yes.'

'Good.'

He lowered his head to kiss me again, cupping my face in his hands. I was flooded with the feeling, the somehow-knowing, that he really cared about me, that this wasn't just physical.

But *boy* did the physical feel good. I only wanted to be closer, so I went with it. I closed the space between us, wrapping my arms around him, tangling my legs between his.

When we finally came up for air, he rested his forehead against mine and said, 'I want to see you again. Are you free Tuesday night?'

'Yes,' I said, without a shred of hesitation. 'I mean, I have to check my work calendar, but I'm sure I can do something.'

He smiled, and kissed me again, and it felt like magic.

But I was aware of tendrils of guilt swimming up like tadpoles in my belly. Why did I feel like I was cheating on Lee? He was just a friend. Barely even a friend.

I took Scott with me to a live music gig. Charlie's band was performing; she played bass and sang all the back-up vocals. We sat on the green at SouthBank, and I sang along with the lyrics I knew.

Scott sat behind me, his chest against my back, running his fingers up and down my arm. It felt like he was claiming me, but not in an aggressive, overpowering way. I liked that he was here, protecting me with his air of natural leadership.

As the sun fell and the air cooled, I shuffled even closer into Scott's space, trying to hold onto every bit of warmth from him. He noticed, and draped his jacket around my shoulders. I smiled up at him.

'What's your favourite of your nicknames?' I asked him. 'I've heard people call you so many different things – Scotty, SD card, PD… That last one has me stumped, I've no idea.'

He chuckled. 'It means "Precinct Dad". Yeah, that's a good one.'

'So? What do you like being called?'

He shrugged. 'I don't know. Never really thought about it. I liked it when you called me Davids. Something about it feels … sexy.'

I smiled slowly. 'Yeah?'

From this angle, we were close enough to touch. He grazed my jaw with his fingertips, gently guiding my head up so he could slant his mouth over mine. My whole body buzzed alight.

'If I haven't told you already, you look amazing tonight,' he said.

'Thanks! It's nice to get dressed up to go out.'

'I think I remember you saying you're not really a party girl.'

'Well, normally I'd rather read a book than go clubbing.' I made a face. 'But always happy to support a friend.'

'So next time, I need to take you to a bookstore,' he said.

I grinned and raised my eyebrows. 'Next time?'

He paused, and a smile tugged at the corners of his mouth. 'I did say that, didn't I?'

The band finished their set, and I ran backstage to congratulate Charlie. 'You were amazing!' I squeezed her in a tight hug. 'You're so talented!'

Scott approached at a much less exuberant pace, passing one of the drinks stalls on his way. When he arrived, he slid an arm around my waist, and passed Charlie a full, unopened bottle of water. He put one in my hand as well, and said, 'Great stuff, Charlie.'

She smiled at him, clearly curious, and took the water. 'Thanks.'

I smiled, happy that he would do something like that to look out for both me and my friend. I wasn't surprised; it was very like him, the protector of the precinct.

'After this, we were gonna go for a walk, maybe get ice cream,' I said to Charlie. 'You wanna join?'

'No thanks, lovebirds! I'm going out for drinks with the band once we've packed up.' She winked. 'You kids have fun now.'

Scott took my hand in his bigger one, and I was amazed at how right it felt. I gazed down at our intertwined fingers, and smiled. I liked how we fit together.

'Thanks for coming with me to meet Charlie,' I said. 'I saw how you brought them a water, too. Trying to take care of everybody.'

'Of course,' he replied. 'That's a sweet thing to say, but it was nothing. If someone's important to you, they're important to me.'

We made our way down to the river and walked along it leisurely. The sun had gone down, and the evening breeze was fresh, carrying the mouth-watering scents of barbecues and restaurants. The lights from the skyscrapers bounced off the water, and a ferry was buzzing along. In its wake, the ferry was creating a thousand sparkling dots and blurs, separating out all the lights and then smearing them all back together, like an Impressionist painting.

I swung Scott's hand playfully, and he laughed. I wondered if he thought of me as being childish. Personally, I didn't care if I seemed childish, because I knew joy is fleeting. It's the reward you win that offsets seasons, sometimes years, of suffering.

Or maybe he didn't mind a bit of childishness because he was one of those guys who loves the idea of the manic, pixie dream girl. In my experience, they usually love that right up until they realise the reality involves as much manic drama as pixie dreaming.

Every few steps, I caught him glancing over at me, and I met his gaze with a smile.

At the steps into my apartment building, I rose onto my toes, touched his cheek, and kissed him. 'Come up?' I asked.

He was wearing his undone face. I felt so powerful, knowing I was the cause.

After a moment, he slid his hands around my waist and pulled me against him again. He tipped his head down and opened my lips with his. My nerves hummed; my heart thudded; my core tightened deep within me. I caught my breath when his mouth left mine. The scent of him filled my senses until I was overwhelmed.

'If you want me to,' he said.

I nodded eagerly.

Upstairs, I poured us both a glass of wine. I felt so overheated that I was amazed my glasses weren't fogging up. We talked. We kissed until I almost lost all awareness of where we were.

'Any STI history I should know about?' Scott asked.

'No,' I said, 'and I'm on birth control, but I prefer if we use a condom anyway.'

'Absolutely, thank you for telling me.'

There was something else I really wanted to ask, though. Like, I was desperate to ask.

Scott ran his thumb over my bottom lip. 'Adrienne, stop biting your lip and say what you want to say.'

'Can I see your wolf?' I blurted out. *Gee, rude. Get it together, Addie.* 'Please? I saw Lee in his wolf form, and since then, I've been dying to know what you look like in your other form. If it's okay.'

He nodded gravely. He didn't seem offended. He let go of my hand and backed away slowly, then shifted.

It was beautiful, incredible. And it confirmed once and for all that he'd been telling the truth – he really wasn't human.

Just like when I'd seen Lee shift, it only took a second. And it wasn't like in those old werewolf movies, where the transformation looked and sounded horrifically painful, all screaming and grunting while tendons popped and bones snapped into a new shape. Instead, he just crouched beside the couch, and his shape rippled and grew. All of a sudden, a wolf stood on all fours, towering over me.

His colours shifted into a rich brown fur, glinting with golden edges in the dim lighting.

With him on all fours and me still sitting on the couch, his head was level with my mine – so he was larger than a normal wolf.

He panted, revealing long, pointed teeth – a lot of them.

There was no doubt in my mind that if this beautiful man-beast ever wanted to do some damage, no one would survive it. If he was the one protecting me, I would always be safe.

I realised I was barely breathing. I inhaled sharply as he moved and the lamp light hit his gold strands. It was so beautiful.

He tensed, not sure what my reaction meant. His tail dropped, holding still, as if he were ready to change back in a second if I showed any hint of fear or disgust.

I wanted to reassure him, but how? I moved carefully, slowly, and touched his shoulder, my fingers tingling. His fur was smooth as velvet, softer than I expected.

He lifted his hand and bumped my hand up to rub his wolfy head.

I stared, then gave him a big scratch with both hands. He made a happy whining sound and a little rumble in his throat, like a big dog would if they were happy and anxious to please. My mouth curved into a shy smile of its volition, and I began to relax. I glided my hands down his back, and looked into his dark amber eyes.

I had to clear my throat to speak. 'What a handsome wolf.'

He padded back, shook his coat as if shaking off water, and he was a man again, with one hand on a knee and one on the ground.

The look in his human eyes made my core tighten delightfully. It was a look that said he liked my reaction to him. He stood until I had to look up again to keep meeting his eyes.

I couldn't have looked away if I tried. I knew my eyes must be wide with wonder. 'Thank you for showing me,' I murmured.

'Thanks for not screaming and running away.'

'Your fur is such a beautiful colour.'

He chuckled, and ran one hand down my neck to my shoulder. 'You're a sweet one. The fur is no colour, really. Just the colour you make it in your head.'

'Huh. Well, then I'm very creative,' I said playfully. 'Because it looks to me like each of the wolves I've seen so far has had different colouring.' I stood to meet him, wanting to be physically closer after sharing such an emotionally intimate moment with him.

His arms wrapped easily around my shoulders, pulling me into him, and lowering his forehead to rest against mine. I sighed in contentment and closed my eyes. I slipped my hands around his neck, enjoying the way we fit together, the way our breath mingled, the way his shoulder muscles tightened under my hands.

He picked me up easily and my legs wrapped around his waist instinctively. Against my neck, he growled, 'Enough sweetness. Take your top off.'

I smiled, already breathing more heavily. The energy between us had shifted, quickly but undeniably. He was in control now, and I liked it.

I let go of his shoulders, and he held me up easily, his hands under my butt, squeezing hard. I practically tore my shirt off, eager to have my skin against his.

His eyes roved my body, his gaze showing his delight in my form. He had a smug smile at the corner of his mouth. He kissed his way down my neck and ducked his head to brush his lips across my chest. As his tongue slid between my breasts, I gasped for air.

'You like that?'

I nodded wordlessly.

His eyes twinkled. He kissed me again, so deeply I lost my breath, and as I panted against him, he started walking, carrying me to the bedroom. He tossed me on the bed, in the way that only strong men who are really paying attention can, so that I landed safely on my back in the nest of pillows.

He slid one hand up my skirt and grazed his fingers against my panties, and I buried my face against his neck, trying not to be embarrassed because I knew what he would feel there. He ran his fingers between my legs, and I shivered. 'Already wet for me?' he rumbled.

'Mm-hmm.'

'How long have you been wet, ready and waiting?'

I whispered, 'Since we were at the park, listening to the band.'

'This whole time?' He pulled his head back for a moment, pinning me with those dark eyes. 'You've been waiting so patiently! I'll have to reward you.'

I pushed myself against his hand, and moaned as his fingers stroked just the right spot.

'Will you use your cuffs on me?' I asked cheekily. My blood was humming beneath my skin from the strength of the dominant energy he emanated.

He chuckled. 'I don't need to.' He grabbed both my wrists and pinned them above my head. 'There you go. Now you're all mine.'

I pulled him close against me with my thighs, and gasped, 'Only if you're all mine, too.'

14
Scott

Walking out of Addie's place the next morning, I finally allowed myself to open the piece of paper someone had handed me last night when I went to get water for Addie and Charlie.

A younger guy had walked up and stood next to me in the line. I immediately smelled that they were a lyko I didn't know, so I just eyed them up and down, not trying to hide my wariness. They had a buzz cut. It was a haircut a lot of lykos used when they first began turning, because for that first year or so after turning, our hair grew thick and fast. So they were young, and freshly turned.

They didn't speak, so I grunted, 'What?'

'Grendel wants to talk to you.' Their voice didn't shake, but I could see them pressing their thumb against their fingers, a nervous tic.

My eyes narrowed. 'So he can talk. What's he doing sending me a carrier pigeon?'

The lyko made a frustrated, scared sound in the back of their throat. I understood what they feeling. They knew I was the alpha of my pack; they knew I didn't need to listen to them if I didn't want to. Eventually, they just stuck out their hand.

I stared at it for a second, then realised they were clutching a piece of paper in their fist. I took it and shoved it into my back jeans pocket, not worrying if it got crumpled.

Now, sitting in my car outside Addie's place, I pulled it back up and smoothed it out on the dashboard.

You've had your final warning. Now I call for a blood challenge. Face me. And when I kill you, I'll run your pack out of town, and I'll run this whole damn city.

I swore.

Then I sighed and started the engine. This was going to be a real problem. I needed to gather the pack and get some more intel before we acted on this.

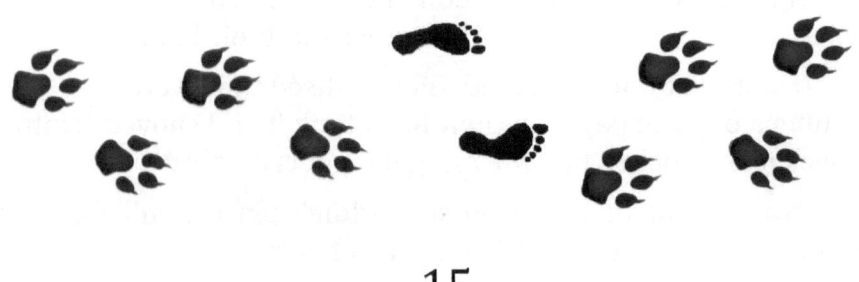

15

Addie

To keep me safe from Grendel's pack, Scott invited me to hang out with him and his pack that weekend.

'With us, you can hide in plain sight,' he said.

We went to the beach for a bonfire night with the pack, and my heart was thrilled at the way he stuck by me, protective of me.

Finally, a friend approached us that I already knew. 'Vicki!' I turned to Scott in shock, realising what it meant that she was here with all of them. 'Vicki's in the pack, too?'

'You bet,' she said easily. 'Good to see you, Addie.'

She sat on a dune next to another of the female lykos, and slid her hand into their back pocket. The woman smiled up at her, white teeth gleaming against her dark skin and hair, and leaned in to kiss Vicki deeply.

I looked away shyly. I hadn't known Vicki was a werewolf; I hadn't known she was into women; what else didn't I know? I prided myself on knowing everything about everything, and now I realised I knew nothing at all.

After a while, Scott lifted something out of his back pocket and held it up. 'I forgot to tell you yesterday, I found this. Thought you might want it back.'

It was my Dara Knot pendant.

All my breath left me in a rush. 'Oh my gosh, thank you! I was wrecked when I lost it. It's just really precious to me and Elle – my sister.' I rose onto my tiptoes to kiss his cheek. 'Thank you.'

'Shall I?' He gestured, indicating he could put it on for me.

I nodded, eager to have it around my neck again, back where it belonged.

He moved behind me and lowered the necklace around my throat. His fingers on my neck made me tingle. Then he ran his fingers over the necklace chain, laying it flat against my collarbone, my chest… His fingers ran past the pendant and down between my breasts, and I trembled, my core tightening. Suddenly, it was hard to breathe. He didn't seem bothered that other people could see us in this intimate moment. He was sending a pretty clear message to anyone watching.

Just then a volleyball hit me in the foot. 'Ow!' I caught it and looked up.

Lee was standing near us, all his weight on one hip. 'Come on, enough standing around already! Give you a game?'

'All right!' I was always up for a challenge, and beach volleyball sounded like fun. And I'd worn my contacts for the beach, so I didn't need to worry about breaking my glasses if any balls went flying. *Volleyball or otherwise.*

I joined the team playing against Lee's, because of course I would. Our rivalry seemed to please the other pack members – they played into it and pit us against each other. The lykos were all a match for each other, and I did okay, even if I was obviously not as strong or fast as the rest of them.

When we lost to Lee's team, I pouted and headed back to where Scott was sitting in the dunes with a couple of the others. I nudged my way into his lap rather than just sit in the sand next to him. He let me, smiling.

'Can you believe he beat me!'

He shook his head good-naturedly. 'Totally shocked.'

Vicki joked, 'He probably cheated.'

'Right,' said Scott. 'Because without cheating, he only has the advantage on you in size, speed, strength—'

'All right, all right!' I dug an elbow into his ribs. 'Rub it in, why don't you?'

He ran a sympathetic hand up my back, and I leaned into it.

The female Vicki had been kissing smiled over at me. 'Hi. I'm Radhika. Ray for short.'

I waved. 'Adrienne. Nice to meet you.'

'Beautiful day for it,' she said.

'Definitely the right day for it,' Scott agreed.

'What could possibly be the wrong day?' I asked. The beach was gorgeous.

Scott shrugged. 'Sorry, I guess I see all the rough days. Ten-year drought in this area, then a flood up to the roof of most houses the next year, then bushfire after bushfire. Those were hard times to be here, seeing everything all black and red.'

I made a regretful noise. 'And you all were out in it, I guess, looking for people?'

'Gotta be done. I told you we don't feel the heat or cold, right? But still, that was a long week. The crisis is the easy part, in some ways. It's usually over quickly, for better or worse. It's getting everyone back on their feet afterwards that's the real challenge.'

'Give it a rest, Scott,' said Vicki. 'We're off the clock, don't be a downer.'

We laughed, and the conversation moved on. Ray was in some trouble with her landlord for having a small dog at her apartment without getting formal approval first. Technically, the law in our state was that landlords couldn't refuse a request to have a small dog or cat.

'Definitely sucks,' I said. I started asking questions about the case.

But it sounded like Ray had asked for permission, and the landlord had just ghosted her. So I offered, 'I could probably help you with that.'

Ray looked surprised but genuinely excited. 'You'd really do that?'

'Of course,' I said. 'You're a friend of Scott's, and they haven't treated you fairly. I can't represent you in my role, but I could help you prepare a submission and file it with the court.'

We exchanged numbers, and I went back to watching the ocean. I could feel Scott's approval like a warmth radiating from him, and I basked in it. I was glad it made him happy that I could help one of his pack.

The rhythmic stroke of his fingers on the bare skin of my back was relaxing and enticing at once, and I found myself just watching the others laughing together instead of trying to join in the conversation. It was like being in a dream – a wonderful, sexy dream...

I was completely captivated, caught up in his touch, drenched in his smell. Hypnotised by the timbre of his voice rumbling through his chest and into me. He seemed so intuitive that I was sure he must know how much he was turning me on, how I couldn't *think* with the way he was touching me. And I didn't want to think.

He looked down at me, caught my eye, and gave me a small, knowing smile.

After a bit, Vicki and Ray stood up. Vicki winked at me as they walked away.

I wondered if I should be embarrassed that they'd seen how much I was enjoying myself physically, but I'd already seen them making out. So when Scott locked his arms around me, turning me in his lap so we could make out easier, I couldn't find it in me to feel embarrassed. Instead, I leaned into him, enjoying his heat.

He tugged on my elbow and I lifted my face to his so he could run his nose along mine. I inhaled deeply, dragging his smoky scent into me, lost in the feel of him.

Eventually, I almost forgot there were other people around at all. I slid my hands under the back of his shirt and ran my fingers around his ribs to his abs. He smiled slowly and kissed under my jaw.

He lifted me to straddle him, and my thighs squeezed around him. He ran his hands up my calves, over my knee, and up the underside of my thighs. I gasped into his mouth. His fingers skimmed the hems of my shorts, and my skin lit up under his touch.

He gripped my hair and tilted my head to kiss my mouth deeper. There was something hot about how confidently he held me, touched me – gently but firmly – and every move was turning me on more. I could feel his hardness growing, too, so it wasn't just affecting me.

I kissed his cheekbone, then his jaw, before kissing his mouth again. 'You feel so good.' I melted into his hold.

'I like having you this close,' he murmured against my earlobe. 'I'd like to keep you here a good long while.'

I was surprised how much I wanted that, too. Was it too soon to be feeling so much? To be feeling so certain about him, and not just physically? I couldn't help the doubt that was rising up, not because I doubted it, but because this felt so right. Being with him felt so good.

He was older than me. Was I just hung up on him because he was more worldly, more experienced, and a powerful person in my line of work?

But he was good at communicating. Since I'd found out he was a werewolf, he'd told me everything I wanted to know, and some things I hadn't asked about, some things that I didn't really want to know but needed to know.

He was reliable. When he said he would call, he called. He showed up where he said he would. And at work, he was one of the people that I trusted the most, and one of the most respected people in the precinct, for good reason.

And as I'd already established, he was sexy as hell.

His lips travelled to the top of my shoulder, then the strap of my bra.

Something very like a moan of pleasure escaped me, and I squirmed. I needed a break or I was going to push him down right there in the sand and lie my body on top of his. And even if he didn't mind getting that frisky in public, I did. I stood and shook myself a bit, catching my breath.

He just smiled up at me.

I ran my hands through my messed-up hair, and wandered back over to the volleyball game.

'Had enough lazing about?' Lee teased.

'I thought you looked like you needed some help,' I said. Then I walked right over to join the opposite team again, and stuck my tongue out at him.

He shook his head and laughed.

I had fun playing with the pack again, but I was a little unnerved that I could go right back to hanging out with Lee right after practically straddling Scott in public just a few metres away.

When I spiked the ball right at Lee's head, he dodged and said, 'Right, that's it! Game over!' He ran around the net, clearly intent on tackling me, a big grin on his face.

I squealed and ran for it, dodging the other players as they laughed. I headed for the water.

Just like the night of our drunken bridge race, he was too fast for me, and his hands went around my waist and lifted me right up in the air. I dangled for a second, screaming and laughing at the same time, before he threw me in the water. I'd had enough warning to brace myself and hold my breath, so I tumbled through the water for a second. When I felt the sand, I pushed off with my feet and broke the surface. I gasped for air, swiping salt water out of my eyes.

Most of the pack were watching, waiting to see if I would be angry.

I ignored them and pointed at Lee. 'Dead man walking!' I shouted and started splashing towards him.

Lee pranced away backwards, laughing.

We were halfway up the beach when someone ran up beside me and grabbed my arm. It threw me off balance, and I staggered back, thinking it was just another pack member joining in our game.

It was Grendel.

I froze, and he tackled me to the ground. I hit the sand hard, landing on my back. All the breath *whooshed* out of me, and I could only stare up at him for a moment as he sneered down at me.

'Hello, Red.' He wrapped one hand around my throat. 'Told ya I'd be back.'

One word escaped me. 'Fuck.'

His grin was inhuman. 'If you want.'

I shuddered in horror.

That's when Lee hit from the side in wolf form, ripping Grendel off of me in a flying mess of black fur and claws. I scrambled to my feet while they faced off, man against wolf, both of them teeth bared and snarling. Lee snapped at his arm, and Grendel punched the side of Lee's wolf head.

Lee staggered sideways for less than a second, but it was all Grendel needed to run out of his reach.

There was the howl of humans and wolves from around us – the lykos Grendel had stolen from other packs. Our pack and theirs crashed together in various forms.

'You don't need to fight!' one of the strange lykos said. 'He only wants her.'

Scott grabbed my hand and ran for it, pulling me with him.

'You can run, but you can't hide her forever!' Grendel yelled after us. 'And if any of you feel like a new leader, you know where to find me.'

When I looked back, I froze as I saw Lee haul off and snap the neck of one of the strange lykos in human form. He turned to the next one, who was in wolf form. Morphing into wolf form himself, Lee ripped at their throat with his teeth.

When he turned to a third one, I made a strangled cry – a wordless plea to stop. These guys weren't monsters, even if Grendel was crazy. You don't kill someone just because you disagree with their leader, especially if they were just tagging along because they were young and stupid. Sure, they'd attacked first, but surely there was something we could do to get them to back down, to spare them.

Lee heard me and turned. He saw me watching and stopped short. His tail fell between his legs.

The tide had turned, and Grendel and his strange pack fled, bleeding and unsuccessful.

Shifting to human form, Lee shouted, 'Why did you stop me?'

'They didn't deserve to die,' I snapped. 'You'll thank me later.'

'Not bloody likely,' he growled, and walked off.

'Are you okay, Adrienne?' Scott asked me.

I shrugged. 'No. No, I'm not okay.'

I could feel tears welling up. My limbs were starting to feel heavy and shaky, with the shock and fear of the attack. Between that and the horrible, sinking feeling of guilt that this was all my fault, I was starting to feel sick in my stomach. I tried to say something else, and my lip wobbled.

Scott pulled me into his arms, wrapping me in his warmth.

Vicki came close enough to pat me on the arm. 'Don't worry, Adrienne,' she said grimly. 'We'll take care of that dickhead for ya.'

16

Lee

As we left the beach and walked through the carpark, Scott pulled me aside.

'I want you on Addie's protection detail,' he said. 'She can stay at your place, safe-house style. I'll drop in on her when I can during the day, while you and Gal are out working, and I'll make sure your roster has you off nights for the week. That way we can have someone on her detail 24/7. She might not like it, but I think it's the best way to keep her safe until we catch the feral and end this. Reckon you can handle it?'

I gave him a mock-offended look. 'Of course! Can *she* handle all of *this*, is the question?' I gestured to myself.

Scott punched me in the arm, not bothering to hold back. 'Piss off, that's my girl you're talking about!'

'All right, all right.' He still looked worried, so I added, 'She'll be fine, man. She's handled herself pretty well so far, even though it's been a shit-show.'

'Promise me, no matter what happens, you'll protect her.'

I was really surprised he was taking this so seriously, but Scott never said things he didn't mean. So I said, 'Of course, man. I promise.'

I wondered if I would eventually regret that promise. Keeping this chick safe from danger was a full-time job so far. But I liked her, and she had a good sense of humour. And she was damn fine to look at, although I tried not to think about that when Scott was around.

Maybe being on babysitter duty wouldn't be all bad.

And it was Scott asking me. I would have burned the world down for that man, that's how much I loved him.

As I walked up to Addie, Gal raced past me and pushed her snout right between Addie's legs. I hooked Gal's collar with one finger to pull her out of the way. Addie just laughed, thank goodness.

'Come on girl, in ya hop,' I said firmly.

Gal leaped straight into her sidecar and sat up while I clipped her collar into its special bike harness. From there, she watched us keenly like a self-appointed parking inspector.

Addie stared down at the spare helmet I handed her, looking uncertain. 'You were going to kill that guy, weren't you?'

'Absolutely.' No point lying. I don't believe in telling little white lies. I have to live in integrity. I know I'm not a good person, but if I don't say what I mean and do what I say, then I'm the person who ends up in trouble. I take care of me, and I take care of Scott, and I take care of the pack, and I do it without glossing over the hard truth of who and what I am.

She put her hands on those generous hips of hers. 'And you don't see a problem with that?'

'I stopped them from hurting you. Or anyone in the pack. And you made me let them go.' *Surely she can't argue with that.*

'It's the *way* you were stopping them that I have an issue with.'

'You're very argumentative, aren't you, counsellor?'

She rolls her eyes. 'It's literally my job.'

'You don't get it. It's a lyko thing. They attacked; we had to subdue them. Physically. And we did.'

'So how can I trust you?'

I scoffed and put on my own helmet. 'Never trust anyone, Address! You should know better than that.'

She nodded slowly. 'But am I going to be safe with you?'

'Yes,' I said firmly, without hesitation.

'Fine, then.' She handed me her sunnies so she could put her helmet on, then put her hand out for the sunglasses again.

I thought about keeping hold of them for a moment, just for a joke.

She shifted her weight to one side, and put her fists up, pretending she was ready to fight.

I laughed and surrendered.

Driving with Addie was torture. Her arms were wrapped around my waist from behind, her thighs clenched on either side of me, her soft front pressed against the hard plane of my back. Within a minute, I was hard and aching, and I was sweating trying to hide it from her. I shifted uncomfortably in my seat, trying not to change the centre of gravity as we rode.

I'd made it very clear we weren't going back to her place to get anything, since the feral knew where she lived. Girl was pretty blind without her specs, so I would have to go around there tomorrow to get her glasses for work. She called me an over-protective jerk about it, but I knew I was right.

'But I need more than just my glasses,' she said. 'Can we just stop at a servo for some emergency supplies?'

I gave in. 'Okay, fine!'

At the petrol station near my place, she browsed the tiny racks and picked up a bunch of chick stuff, like deodorant, hairbrush, make-up remover wipes, a razor. They even had phone chargers. By the time she had everything, her arms were full and she was doing some hard-core juggling to avoid dropping the lot.

'You know, believe it or not, I've actually got toothpaste and a razor?' I said, coming up behind her.

She nearly jumped. 'Geez, you're so quiet. I always forget how quiet you are. Anyway, your man razor is probably designed for man faces. I like the five-blade – gets a nice, close shave.'

That made me look at her legs – those lovely, thick thighs and curvy calves, and the delicate lines of her ankle. I raked my gaze back up, and a flush began lighting up her skin. God, she was beautiful when she blushed. 'I'll get this,' I said, and grabbed the lot out of her arms. 'Meet you at the bike.'

'Oh, okay, are you sure?'

I jerked my head to the door. *Let's just get out of here already. Enough shopping.*

'Okay, thanks.'

Waiting at the check-out, I checked out her ass as she slid on her sunnies and walked out to my bike, highlighted by the setting sun. *Fuck.* Thoughts like that were just plain unhelpful. I paid as quickly as I can, but I still saw some of what happened next.

Some older, overweight guy was walking around the Yamaha. Addie slowed, clearly not wanting to get too close.

The guy eyed her. 'This your bike, sweetheart?'

She stiffened. Everyone knows a guy who starts a sentence to a stranger with *that* look and says anything at all is thinking only one thing: 'fresh meat'. Addie turned to go straight back into the service station, but the guy's fat fingers grabbed her arm.

That did it. I grabbed the stuff, and leaped out of the servo. It took effort to manage to stay in human form, and I crashed into the guy, ripping his hand off Addie's arm.

There was a sick smack of flesh on concrete as I hauled the guy up against the wall, holding him by the throat. The guy was literally dangling, feet in the air, choking, his eyes getting wider and wider.

I snarled, a low, rumbling growl. With teeth.

'Lee!' Addie gasped my name.

My eyes snapped to her, seeing her shocked expression. I tried to decide whether killing this douchebag would be worth the satisfaction if it meant Addie looked at me with fear in her eyes. No, it wouldn't. So I opened my fist, dropping the guy like a rock. The guy sagged onto the concrete, then scrambled to his feet. He ran to one of the cars without looking back, snivelling in fear.

'Thanks,' Addie was saying. 'Not sure that was reeeally necessary, but—'

'Not necessary?' I snapped. 'Didn't we *just* have this conversation five minutes ago? I know you know how lucky you just got!'

'I had it handled,' she protested.

'He was handling you!' I stalked past her and bent to pick up the bag of supplies I just bought for her. Hopefully none of it was breakable, since I'd dropped it on the ground as soon as I got near the guy. 'You're a magnet for trouble.' I popped the seat of my bike open and shoved the bag inside. Hard. 'Get on the bike,' I ordered.

I filled the words with just a tap of lyko power. I wondered if the feeling would zip through her, like it did when Scott asked me to do something. I couldn't compel her to do anything she didn't want to do. I just wanted to get her back to my place, where I knew she would be safe.

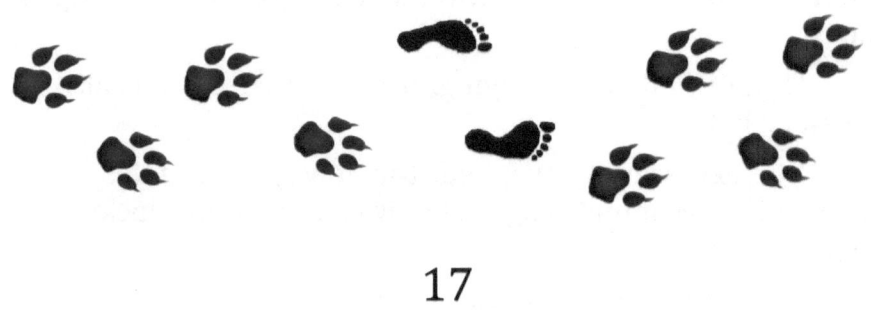

17

Addie

At the door to Lee's apartment, Gal ran in ahead of us, her tongue lolling out happily. She *whuffed* and pranced back far enough for us to get in, then began sniffing around the kitchen for food.

I put my bag on the living room floor and looked around while Lee put out a bowl of kibble for her. He had a big, open-plan living room and kitchen area. Almost no furniture, just a long, saggy couch, and two bar stools against the kitchen bench. I'd have to find space on the kitchen bench for my work laptop, since Scott said I should plan to work from here as much as I could until they cleaned up Grendel and his pack.

Down the short hallway, there was a bathroom with a weird-looking door, and one bedroom, which I snuck my head into for just a moment. A queen-sized bed with lots of big cushions but no blankets. He wouldn't need them, I realised, being as warm-blooded as werewolves seemed to be.

He saw where I was looking. 'I'll sleep on the couch. Unless you want to share?' He winked.

I laughed easily. 'Nah, it's your place, and I'll be happy on the couch. Thanks.'

He shrugged. 'Up to you.'

Having a safehouse and a bodyguard felt special and painful at the same time. No one ever had been around long enough to protect me from the evils of the world; even my dad had been absent for most of my waking hours, walking the city streets far from our home. And now I knew I wasn't even safe in the one arena where I'd become strong enough to put on my armour and take up a sword: the courtroom. I'd been fighting to make sure misguided people were redirected and truly dangerous creatures were secured behind bars – and now I was in danger because of it.

But Scott and Lee… I had a feeling both of them would do anything and everything they could to keep me safe. For whatever reason, I mattered to them.

Suddenly, I felt the urge to cry, overwhelmed with both gratitude and fear. I pressed a hand over my mouth and sat on the couch. I cleared my throat, forced down the tears, and began unpacking my plastic bag of stuff from the servo.

'I'm going to UberEats us some Chinese,' Lee said.

'Yeah, great. Let me know your email, and I'll PayPal you my share.'

Lee crashed next to me on the couch, heating me up along one side where his elbow and knee bumped against mine. We sorted out dinner, then Lee got a look on his face.

'What are you thinking?' I asked.

'What was your plan?' he said bluntly. 'Back there, at the servo. If I hadn't got there in time, what would you have done?'

I blinked, surprised, but I had an easy answer. 'Well, I would've either used my dad's self-defence lessons – rip my arm free and then run back inside – or I could've tried hitting the guy in the nose, get him to let go.' I shrugged. 'I probably would've just run, though. I'm not 100% confident that I would've been strong enough or fast enough to land a hit on him. And if he pressed charges, it would be my word against his that it was self-defence.'

Lee nodded slowly. 'Good. You might've got out of that situation all right. But if you want to learn some more tricks, I can show you.'

'Like self-defence?'

'Like getting out of any hold they can throw at you, then beating the ever-loving shit out of the guy.'

He wanted to train a cop's daughter in self-defence? I nearly laughed. But given how my day had been going, between the werewolves and the usual predators of this world, maybe I could use as much help as I could get. I nodded.

He stood and gestured for me to get up, too.

'You already know how to break a simple hold, when you have a hand free, and you can see your attacker. What about if the attacker comes at you from behind?' He spun behind me faster than I could move, and wrapped his muscles around me, pinning my arms to my sides. He was so fast!

So I ran him through the techniques my dad had trained me in, throwing in the principles he'd taken pains to instil in me.

- Run first, if you can.

- If they grab you and pull, you push towards them, which they won't be expecting, and then rip away.

- Always keep your eyes open, especially during a fight.

- Guard your head before anything else.

- Scream like your life depends on it, just in case there are any wannabe heroes nearby. There usually won't be, though, so you need to be prepared for that.

- Use the heel of your palm to strike, rather than punching with a fist, which risks breaking your fingers if you're out of practice.

- Aim for weak points that give you more time to run: eyes, nose, solar plexus, groin, toes, jaw.

- Always wear a few rings with stones you could use to scratch an attacker's face.

- Incapacitating points to hit if it's life or death: throat and temple.

- If you fall down on your back, kick upwards, then get up and run again.

Lee wanted to add to that last one. 'If you're pinned down, you can use your fingernails – depends on the angle.' He took my hand and slid my fingers around under his ribs. 'Here, I'll show you. Hop back on the couch again.'

I tried to breathe normally and not think about the fact that my whole body was tingling because I was getting horizontal on the couch with a hot guy.

'Not quite there.' He dug his fingers under my ribs to demonstrate, and I gasped. 'Here, but harder, obviously.'

It didn't hurt, exactly – he was being gentle with me – but it made my body squirm under his, trying to get away.

He grinned wickedly. 'Oh, ticklish?'

Danger! Danger! I didn't answer, and instead I jammed my hand like a knife up under his ribs.

He grunted in pained surprise.

Satisfied, I asked, 'What if you didn't have your hands free, though?'

He grabbed both my hands and dragged them up over my head, pinning them to the fabric of the sofa with one hand.

My mouth dropped open.

'Now you have a problem,' he said slowly. 'They have a hand free and you don't. If you don't stop them, they can do whatever they want.' He wiggled his fingers at me, then pulled my shirt up an inch and tickled my tummy.

'Leeeee!' I screeched.

He tickled me until I couldn't breathe, wriggling under his weight, not letting me go. Finally, he stopped and sat up, and I sagged in relief.

I let him see the absolute fury in my eyes.

'What do you do now?' he asked, his eyes flashing at the challenge.

'I don't know, it's easier when someone's not *tickling* you,' I ground out. 'Dickhead.'

'Sure, sure.' He lowered himself again, keeping his weight off me this time. That didn't change the fact that his whole body was pressed against mine, his hips pinning me, one of his legs between mine. 'Show me.'

'Knee to the groin.' I demonstrated, without any force. 'Bite something, anything.'

'Yep, you could bite the shoulder. Bite the neck or the ear, even.' He brushed my hair aside with his free hand, and I gulped. He trailed his fingertips from behind my ear, all the way down my throat to my collarbone. 'All of this flesh is so, so weak. Your attacker is vulnerable anywhere along here.'

'Right. Okay.' I was blushing from head to toe, I just knew it. Honestly? Lee giving self-defence lessons was hot as fuck. 'Well, uh, great lesson.' I shoved his chest a bit. 'Let me up, dude.'

He rolled us so I was on top. Then before I could move off him, he sat up, so we were pressed against each other, and I was straddling his lap.

'Umm,' I stammered.

His eyes widened; he seemed as surprised to find us in this position as I did. At first, he didn't move. Then he tilted his head just a fraction, bringing our mouths just an inch apart. I could feel his breath stirring the air against my cheek.

I was barely breathing. If I moved, we would kiss, I just knew it. I could feel him hard beneath me. I had to admit, it made me feel better that this was turning him on as much as it was me. But we weren't supposed to be turning each other on.

You're with Scott, remember?

'Shower!' I yelped. 'I'm gonna go shower.' I started untangling us, pushing myself up to standing.

He let me slide out without saying anything.

I eyed Lee's shower critically, and ran a hand through my hair. Then I looked back at the bathroom door again, groaning. It was one of those swinging ones like you get in restaurant kitchens, where you can swing it open from either side.

Whoever designed this place was really fucking weird.

Or they didn't always have opposable thumbs…

I pushed the door open and stuck my head out. Lee was in the kitchen, putting stuff in the dishwasher.

'Dude, your shower doesn't have a shower curtain,' I called. 'And your bathroom door doesn't lock!'

'Bit hard to manage that kind of thing when I'm furry,' he called back.

I tossed my hands in the air, frustrated. 'Well, that's just—'

'But don't worry, it's all clean. It doesn't get used much. Remember, I told you we don't like baths.'

I laughed in spite of myself. Well, if I didn't want to spend the next day with the stink of Grendel's BO on me, I was just going to have to get over it. 'Okay, well, don't come in!'

I heard Lee laughing as I let the bathroom door swing shut behind me. The back-swing nearly whacked me in the butt when I didn't get out of the way fast enough.

At least the exhaust fan worked, so my glasses wouldn't get all fogged up sitting on the edge of the sink.

Showering while knowing that he could hear me – and basically see me as well, if the door swung at the right angle – was a really weird sensation. I felt vulnerable, not wanting to be seen, and I tried not to think about it, but some tiny part in the back of my brain wanted to imagine him coming in. Maybe even watching… Or helping… It was a strange kind of thrill.

Once I got over the idea that he could hear me showering, it was almost comforting, knowing that he was out there. Like he was keeping me safe while I was naked and at my most vulnerable. Which I knew didn't totally make sense. But then again, not much had made sense since I'd found out werewolves were real.

I put on my moisturiser but no makeup. With my pale complexion and red hair, I usually always wore at least some mascara around other people, so that I didn't look like a flushed ghost with no eyelashes or eyebrows. But Lee was a friend. *Right?* So I didn't need to be all fancy around him.

When I opened the bathroom door again, Lee said without looking, 'I put some sheets and a pillow on the couch, but let me know if you need anything else.'

'Great, thanks.' I came out in the clothes he'd given me for pyjamas – again, because he hadn't let me get my own from home. His T-shirt was big on me, which honestly felt comfy as – and it was so soft it must be made of bamboo. It even smelled like him, like sunshine. And there was a pair of cotton bike shorts that almost fit. I walked through the living room so I could put my dirty clothes in his washer-dryer overnight. I'd decided I wanted to have my own clean undies again in the morning, at least.

He was saying, 'I don't really get cold, so I don't have a lot of blankets…' He trailed off, and I felt his eyes on me. I couldn't help but look back over my shoulder.

His eyes raked up and down me, then met mine. My whole body heated, as if I'd walked into a sauna. The air crackled with tension between us.

He smiled slowly, wickedly, and said, 'Chinese should be here soon.'

'That's great,' I squeaked, and ran into the laundry alcove. I chucked my clothes in, then leaned on the machine, trying to get my breathing under control.

Get it together! You're with his friend! He's just supposed to be your bodyguard, not a … hot distraction.

I put the clothes on for the half-load cycle and shook my hands out, bracing myself for another round of nerves.

When I came back out, Lee was sitting on the couch with two Nintendo Switch controllers. He waved one at me, and I spied a tattoo sneaking out of his T-shirt. 'Race you?'

'Oh, not this again!' I threw myself onto the couch and curled up next to him, close to his warmth. 'It's definitely my turn to win by now.'

We Mario Karted our way around a few courses, trading trash talk and red shells. At some point, the food arrived, and we took a break to eat.

'So what's your tattoo?' I asked in between mouthfuls of honey chicken and steamed vegetables.

'Which one?'

I poked one finger at the dark marks stretching out from under his sleeve and down his bicep.

'Oh, the wolf.' He pulled his sleeve up over his shoulder muscle, revealing a dark etching of a wolf silhouetted against the moon, howling. 'Got it at my twenty-first. One of my mates did it for me. They were an apprentice then; they've got their own tattoo studio now.'

'It's gorgeous.' I regretted the choice of words immediately, because it brought his gaze up to meet mine, our eyes locked, and I couldn't look away. I licked my lips, and his eyes dropped to my mouth.

He looked away. 'Halo?'

'I've never played that one before.'

'It's easy, you'll pick it up.'

'Okay, sure.' I clapped my hands, trying to break the tension with a different kind of excitement.

He showed me which buttons to use, and rattled off a great number of words about characters – the Chief, Cortana, and Spartans… I glazed over and started spamming the buttons.

Eventually, I scowled. 'This is hard. I can't keep it straight how you do anything! Like what button does what… Which is ridiculous. I have a law degree. I remember everything I need for work, plus a bunch of random legal crap I had to learn at law school but I'll never need.'

He shot something he'd told me was a 'high value target'. 'Yeah? Like what?'

I ran behind a building, something shot me, and I disappeared in a red mist. I sighed. 'Like, you can get sued for private nuisance if Gal was barking after 10pm or before 7am. But only in our city, because of the by-laws. Move to another city, the noise curfew changes.'

'Gal would never. She's a good girl.'

Gal heard her name and leaped into my lap. She stuck her nose in my face and gave me a sniff – of course – and I roughed her up a bit until her tail was wagging with almost hysterical happiness levels.

When she hopped off, I said, 'And there's other random stuff stored in my brain for no reason, too. Like ants always fall onto their right-hand side – or right-legged side, I guess – when they're drunk.'

'Why do you know that?'

'Dunno, *World Around Us*, probably. Anyway, I think I'm done gaming for the night, thanks.' I yawned and rubbed my eyes.

Lee went to the fridge and came back with two bowls of frozen cookies-and-cream, and two beers. He offered me one, and I tried not to brush his hand as I took it. Gal curled up on her doggie bed and appeared to go to sleep, twitching her ears and nose every now and then. Dreaming of catching criminals, probably.

In between bites of ice cream, I noticed how late it had gotten. 'So you're a night owl, huh?' I said.

He nodded. 'Most lykos are. But I do my best to be awake during the day because Gal and I do a lot of afternoon-evening shifts. Sometimes we'll track something way into the night, which is fine for me, but not great for Gal. But those first few hours of scent, you gotta catch it while it's hot.'

'Yeah, not much you can do about that, I guess.'

He nudged me with an elbow. 'And you?'

'I have really long work hours at the moment, but I'm hoping it'll ease off in my second year, when I'm more used to this job and I can get the paperwork done faster. These days, I'm just like, eh, I catch up on sleep on the weekends. Except for when I have to work the weekend.'

'Oof! That's rough.'

I shrugged. 'It is what it is.'

He frowned. 'Life's what you make of it. You could get out, if you wanted.'

'I don't know. After being dealt a bunch of rubbish hands in a row, I'm not sure you can fix a broken life, even if you want to.'

'Well, shit. I've done a lot of things I'm not proud of, does that mean my life is broken? Should I just be miserable for the rest of my life now?'

'That's not what I meant,' I protested.

'You shoulda met me ten years ago,' he said ruefully. 'Maybe you woulda liked me better.'

'Oh, come on. You're just fine now,' I said. I'm pretty sure I meant it like a friend, but Lee's eyes caught mine when I said that, and it became hard to breathe again.

He grinned. Seemed like he always had a grin ready and waiting, just below the surface. 'Thanks. You're "just fine", too.' He caught a lock of my curls and twirled it around, brushing past my neck with the backs of his fingers. 'You're funny … take good care of your friends … don't take any shit from anyone … and you're smokin' hot.'

Ohmigod. 'Th-thanks.' I cleared my throat, all confidence gone. What was it about this guy that made me want to jump him and run away from him at once? Could I blame it on werewolf vibes? 'Umm, so I'm going to brush my teeth and get to bed, I think.'

He jumped up, muscles flashing. 'Yeah, I'll leave you to it.'

I popped my bowl in the dishwasher and headed to the bathroom. 'Thanks again for letting me crash here.'

'Anytime. Sweet dreams, AstroGirl.' He strode into his bedroom, which didn't have a door.

An hour later, settled into a comfy spot on the couch, I couldn't sleep. I'd taken my meds, brushed my teeth, and my glasses were on the coffee table so I could find them easily in the morning. But Lee was right, he didn't have enough blankets here to keep me warm. And I kept thinking about how he was lying *just over there*, with his body all warm, like a human hot water bottle… A shirtless, inviting, space heater.

I rolled over, trying to find a patch of couch I'd already warmed up, so I could stick my cold feet in that spot. Then I rolled onto my back and let my breath sigh out with frustration.

'I can hear you not sleeping,' he said. 'You wanna come to the bed?'

I startled. 'I'm fine,' I said automatically. *No, I'm not, why did I say that?* I rolled back onto my side.

'You sound uncomfortable,' he said. 'But you know, up to you. I might just put in earplugs, so I don't hear you thrashing around over there.'

I sat up, indignant. 'I'm not thrashing around! I'm barely moving! Anyway, it's cold in here!'

I saw him sit up, too. He patted the bed beside him. 'Come on, Apricot. It's late. Just get over here already.'

I gave in. What was the point of fighting? I was cold, he was warm – it was an easy fix.

'Fine,' I muttered, not at all graciously. I tugged my blanket around my shoulders and dragged my pillow over to the free side of his bed, not bothering to bring my glasses with me. It was dark; I wouldn't be able to see anything with them on, anyway. 'Thank you.'

I shuffled into the bed, as close to his delicious warmth as I dared without actually touching him.

After a moment, Lee rolled over and put his hand on my arm. My heartbeat started tap-dancing, until he said, 'Hey, let's spoon.'

'*Whaaat?*' I tried not to screech.

'It'll help us relax. Co-regulation, you know? Two nervous systems relaxing each other. Fall asleep faster.'

'Oh.' That actually did make a bit of sense. Still sounded like boy talk for 'I'm horny', though.

'Your necklace isn't silver, right?' he checked. 'I don't wanna burn myself in the middle of the night.'

'Why would you be touching my necklace? Whatever, no, it's white gold.'

'Okay, good. How 'bout this?' He shook his shoulders, and morphed into a dark, black wolf. Within a second, there was a lot of his very soft, very warm fur rubbing up against my body. He was just as big as a wolf as he was as a human, taking up most of the bed. He stuck his tongue out, panting, and rested his chin on my shoulder, as if to say, *Happy now?*

I tried not to freak out, so I could think it through. It was dangerous, giving in to him. Every time I gave an inch, he took a mile. But at least as a wolf, he couldn't do anything that would get me in trouble with Scott. And he was warm. So warm. It was purely a practical decision.

Think of him as a big dog. You can let a dog in the bed, right? No big deal. And he doesn't even smell as much as a dog would.

'Okay, thanks,' I sighed.

He yipped, happy, and plopped down, half on me, one paw stretched out over my arm, his tail curled over my knee. I shoved him over a bit, so I could roll onto my side against him, becoming the little spoon. Honestly, even though lying next to a man-sized wolf was the weirdest thing ever, it also felt amazing. I have never been so comfortable in my entire life. My toes began to thaw with his warmth, and my legs relaxed at last.

His warm breath hit the back of my neck. He touched his nose gently to my ear.

'Go to sleep,' I told him. I shoved him back a bit again, but he didn't budge, all heavy muscles and fur.

His chest breathed in and out against my back. Together with the warmth, that motion and sound lulled me very quickly into a deep relaxation.

What had I been so freaked out about?

Whatever it was, it could wait until morning.

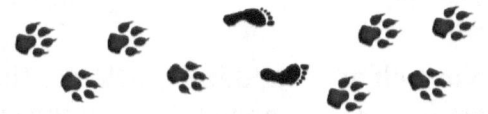

I woke up slowly. I was cuddled against someone. *Lee, right.* He was so warm, and he smelled incredible… I let out a little sigh of contentment, then realised where I was, and that woke me up all the way.

He was in human form again, our legs tangled together. His arm rested over mine, his hand cupping my breast.

Holy shit! Talk about co-regulation. He was getting way too comfortable around me. And as for me… *Holy shit, that feels good.*

I wriggled a little, trying to shift his arm off my boob, but with the movement, I felt a wetness between my legs that had nothing to do with excitement. I groaned with realisation: my period was here. *What perfect timing, as always.*

I didn't want to get out of bed and wake Lee, but the first day of my period was always the heaviest. I needed to put my menstrual cup in now, or we'd have a bloody mess to deal with in about an hour. I shoved his arm off, found my cup in my bag, and went to the bathroom. By the time I got back to the bed, Lee was gone. That was fine by me. I turned the alarm off on my phone so it wouldn't wake me up, and put the pillow over my head.

I stirred again when I heard Lee and Gal leave for their morning run, but I couldn't bring myself to hurry into the day. Unfortunately, my body's demands were insistent. Every part of me was aching, from my head to my belly and legs. I needed water, and painkillers.

Nooo, don't get up.

But I have to.

I swore to myself as I wandered back into the living room to find my glasses. Then I rummaged through the cupboards, looking for painkillers, but I couldn't find anything.

Fucking werewolves, they probably just have fucking healing powers. Fucking human periods. Whose idea was it to give us periods, anyway? Fuck.

Eventually, I remembered I had a spare card of paracetamol in my wallet. I fished it out and downed it with a full glass of water. Good old pharmacy home-brand, coming through in the clutch.

Satisfied, I made a cup of coffee and took it to the couch. Wrapped in a fuzzy throw, I pulled up the journaling app on my phone and started writing. There was a lot to think through. And even if tapping out the words 'werewolf', 'danger', and 'bodyguard' felt insane, it actually did help me feel a bit calmer to record my thoughts about everything that happened this week.

When Lee and Gal trotted back up the stairwell, they found me staring out the window into space. Lee smiled and came straight over, carrying a brown paper bag.

'I brought treats,' he said, handing it to me.

'Hmmm, smells amazing.' I peeked inside, and almost squealed with delight. *Donuts! A girl's best friend.*

'Scooch.' Lee lifted up my legs so he could sit down, then put my legs straight back down again, in his lap.

I tried not to freeze up. Normal friend behaviour. Normal, *friendly* and definitely not at all sexy, behaviour.

Lee sniffed and sat up straighter suddenly, running his hands down my legs. 'You're bleeding. Where are you wounded? What happened?'

I stared at him, then burst out laughing – and once I started, I couldn't stop. He stared at me, then relaxed a little bit, but he was still eyeing me up and down.

'It's my period,' I said plainly. 'Just that time of the month.'

'Oh shit,' he said, startled, then sank back against the couch with a huge sigh of relief. 'Okay, right.'

That threw me into another laughing fit, seeing this big, burly, hunk of a man stumped by the inner biological workings of a woman.

He eyed me side-long. 'Are you … okay? Do you need anything? I've got some tampons in the bathroom drawer in case anyone has an emergency.'

I shook my head, impressed by his thoughtfulness. 'I'm all good for now, but thanks.'

I worked on the couch, trying not to hunch over my laptop, occasionally swearing when the VPN dropped out. The day's work passed in a pain-hazy, exhausted blur.

I took a lunch break for once, and used it to take a nap on the couch. I could have sworn I felt someone brushing my hair out of my face while I slept. It felt really nice, really peaceful and warm and calming.

As the sun dipped into the horizon, I logged off for the day. I leaned back, stretching everything out with a huge groan. Tomorrow would be better, as long as I could get a good night's sleep – the rest of my period was always easier than day one.

'What do you want to eat?' Lee asked, standing in front of the open fridge.

I wandered into the kitchen. 'Anything you have is fine.'

He took me by the shoulders and walked me straight back out of the kitchen. 'Uh-uh. You relax, I'll get this. I can't do anything about woman troubles, but I can make sure your day ends well.'

Tears of gratitude welled up in my eyes. That was normal for me at this time of the month – every emotion was a lot closer to the surface than usual. 'Thank you.'

Eating on stools at the kitchen bench, I kept looking up to see Lee watching me. Eventually, he said lightly, 'So, any dreams about me last night?'

'Lee!' I scolded, slapping his arm. 'If I had any dreams, they would've been about your wolfy snoring.'

He caught my hand, and held it, suddenly mock-serious. 'Addie Bear, come on.'

'Come on what?' I leaned in, not buying it.

'You can't deny you're drawn to me.' He winked. 'I bet you find yourself thinking about me all the time.'

That annoyed me, so I had to shut it down. 'Look, I'm sorry, I can't tell if this is just a little, pretend, competitive thing or if you're actually jealous that I'm with Scott or whatever, but I can't get in the middle of it, Lee. I can't. You need to stop flirting, and looking at me, and…'

'Why, how do I look at you?'

'You know, that eye thing you do.'

'What eye thing?' Lee narrowed his eyes at me, all hot and brooding – exactly what I was talking about.

Annoyed, I said, 'Stop it!'

He gave a big, exaggerated sigh, and tossed his bowl into the kitchen sink. It clattered around but didn't break.

I flinched, even though he hadn't thrown it angrily or anything. I remembered how he and Scott told me an angry, out-of-control lyko can turn into fur and claws in an instant, if provoked. But he didn't make any move towards me.

Instead, he just kept talking. 'You know what, Addie, yeah. I flirt with you. Because I like you. Who cares? I like lots of people. Monogamy's crazy.'

I held a hand over my chest and took a deep breath, trying to calm myself down. 'Please. Listen to the point I'm making. Don't make me regret being your friend.'

He watched me silently, his eyes hard to read. I didn't want to hurt him, but he was hurting me! And I wanted to be clear.

Finally, he shrugged. 'Yeah. Right.'

Trying to pull myself together, I went to lie on the couch for a bit while I waited for the next round of painkillers to kick in. I had never been so confused in all my life. I was mad at Lee and mad at my period, but my pulse was racing from him flirting with me.

I checked my phone, an automatic action. I was shocked to realise I hadn't touched my phone in hours. I'd been so wrapped up with Lee that I hadn't even thought of it.

There was a missed call from Scott, and he'd left a voicemail. My core tightened gently. I couldn't tell if that was because I was happy to hear from him, to know he was thinking of me... Or wracked with guilt, because I was tied up in knots over one of his best friends.

I pushed the big window open, then lay on my stomach on the couch to help with the cramps. The scent of jasmine blooming outside calmed my nerves a little. I hesitated, then hit play on the voicemail icon.

'Adrienne, it's Scott. I've been missing you. Hope you're doing well. If you haven't tried to strangle Lee by now, I'd say it's a total success. Anyway, I was just passing Zeus's where we had the lamb that time, and thinking about all the things I'm going to do when I get to see you again... Hopefully, this should all be wrapped up by the end of the week. No promises, though. Okay, talk to you later, Adrienne.'

I grinned at my phone. I was starting to really fall for this man. Then my smile faded, because there was another man rummaging around in the bathroom right now, and I didn't know what I felt about him.

And even if I did feel something genuine for both of them, I didn't want to mess up their friendship. It really seemed like Lee didn't have many people he could trust, and likewise, Scott seemed to really enjoy having Lee in his life.

Torn, I hit 'play' again, and closed my eyes.

'Adrienne, it's Scott. I've been missing you...'

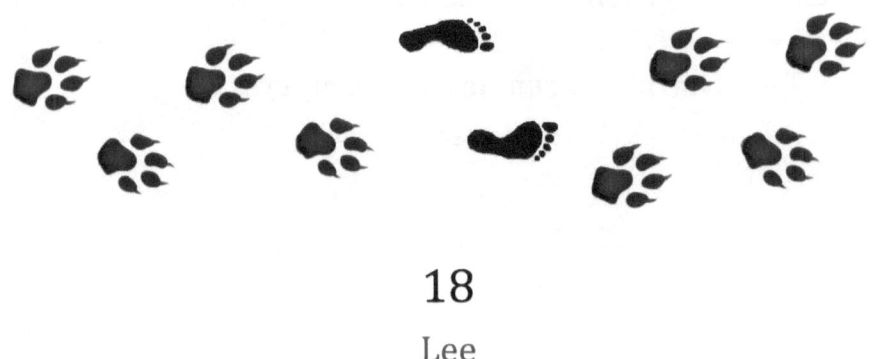

18

Lee

I discovered a few interesting things about Addie over the next couple of days of living together.

She liked to listen to electronic trance music while she worked, but with headphones on so no one but her could hear it. I know because I put her headphones on one time when she stopped typing to take a phone call. She fake-scowled at me and tried to tickle my abs to get me to put it down. Honestly, she was adorable.

But then over dinner, when I put the bluetooth speaker on for a bit while we ate, she stole my phone and switched the track to Taylor Swift's Delicate. I smiled, remembering how we'd bonded over TayTay the first time I'd come to see her at her office.

She was always drinking cups of the chamomile tea I always kept in my cupboard.

She had a rosary that she brought out every morning after breakfast for a few minutes, sitting silent on the couch, her fingers running over the beads.

The first time she did it, I eyed the two medals on the rosary with curiosity. 'Who you praying to over there?'

She answered while her fingers kept moving. 'Saint Teresa, for wisdom to do the next right thing. Aaaand Saint Anthony, patron saint of lost things.' She paused, and grinned at me.

'What's that look about?'

'Oh, nothing.' She stifled a laugh. 'I was just thinking about lost things... Lost boys.'

'Who, me?'

She said, 'I'm Irish – are you really surprised I'm Catholic?'

I was in the kitchen, loading the dishwasher, but I came over and sat on the arm of the couch to stare at her for a minute. 'I'm not *surprised*. You kind of have that vibe, that you might be kind of spiritual. Surprised at the religious thing, though.'

She made a face. 'Did you see me at mass on Sunday? I'm not religious. I'm not even convinced my faith is that strong. Why, you?'

I burst out laughing. 'Fuck no. Don't believe anything anyone says about what's out there. There's no way anyone can know *anything* for certain.'

'Right, exactly. Like, a hundred years ago, nobody knew if it was possible to fly to the moon. Heck, just a few years ago, I had no idea werewolves were a real thing. I thought that was just a *Twilight* fairytale. But—' She lifted the rosary and shrugged. 'This gives me some peace, and I need that. Especially after the week I've had.'

I thought that was promising. If she could be Catholic and not try to change me, I could be happy being friends with her. *Well, friends with benefits, maybe…*

I could tell Scott was getting angsty about being away from her. He hadn't shown up in person to check on her, though, unless he'd done it while I was out on shift with Gal. So since I knew he cared about her, I texted him an update every day. Nothing serious, just random things:

what is it with women and toilet seats?

she showed me how to cook eggs properly, you're one lucky s.o.b.

gal's pissed there's less room on the couch for her now, keeps trying to push me off

By the time we'd been staying together for five days, I was barely keeping it together. She was driving me crazy.

It wasn't that she was working from home. Her papers and laptop and everything were already spread out all over my whole living room by the end of day one, but I liked it.

No, the things that bothered me were less concrete.

Like the way she talked to her coworkers and clients over Zoom – she talked to a person like they were the only one in the world. It made me want to shift and climb my furry weight onto her, pin her there, steal her attention from them.

When speaking to a group, she spoke with all the weight of her expertise, and a wisdom beyond her years. That made me want to roll onto my belly before her and show her my neck in submission, and *that* was crazy. I wouldn't submit to anyone, not even Scott – unless he asked nicely and I wanted to show him how much I respect him as a leader and a friend.

Her personality was adorable. She talked with her hands. She frowned and swore at her computer whenever it didn't load a page quickly enough. Whenever she got anxious, she jumped up from the couch and made endless cups of tea.

She complained endlessly about not being able to go outside the apartment, but she also said a hundred times a day how nice it was to have a great view while she worked.

And she was so fucking sexy. I'd brought a bunch of her clothes and stuff over on that second day, so when she was working, she wore professional office-type clothes. But she always took that off the second she finished her last Zoom call of the day. Every day finished with her only wearing this tiny tank-top-singlet-thing and sleep shorts or her skinny jeans.

That singlet was going to be the death of me: a tight-fitting, white singlet that showed the edges of her bra and the perfect curve of her breasts. Mouth-watering. Made me wonder if she normally wore a bra around home, or if it was just because I was here.

The soft, vanilla scent of her never left my nostrils, even after I pounded the streets for hours with Gal on shift. Her long, curly hair was a curtain of red silk when she unbraided it every night, and it draped around her shoulders and over her chest like a rich, silky scarf. That hair made its way onto my shoulder every night when we curled up together in bed.

And then there was the way she leaned her head on my shoulder when we played video games in the evening. Like she knew she was safe around me, like she knew I wouldn't do anything, even when she got all up in my space.

I'd never had so many cold showers in my whole life. Rubbed one out a few times, but tried to do it quietly so she didn't hear.

I figured we'd both survived the fall-out of our little barney over her being 'taken', when Scott gave me a call.

'We've patrolled the perimeter thoroughly, and there's no sign of movement. No more feral tracks to follow, just dead ends.'

'You think they're gone?' I asked.

'Yeah, as far as we can tell. It should be safe for you to take her home.'

Dropping her off at her door, I felt the end of our amazing few days together crashing down on me. I knew I had to say something. This might be my last chance to talk to her one on one, if she was going to spend all her free time with Scott.

I reached out to hold her elbow. She smiled and lifted her forearm to rest on mine. That simple touch on my arm was like a jolt of electricity.

'I had a great time with you this week, Addie,' I said. For the first time since meeting her, I couldn't think of a cute nickname to add. But I guess this wasn't that kind of moment anyway. I wanted to be serious.

'I liked seeing you smile so much,' she said.

'I liked seeing you. Being around you. I like it.' I stroked one hand down the side of her cheek, then her arm, to hold her hand. 'I like you.'

'I don't—' She stopped and looked down at our hands, as if she couldn't lie to me. 'I'm not sure what I feel. I just know this would hurt Scott if he knew.'

Well, fuck. That hurt, real bad. Especially because I knew she was right. I sighed. 'Great, well, I guess that's it then. Not your fault you picked Scott. Not my fault I want what I can't have.' I was still holding her hand. 'Unless you want to see what it'd be like to have both of us?' Slowly, giving her time to pull away, I leaned in closer.

She didn't pull away. She tilted her mouth up towards mine, and all conscious thought stopped.

I kissed her. Her mouth was just like I'd imagined it would be – all plump sweetness that tasted like the vanilla lip balm she used. Her hair drifted around us like a waterfall, shutting out the rest of the world, and then, *thank fuck*, she was kissing me back.

I wrapped my free hand around her waist and pulled her hard against me. Damn, she was soft. She was so soft, from head to toe. She whimpered against me, and my wolf just about went wild, wanting to claim her. I nipped at her bottom lip, not biting into the skin – I would never risk that. She opened her mouth to me, and I tasted her, all of her, desperate for more.

She broke away, breathless, and pushed against my chest as she stepped back.

I ached, feeling cool air against me instead of her soft, warm body.

'We can't do that again,' she gasped.

You could have shattered me with one punch in that moment. I took a deep breath, everything aching with desire and devastation all at once. Then I nodded. 'Okay. I'm not saying I won't.'

She gave me a pointed look.

'But I'll try not to.' I shook my head slowly. 'It's right, you and me. It's just not right now.'

Then I backed down the steps and hopped on my bike. In the sidecar, Gal looked up at me and whined, not sure why I was sad. I couldn't comfort her.

I just rode until I couldn't feel anything anymore. Then I shifted, and let Gal and my wolf take over. The wolf was disappointed, too, but his sadness was simpler.

No guilt.

No regret.

No 'what if's.

19

Addie

I had to tell Scott that I kissed Lee. That we kissed, I mean. He kissed me. But yeah, I kissed him back…

The whole situation sucked. I felt sick to my stomach. I didn't know what to say, how to tell him – I just knew I had to. Was there any way I could tell him that didn't end in him hating me?

We'd planned to go out for dinner once I was out of lockdown and we were both done with work for the day, so I met him at Zeus's. I couldn't decide whether to tell him up front, so that he might stay to talk about it with him, or to wait until after we'd ordered and eaten to tell him. But how could I eat when I felt this sick? I kept twisting my pendant back and forth between my fingers, until I was worried I was going to break the clasp or the chain with all my fidgeting.

So as soon as he arrived, before we even went inside the restaurant, I blurted, 'I have to tell you something.'

He gave me a curious look. 'All right.' He strode straight into my space, pulling me flush against him for a spine-melting hug, which turned into a breath-searing kiss.

I trembled, not wanting it to end, just so glad to be close to him again. *Adrienne, don't be an idiot. Don't tell him.*

Then he pulled back, just far enough to see my face. 'Shoot.'

Oh God, I don't want to. I'm about to shoot him right in the heart.

'This is so hard, and I'm so sorry that I have to tell you this.' I shuddered, hating the sad, fearful shame that swamped me. 'This week, while I was staying with Lee... We kissed.'

His face went grim immediately. 'You kissed.'

I rushed to explain, 'I didn't mean for it to happen. I didn't start it. I stopped it as soon as I realised what was happening.'

Scott's eyes hardened. 'So he forced it on you?'

'No, no! I mean, it wasn't all Lee's fault, but I mean, it wasn't my idea. You know, he's hot, and he's funny, and I just wasn't thinking straight, so I let him kiss me.' My voice ended on a whisper. 'I'm so sorry.'

Scott had pulled away completely from me now. 'Well. That's hard to hear, but... I mean, I knew you two might have trouble staying together, I just thought you would kill each other, not... Did you kiss him back?'

I swallowed, hard. 'I ... I—' I couldn't think of anything to say. I couldn't believe I'd once imagined that he might be open to a polyamorous type of situation. I should've communicated better about what I might want; should have asked him earlier what he wanted; should have just *not kissed* Lee.

Scott's gaze turned dark, and sad. 'I mean, maybe we both

knew this was…'

'What?'

'Temporary.'

My shoulders slumped. 'Scott, no. It was an accident. It won't happen again.'

'The thing is,' said Scott quietly, 'I see how you are when you're around him. He makes you happy. Those kinds of feelings don't just go away.'

'But, but, you both make me happy, just in different ways,' I protested. 'When I'm with Lee, it's unpredictable. He makes me laugh but he also drives me absolutely crazy, he makes me so mad!' I rubbed my hand up his arm, but he didn't respond. 'And when I'm with you, I feel safe and happy and excited, all at the same time. You're incredible, and I just want to spend all my time with you. I love both of you.'

He sighed, and when he spoke, he sounded so weary. 'Adrienne. I would feel a lot better if you wouldn't say you love me after you kissed my friend.'

'But I—' My voice broke, and I started crying. I tried to stop, but it was taking control.

He took pity on me. 'Come here,' he said gruffly, pulling me into his arms again.

I sagged into his embrace, weeping against the collar of his uniform. I wrapped my arms around him, pressing my head against his chest. His arms came around my shoulders, and I breathed him in, still hoping it wasn't the last time. Memorising his spicy scent just in case.

I felt him kiss the top of my forehead, and I pulled back,

looking up at him.

He was very close; I could see his concern for me in the crease in his forehead, and the yearning for him swelled in me until I couldn't hold it in. I lifted my head an inch and kissed him. He let me, but then he broke away, freeing his arms and stepping back.

The sting of shame and rejection hit hard and fast. 'I'm sorry,' I repeated.

'I know. I'm sorry, too.' He rubbed the heels of his hands against his forehead. 'Trying not to make this harder than it has to be. I just need some time to think.'

I tried to catch my breath, fumbling in my handbag for a handkerchief. 'Yeah, sure, sure. So, that's really it?'

His hand reached out, brushed the side of my arm with his knuckles. He was always so gentle with me. 'Are you going to be all right?'

I shook my head. 'No! I'm ... I mean, how can I be all right? I'm so disappointed. Aren't you?'

'Of course,' he sighed.

'I'll go.' I wrapped my jacket around me, over the dying warmth where his arms had been around me. I swallowed past the big lump in my throat. I couldn't meet his eyes. 'Goodbye, Scott.'

His deep voice rumbled one last time. 'Goodbye, Adrienne.'

I cried the whole way back to the train station, trying to choke my sobs in my handkerchief, tears running silently down my face. I had shattered my own happiness into a million pieces.

As the train door opened for me, I flinched at a sound I

recognised.

A wolf, howling alone in sorrow.

Two thirds of the way through a bottle of the bad stuff, I realised what I was doing, and drunk dialled Elle. I let it ring a couple times, then remembered she'd be with the kids. *Shit, they don't need to know their aunt's crying drunk.*

I hung up, then called Dad.

'Hello darlin', he said. *'Conas atá tú?'* That meant *how are you?* in Irish Gaelic.

'Hey, Da.' I slipped into the Irish word for 'dad' without thinking about it; I always did with my dad. 'Not so good.' My voice wobbled.

'Oh, what's wrong, love?'

I swallowed to stop myself from sobbing into the phone, then said, 'I had a hard week. Lots of tough cases. Had a fight with some friends. And I've … I've had a bit too much to drink.'

Dad didn't hesitate. 'You at home? I'm on my way over. You stay there, I won't be long.'

He said something more, but I started sobbing again and couldn't hear it.

I faded into a haze of ugly crying. At some point, I pushed the whisky bottle away, then lay down on the kitchen floor. I was still there, staring at the ceiling, when I heard footsteps, and then my Dad was crouching down beside me.

'Oh, Da,' I said, starting to realise how pitiful I must look.

'You all right?' The eyes beneath those bushy eyebrows looked concerned.

I shook my head. Better to be honest, if I wanted help.

He nodded and made a face. 'Well, let's get ye sittin' up, then, and we'll have a good, long chat.'

I sat up with his assistance, and wiped my eyes on my sleeve, then popped my glasses back on. 'Thought I locked that,' I said, pointing to the door.

He shrugged. 'Oh, aye, well, needs must.' Every cop worth their salt knew how to get through a locked door in case of emergency.

I wobbled up onto my feet, his hand under my elbow. Embarrassed, I made my way to the couch and slithered onto it. I tried to stay upright for a minute, then slid down horizontal on the couch cushions while the world spun.

I heard Dad fussing about in the kitchen for a moment, the kettle clicking on, and then he came back out, holding two big glasses of water. 'We'll start with this, then have us a cup of tea, eh.'

'Thanks, Da.' I took a long sip, then grimaced. I waved my free hand. 'Sorry about all this.'

'Ah, it's nothing.' He fiddled with his wedding ring for a moment. 'Now, look, you know I'm not big on talking, but uh, when you're knee-deep in a bottle, it's gotta be done. Better out than in, that's what your Ma always said.'

'I didn't mean to drink,' I mumbled. 'I never drink on a work day.'

Dad's 12 years sober, which I've always been so proud of. He made the switch towards the end of his already-illustrious career, and it only made him a better cop.

He waved a hand dismissively. 'Every O'Connor alive has been there. We'll dry you out, get ye back on the wagon. You were doing so well!' He gripped my hand in his. 'Adrienne. Who did this to ye?'

That got to me. Normally, I was the rock of the family. I'd helped Elle make friends and get used to the culture when we'd first moved here from Dublin. Then I was there for her and Dad when Ma died. And then later, I'd helped when Dad was getting sober. And when Elle was leaving her abusive ex.

Usually, if I was hurting, I hid it. Everyone else had bigger problems than me.

I sniffled, then said, 'Don't laugh, but it's man trouble.'

He smiled grimly. 'Jes' tell me who, I'll make 'em disappear.'

My mouth twitched towards a smile in spite of it all. 'Nah, it's not that bad. Thanks, though.'

'All right, I'll put me shovel away,' he said.

We laughed together for a moment.

After a beat of silence, I said, 'There's these two great men, and they tried to get me to choose between them. And I can't. I couldn't.' I shrugged. 'So the one I was dating broke up wit' me, and now I don't have either of them. And they did that thing in a new relationship where they draw you into their world, into their lives, you know, you meet their friends and they become your friends, and now… I'm just alone again, and they're gonna just move on, back to life as normal, without me.' I left off the part about them being lykos. Dad really didn't need to hear that part.

Dad sighed. 'I'm sorry, honey. Men are arseholes, we really are.'

I nodded, and blew my nose.

'Just so you know, you can talk to me anytime. About anything.' He drew me in for a hug, and I felt safe and loved again, for the first time all day. 'I'm here for you. No matter what.'

20
Lee

After I'd run around as a wolf with Gal in our local national park for a few hours, I wasn't exactly calm, but that stabbing feeling of guilt and sadness and painful longing in my chest had been replaced by a searing rage. I'd upset both of the people I loved in one day. One terrible, no good day.

But this had all started with that feral. That *fucking* feral.

Grendel.

Now *that*, I could do something about.

I was going to hunt him down.

Tear out his throat.

Slice him to pieces.

And then I'd probably let Scott know where I'd left the mess, because he'd want to clean it up, just in case. He'd be mad, but what did that matter, at this point? He was probably already mad at me.

He hadn't said anything about Addie ... yet.

Then when it was all over, I'd go look for some fun and try to forget this whole, awful week.

The last place we'd seen the feral was running around the containers at the docks, so that's where I drove next. I parked the bike and Gal and I wandered down the main pier until she caught a faint whiff of wolf. She alerted me, and we started tracking it.

The feral's wolf musk smelled sick. I'd noticed it before, but hadn't thought about it. It smelled like a mix of burning flesh and vomit.

Stupid bastard.

Night fell, and I shifted forms. You had to avoid getting in range of CCTV in these populated areas, but I'd had plenty of practise. I was human for every single shift I ran with Gal, but we'd run together on all fours a bunch of times off-duty.

Traces of their footfalls, not enough to be called footprints, changed from wolf form to human form and back again. I traced their sick scent to an open container. My approach was silent, but I knew they would smell me coming.

Fur flicked as they tried to run out and away.

I pounced.

–you hurt her– I accused them. *–why?–*

–she put me in jail, horrible, no moon, no sun– They trembled under me but didn't show their throat in submission. *–escaped, and she came to me, ran right between my paws–*

Somehow, he wriggled out from under me, and we tangled, fighting with teeth and claws, snarling.

I ripped into his belly with my claws, not holding back. I tried to get his neck between my jaws, but he was moving too much to get an easy grip.

Gal leaped on his back and helped pin him down with her weight. She wasn't nearly as heavy as either me or the feral, but it was enough to give me the upper hand.

When I finally got a hold of his jugular, I tore and shook until he finally went limp. I let go, and his dead body dropped to the ground.

I lay there panting for a moment, registering that the fight was over, that he wouldn't bother me or Addie or anyone else ever again. Gal licked my muzzle, trying to calm me down and get me clean.

I could have justified it to myself. Grendel was feral. He would have just killed his fellow prisoners, if I'd taken him back to a cell.

But to be honest, that didn't really matter to me at the time.

He'd hurt her, so he had to die.

When the bloodlust cleared, and I found myself human again, washing up in my bathroom at home, I wasn't even sorry. I checked down the length of my own body for wounds, but I was fine. He'd inflicted no mortal wounds, just scratches and bites that would heal in time.

I also checked Gal from head to toe, but she was perfectly clean. He hadn't gotten a single claw on her.

I called Scott, and it went straight to voicemail.

'Found the feral. Dead now.' I paused. 'Look, man. You know I don't mind being the bad guy most of the time. I'll make the life and death moves, while you're busy worrying about collateral damage and managing the pack and all that. And I'll even let Addie hate me for being too pushy, too violent, for wanting her even though she's with you. But at the end of the day, she's alive, right? So, fuck it… Anyway, feral's dead. I'll see you at work, mate.'

Then I texted Addie:

I'm sorry. Don't worry about the feral, it's been taken care of.

PART TWO
now

21

Addie

It's the last day of my week off before I go back to work and back to court.

My last day of unpacking into this sad, tired apartment. All those fucking law school fees. I could've been in a penthouse by now, on my wages, if it hadn't been for student loans that grew faster than I could pay them off. Instead, I'm in a dodgy, little apartment with a dishwasher that leaks every time you run it, and air-con that's only cold for 15 minutes a day.

I really don't want to be here. Not just this apartment, either. I can't believe I'm back in this *city*, after spending three full years away. I lived here for years, until everything went down.

But this is where the job is, so this is where I've come. I've finished my secondment in the sticks, up on the big dividing mountain range. And I didn't really want to stay there anyway, so far from family and friends. Turns out, this is the only city with an opening for a DPP anywhere within three hours' drive of my dad, Elle, and Charlie.

Tomorrow, I'll be back at work, going from the pristine law offices with free coffee, to the courtroom, and back to the one place I'm truly dreading – the precinct station.

I need a drink.

And I know exactly why I'm not going to have one. Because just like everyone else in my family, I now know that one shot ends up arriving in a dozen shot glasses, one after the other. It makes all the hard feelings start feeling a bit blurry, sure, but then everything starts *looking* blurry as well, and that's no good.

So I pack my bag, and head off early on my assignment. I'm picking up Dad on our way to my sister's house for dinner. Eloise has two kids, so we try to make sure we travel to see her, rather than the other way around. Besides, the kids love it when their Pappy runs them ragged before bedtime – they fill up the house with screams and giggles until all of them fall asleep together on the bedroom floor.

Butterscotch greets me at the door with a sloppy, excited kiss. She's 12 years old and gorgeous, a Golden Retriever-Lab cross, all big paws and long, fluffy tail. I've long since given up trying to persuade Dad that she needs a grown-up name, not a puppy's name like Butterscotch.

'Butters!' I say delightedly, making sure she knows how happy I am to see her.

He met her while he was still working in organised crime, and they've been inseparable ever since. She had an injured leg that meant she could no longer work in the search and rescue squad, and he had just quit his drinking problem and was angling to move into a desk job. Together, they've helped each other

197

adjust to the life of a detective inspector, spending half their time talking with people and half their time sitting in the office.

Although, based on what I heard today at the precinct, they won't be spending much time in the office anymore.

'Hey Da,' I call out as I follow Butters into the house. 'What's this I hear about you retiring?'

'Hello darlin',' he says, giving me a big hug and ignoring my question. *'Conas atá tú?'*

'Good, good.' I hold him there for a moment, breathing him in, all peppermint gum and Old Spice cologne. I close my eyes tight for a second, remembering. I'm 10 and I'm wishing him luck at work, my smaller arms around his big shoulders, and the world is all sunny side up.

He roughs Gal up behind the ears and leads her into the kitchen. The scoop scrapes in the box of dog biscuits and he rattles some into her bowl. As she starts crunching it up, he turns to me. 'Tea?'

'Yes, please.'

He pours us both a cup, and I try again.

'So … retirement?'

'So they told you. I'm not sure it will take, but it's a legal requirement for police officers in this state, you know.' He shrugged. 'Turn 60, you gotta retire. But I'll start a business, mebbe. It's time.'

I'm not surprised he's unsure about the idea of hanging up his boots. Coppers are drifters; for most of them, being on-duty is the same as being awake. In organised crime, Dad had often gone to work with the sun high in the sky and crawled into bed just before it rose again. When I was a kid, he used to sneak into the house as quietly as he could so he wouldn't wake me and Mam (the Irish term for mum), but I often slept lightly, hoping to hear him come home. Hoping that he *would* come home.

These days, he's mellowed for the better. He doesn't drink, barely smokes, and gets up early to go jogging with Butters. I think he even lets Butters sleep in the bed with him.

I run a hand over his head as I slip past him on my way to the sink. 'You've lost some of that orange fuzz you used to call hair.'

'It was jes' slowing me down. Better to be bald, mebbe.' He sits down when I do. 'I haven't seen you in a couple of weeks.'

'Yeah, we hit a busy spell.' He nods; my team out in the back country was used to being overworked. Maybe being back at the DPP here will be different. I tilt my head at him and pull aside my braid, the same copper-red colour as his remaining fuzz. 'Well, I'm glad *they* told me, since apparently, you weren't going to?'

He shrugs. 'It's time. It was probably time five years ago, but...' He pulls a cigarette out of the drawer, and I groan.

'Da, nooooo. That'll kill you, you know.'

'So will a million other things,' he says, 'including that fecking covid, and the asthma from the pollution.'

He takes his hand off the table and clenches it into a fist a few times, probably trying to ward off the ache of old wounds. He's got plenty of them, from his undercover days.

'You need a Panadol?' I ask.

'No, no, this is just fine, thank you.' He waves the cigarette at me.

'I didn't think doctors still prescribed cigarettes for pain management.'

'I don't have a problem with pain.'

I open my mouth to argue, but he looks down, and I stop myself. My hair may come from him, but my mouth and my stubbornness are my mam's, especially when I'm annoyed.

He makes an exaggerated sigh and stubs the cigarette into the ashtray. Unfortunately, that lights one of the old butts up, and the overflowing ashtray bursts into flames. We both jerk back, but the blaze is brief, although spectacular.

I burst out laughing at the look on his face.

He smiles sheepishly and lifts his glass. 'Want anything else before we head out?'

I shook my head. 'We should get going, get on to Elle's.'

In the car, he asks, 'What about young what's-his-name, who took you on all those long drives around the mountains?'

I pull a face. 'Max. I stopped seeing him.'

'Don't tell me. He was boring.'

'He was an IT guy, more in love with code than with me. We didn't have that much in common to begin with. All the interesting men are already taken.'

'Och, *interesting?*' He shakes his head, his brogue thickening. 'If your mam had bin so hung up about "interesting", ye'd never've bin born.'

I just grin and thicken my own accent to match his. 'And ye'd still be missin' me, though we'd never'a met.'

At Eloise's place, her kids scream an excited hello and drag their Papa into the living room. Penny – Penelope – is 6 and wants to be a firefighter when she graduates from preschool. Meanwhile, 4-year-old Jazz – Jasper – still only cares about Paw Patrol, and doesn't care about grown-up things.

Elle pulls me into her arms and hugs me as hard as she can. It's always like that with Elle, and has been even before she separated from her ex last year. She needs regular doses of loving words and physical affection like other people need regular breaths of air.

Unfortunately, her ex's flowery words of praise and love kept her blinded for many years, even when his actions didn't line up. Now that she's free, I always wish I'd said something sooner, before they got engaged, or before they had kids together, at least. She's told me about red flags from as early as when they were dating, how he wouldn't stick to any of the boundaries they talked about, but showered her with attention.

I know she still blames herself for not leaving sooner, but anyone would've done the same, especially once the kids came along.

I've seen enough of human nature to know none of us can predict what another person is capable of. It's impossible.

When she got the courage to leave, I'd just gotten out of law school at the time, so I found her the best lawyer I could and helped her navigate the hellish maze that is the court system. I still wish I could've done more. If only I'd got her out of there sooner – both for her sake and the kids' sake. They've come out of this mess with more trauma than any child should have.

'How's work?' I ask as we follow the kids and our Dad into the living room.

'Good,' she says. 'I mean honestly, right now it's a bit frantic, trying to get back up to speed. But it's great to have a job again.'

Now that she's getting back on her feet, Elle has been able to return to work part-time, as a forensics specialist.

Dad waves a finger. 'The apple never falls––'

'Far from the tree,' Elle and I finish his quote at the same time.

We all chuckle at that, but it's only to be expected that the children of a police inspector are now a prosecution lawyer and a forensics technician. And Elle really does love her work.

'Excuse the mess,' she says. 'Just making decorations for Jazz's birthday party.'

'That's coming up quick.' I finger the Celtic pendant around my neck. Elle has a matching necklace – the Dara Knot. Our mum gave them to us before she passed away. It looks like an interwoven, never-ending circle, which is the Celtic symbol for strength and courage.

Elle sees me rubbing the necklace, and smiles sadly. 'Mam would've loved this; she'd have been here in a second, helping make bunting and other crafty bits. Jazz wants a Paw Patrol party, of course.'

I hug her again, quickly. 'She would have been so proud of you, Elle. You're a great mum.'

Penny grabs my hand. 'Aunty Addie, you want to see my new jigsaw puzzle?'

I smile. 'Sure thing, cutie pie!'

Dad's telling his news about retirement to Elle, and it's clear from her enthusiasm that she's imagining he'll use some of that time to help her out around the house. 'You can come babysit Jazz one day a week, save me having them in daycare every day, and then I'll be able to afford to go back full-time at last.'

Dad looks awkward. 'Ah, jayzus, Elle, I'm not sure. You know I'm not great with all that business, the toilet training and making lunches. I mean, I love the kids, you know I do. But...'

We can both hear what he's saying. Even I usually only ever babysit them for a couple of hours at a time, and I enjoy handing Jazz and Penny back to their mum afterwards.

From the way Elle's face scrunches before she recovers her smile, I can tell it's hurt her feelings. I feel bad for her; it's an easy assumption to make, that Dad would help out a bit more once he retires and has time on his hands.

'Well, you've got time to think about it,' I say, keeping my tone light. 'Even if you have the kids for the morning on a Friday, maybe Elle could work Friday afternoons from home. Might be a bit hard to do that when you have a lab job—' I waved in Elle's direction and she barked out a little laugh. '—but I think these days, most employers will let you work from home occasionally, right? To do like, the admin side of things at home, without the distractions of the office?'

Elle nods. 'Worth a try. Think about it, Da. No pressure, but it would be amazing.'

22
Scott

I lock the door on my way out, with a silent moment of gratitude to the universe for helping me get this place of my own. On a sergeant's pay, saving for a deposit has been a lot easier than in my younger years. Especially when housing prices and interest rates in this city keep soaring, spurred higher by investors and buyers who live out-of-state or overseas. It's not a big house, but I'm just so glad it's mine. It's even got a small backyard, for when Gal or the neighbourhood kids come round.

Court is crammed full today. I arrive early, since I don't normally spend much time in court these days, and I don't want to mess it up by being stuck on a slow train.

'Morning.' I wave to the bailiff, a big guy named Aaron.

He nods back in greeting. 'Davids. Usual lawyer's resigned. Got a new one today.'

'Funny,' I say. '*I'm* only here because the rostered prosecutor is off sick.' Unlike the DPP lawyers, a police prosecutor doesn't need to hold a law degree, so any sergeant can fill in when needed.

It doesn't matter to me if it's not going to be Jensen, the usual DPP, today. I don't have to know who I'm working alongside in order to get the job done. I'm just here to fill in for a day's work, then get back to the station to deal with my normal job as sergeant: managing ongoing investigations, being a supervisor for the constables and the pit, drawing up the patrol roster for next month, and liaising with our public volunteers when they've got activities and events coming up.

Then I glance up, and my heart skips a beat.

It's her.

Adrienne.

The past comes flooding back to me in a disorienting rush. Three years' worth of memories in one second, and my equilibrium is thrown. My body reacts viscerally. My chest tightens; my gut twists; I can smell every scent coming from her, her shampoo, her warm skin, the light perfume of her fabric softener.

She's scribbling something on a piece of paper, her lips pressed together, her legs crossed. She's wrapped in a plum-coloured pencil skirt that hugs her hips in a way that makes me want to hike it up over her knees and—

It's been three years, but just like that, I'm right back there again, living it all over again. I remember her sitting between my legs at the beach, brushing sand out of my beard. Laughing with me at some stupid show on Netflix, her long curls unbound, draping over that gorgeous chest. Arguing with me about the best way to make spaghetti, the best exit to take off the motorway, everything really. She was stubborn and argumentative – an occupational hazard – but she was also sweet, kind, and more intelligent than anyone I know. I wonder if she's still like that.

Fuck. I could have sworn I was over her.

I blink, resisting the urge to bang my head against the desk. I never imagined we'd have to work together again, not after she moved so far away. It takes me a minute to recover. Better get this over and done with as quickly as possible.

Pull it together, Davids. Keep it smooth. Professional.

I open the gate to the courtroom floor, striding up to the police prosecutor's seat. 'Counsellor O'Connor, how are you?' My voice is firm, confident.

She looks up, and her pen droops slowly in her hand. She gives a small nod, no smile. 'Sergeant Davids.'

She's wearing an oversized white shirt that brings out her chocolate eyes, but I shouldn't think about that. My trained eyes pick up the signs of anxiety – she's tense, fidgeting, avoiding eye contact, and there's a hint of a blush starting in her cheeks. I aim for an unworried air.

'So, you're back in the city?'

'Umm… For now, yes.'

I gesture to the court list I collected from reception. 'Looks like we've got a full line-up today.'

'Mm-hmm.' She looks down again, which is kind of disappointing.

Well, fine. I take my seat at the end of the bench. Honestly, it's annoying that she's acting so cool, so professional, with me. Which is exactly what a lawyer in court *should* do.

But it sucks to realise that she doesn't trust me.

I'm also a bit disappointed in myself. Because after everything we've been through, I still love her. With an intensity that scares the shit out of me. It's like she branded me from the inside out, made me a one-woman man. All I want to do right now is wrap her in my arms, kiss the top of her head, and tell her everything's going to be okay.

The judge also recognises her, and asks, 'Glad to be back in the city, counsellor?'

'Oh, well, it's interesting seeing how much has changed,' she says. 'As I was driving in, there were cranes everywhere I looked.'

'Did you get a bit of a holiday between jobs, then?'

She laughs, and says wryly, 'I got sick, actually, right in time to ruin the break. What can you do, right.'

He looks concerned.

So am I. 'Are you all right now?' I ask.

She glances at me. Hesitates. Nods. 'I'm fine, thank you.'

The judge nods. 'Well, we've got a full sheet today, folks, so let's get started.'

23

Addie

At the end of the day, I'm exhausted. It's not the job, which is fine – it's the change of scenery. It's being back where I started, feeling those old insecurities. And being near Scott again is *not* helping.

As I'm zipping up the files back into my wheelie bag, he strides over. I look up at him, telling my heart to stop beating so fast.

Make him go away.

Make him stay.

'Great work today,' he says.

'You too,' I say, and I mean it. He's always been amazing with people, no matter the situation, and he even had everyone laughing together a few times today in the courtroom.

'I know you must be tired, after the big move, first day back and all that,' he says, his eyes piercing. 'But would you like to go for a burger at the Pig'n'Whistle? You can tell me all about being a lawyer out bush and all that?'

'Sure.' I need to eat, after all.

At the diner, we order and find a booth to sit in.

He asks, 'So, how are you?'

I shrug. 'Tired but good. It's been a busy year. A busy few years, really.'

'I saw you in court today. You looked miserable.'

'What a funny thing to say,' I bite. Then I soften. 'Well, sure. I used to love it. I'm a bit more cynical these days than I used to be. What about you? How've you been?'

'It's definitely been a busy few years.' He stares at my hands for a moment, as if thinking of reaching out. My skin tingles as if he actually touches me, but I don't reach out to bridge the gap. 'I'm glad you're back.'

'Really? Because I never thought I'd be back. Not after getting my heart broken like that.'

'The second you left, I regretted it.' His eyes plead with me.

'So do I.' *Dang, I should have said "did" – did, past tense.* 'But I already apologised for what happened.' *And you never apologised for giving up on us.*

'I miss you,' he says simply.

I don't know what he wants. To get back together? *Impossible.* I bite my lip, and I know I sound a bit cold when I say, 'I miss two of my best friends.'

He nods. 'It's been a long time. Lee and I got our friendship back on track again, eventually.'

I roll my eyes. 'Of course you did.' Doesn't he remember that Lee's the one who started all the drama between us? How could he choose to leave me and stick by Lee? *Typical men and their 'bros before hos' mentality. Well, men, er … I mean wolves. Whatever.* 'So you left me and kept him.'

'He's my oldest friend,' Scott says. 'And you were gone.'

I have nothing to say to that.

'I know that was my fault,' Scott concedes. 'And I'm not trying to start another fight. I'm just taking this unexpected opportunity, to see if there's a possibility you and I could be friends again, as well.'

To be friends with him again … or both of them? I can't picture it. And it's a question of integrity. Could I ever be casual with Scott, when before, I handed him my whole heart and he dumped me? I really loved him. Both of them, maybe.

I don't know if I can do that. Is my heart strong enough to survive if it gets broken again?

But in spite of my frustration, and all the band-aids I've used to cover up the cracks in my heart for these past three years, I still want to give this a try. I'm aching to try again.

Maybe just one more try. I could let him back in. See whether he can make it up to me. See whether he can keep both my name and Lee's at the top of his list at the same time.

So I say, 'Anything's possible, sergeant.'

He smiles. 'I can work with that, counsellor.'

24

Lee

This young lyko is lying to me. I just have to get them to admit it. I've been playing the good cop, asking polite questions. When what I really want is to drag them into the empty alley and pin them against the wall until they agree to talk.

It should've worked, too. They're young, still a teenager. They shouldn't be able to stand up to me, but they're from a pack I don't know. My wolf doesn't seem to have any authority over them, despite me being older.

I caught this one's scent all over the south side near my place. Not from my pack; not from any of the local packs. And no good reason to be here.

Maybe it's time to try a little bad cop.

'Let's try this again,' I say. I grab the side of their head and smack it against the brick wall. It's not *nearly* enough to dent a lyko, just enough to get them to flinch and start paying some respect. As they gasp and cry in pain, I grip their throat in one hand, firm but not squeezing. Yet. 'You were at my apartment. Why.'

'I'm just paid to watch! I'm just watching, that's all, I swear. *Fuck.*'

'Language!' I give them a little shake, like a terrier with a rat. 'Who paid you?'

'The pack, the pack did.'

'Which pack? *Whose* pack?' I squeeze, just a hint of a threat.

'Mara.'

I don't know that name. 'Where'd your pack come from? Why are they here, trespassing on our territory?'

'Mara brought us together, over the past couple of years. She said there were jobs here, for lykos.'

I snarl. 'There are, for people who ask honestly. Tell her to come to The Nocturnals tonight, and ask for Scott.'

25

Scott

Mara's scent wafts into the bar ahead of her – she smells like cigarette smoke and rose perfume, both strong scents that invade my nostrils. I'm surprised any lyko would want to smell like that. She looks like she's got spunk, and under her corporate blouse and pants, I can see wiry muscles that could probably go up against the best of my pack.

Better lead strong. 'I'm Scott Davids, alpha of the inner city pack. Who are you, and why are you coming around here, harassing my pack, my family?'

'I'm Mara Grendel.'

I know that last name. *The feral had a kid?* 'And what the hell are you doing in our territory?'

Her face turns cold as ice. 'My father was Konrad Grendel. He was murdered here, by someone in your pack. Three years ago.'

That stuns me silent for about a second. I haven't heard that name in a long time, and it brings back bad memories. 'He'd gone feral,' I say, firmly but not without some empathy.

Her lackeys tense.

'He did *not*,' she snarls.

My hackles go up. 'Ma'am, I'm sorry for your loss, but he knew the law, and he brought his end on himself.'

'And where is your evidence?'

'I was there. And most of my pack were all there, too.' I wave my hand to the other lykos with us. 'We saw him attacking innocents without provocation, while he was in human form and in wolf form. I can show you photos of his dead victims. I personally interviewed a doctor whom he bit, turning them into a lyko who's now a member of the valley pack. I hope I don't have to remind you that all of that is against the law – not only the law of this country, but also our pack treaties.'

She sniffs, but doesn't say anything. For a moment, her eyes narrow, but not with contempt. Is she actually considering what I've said? I've never been unable to read a lyko like this before.

I ask her, 'And who turned you?'

She shrugs. 'Someone from my father's pack. Nobody important. They're dead now, anyway.'

At her hands? I wonder. Out loud, I say, 'You've insulted me and my pack enough. You need to leave this territory by dawn.' I back my words with power, although it might not work. She's never been part of my pack, so I don't have any mental connection to her.

She spreads her hands. 'No big deal; just hand over the killer, and we'll follow the yellow brick road away from here.'

'No.' She obviously doesn't know anything about me, if she thinks I can be intimidated into giving up one of my own pack members, let alone one of my best friends.

She strides closer to me. She gives me a long, intent stare – a direct threat, in both wolf and human body language. 'So you know who the killer is. Well, if you won't tell me who it is…'

I stay silent.

'No?' She shrugs eloquently. 'Well, you know, there was someone else my father always talked about, when he mentioned this city. He spent some time in a human jail here – even though he was innocent. He told me the name of the lawyer who sent him there.' She taps a painted fingernail against her chin. 'Now, let me think… Who was it again?'

Adrienne.

My hand wraps around her throat before she can blink. I growl, 'Don't even think about it. You wouldn't like me when I'm angry. And right now, I'm fucking pissed.'

'I wouldn't do that if I were you,' she says huskily. Still threatening me, with her life in my hands? Got to give it to her, the woman's got balls. 'Brian over there has a bit of a trigger finger.'

I keep my eyes on her. From the other side of the room, one of her pack has a gun trained on me. *Brian, I assume.*

From next to him, Lee says, 'Guy's got silver bullets, Scott.'

What the fuck? How? A werewolf can't touch silver, let alone hold it long enough to get silver bullets into a gun. Lee and I are the only lykos I know who have a legal reason to carry weapons. We're not naturally creatures of metal. If we're going to hurt someone, we bring out the claws and teeth.

Bottom line, this is a *big* problem. It means her pack can hurt mine a lot easier than my pack can drive them off.

'Threatening people's lives, that's what your dad did,' I say. 'You don't want to be like him.'

Mara taps a manicured nail on my wrist.

I release her immediately.

'I'll remind you,' she says, 'I haven't done anything wrong. I haven't hurt anyone. I just want justice. So give me the killer by the end of the week, so I can press charges. Legally. Or I'll go look up that pretty, little lawyer. And I won't stop there, either. I intend to live in this city. So if I have to, I'll start working on your pack, one by one.'

She leaves, her heels clicking on the bar floor.

I let out a long, slow whistle.

Lee pads over and elbows me. 'You want me to follow her home?'

I shake my head. 'We can look her up in the system at work. And if you go anywhere near her, hide your scent. We need to do some detective work, see if we can shut this down the civilised way. Look for a warrant for her in other states. Maybe she's committed some crime we can put her away for.'

'Or something we can blackmail her for,' murmurs Kenny.

I shoot them a look.

Lee rolls his eyes. 'Kenny didn't say anything. We would never do anything illegal.'

Mara's pack spends the day after my meeting with her doing a bunch of hit-and-run type attacks, trying to scare and weaken my pack. Mara isn't there for any of the attacks, so I can't pin any of it on her. And they're not killing anyone, just scaring people.

I can't find anything to pin on Mara in the criminal or civil system, either. If she did kill the lyko who turned her, that would have been a good way to put her behind bars, but I can't find who it was. So I don't have a way to make her back off.

It makes my blood boil.

Our pack has implemented a buddy system so that none of us is ever alone for long during the day, and everyone's noses are on high alert, and hopefully that's enough for now. But I hate that we're being reactive. We need to confront Mara and drive her out of the city. We need to go on the offensive.

And after last night, I know that I can't do that until we have a plan for keeping Adrienne safe. I call her while I go for a walk in my lunch break, trying to clear my head.

'They know about you,' I tell her over the phone.

'How?' she asks.

'Lee killed Grendel.'

'He did? When?' Her voice sounds distant all of a sudden.

'Right after you left. Three years ago.'

'I'm – I'm just—' She cuts herself off, her voice sounding strangled. 'Lee told me the problem had been taken care of; I assumed you got him sent back to jail.'

Shit. I clear my throat. 'Er… Well, we didn't. Unfortunately. You know, yep, it sounds really bad. I'm sorry.'

'Both of you know better! And Lee – why did he even kill Grendel? Why couldn't you have gone through the proper channels, done it safely, *legally*? Then Mara's pack wouldn't be coming after all of us now!'

'I don't know what to say,' I say. 'I'm sorry we ended up in this position, although I don't know if the outcome would be any different.'

Part of me thinks technically, only *technically*, she's right to blame Lee. He could have tried to capture Grendel, and put him back behind bars again. And that's what Mara says she's so mad about. If he hadn't killed her father, she wouldn't be threatening to get her revenge against Lee and Addie.

But in reality, I know Grendel would never have gone quietly back to jail. He wasn't in his right mind; the only thing he was determined to do was to kill Addie for revenge.

No, Lee did the right thing in taking him out of the picture permanently. If I'd been more of a man, maybe I would have done it myself, instead of moping around after the break-up and distracting myself with precinct work. There was always so much work to do.

I've been thinking if we're all going to cooperate, I may end up having to accept those two being friends again. The idea tastes strange, not as off-putting as I'd imagined. I'm not afraid anymore that he's going to steal her away from me, or that she'll prefer him to me, or that they'll cheat on me behind my back.

But then, she's a lot madder at him now than she's been at me, so maybe I should go back to worrying about them hating each other, not liking each other.

I should find a way to reassure her.

But maybe I'm wrong – maybe she's stronger than I think – because she just waves a hand dismissively. 'Well, whatever. Whoever's fault it was. Or is. We're going to survive this. We always do.'

26

Lee

I have to get back out there. I haven't dated anyone in ages. And Scott tells me Addie is back in town and they're gonna try to be 'friends'. *Pfft. Sure.* But if there's any chance she and I are gonna be friends again, I need to find someone else to play with. So there's no temptation.

So I sign up for a speed dating session. I'm running late from work – as usual – so when I walk in, the host tells me to find a seat on the men's side and sit.

All I hear is 'sit', so I pick a chair and I'm down, ready to go. I notice that it's very binary, and very hetero – a side for men and a side for women. I frown.

I don't know why I didn't expect this. I'm pan, and sometimes I forget there are people who are only attracted to one type of human. I shouldn't be surprised; Scott's my best friend, and he's as straight as they come. Which is a shame. He's hot.

I try to focus on the people in front of me.

The first woman I meet twirls a lock of hair around her fingers. It's not as shiny or vibrant as Addie's red-auburn hair. As if she senses what I'm thinking, the woman says, 'You've got great hair, what shampoo do you use?'

'I don't know. I don't take a lot of showers.'

There's a beat of silence for a moment.

'Umm…' She looks surprised and a bit lost, like she doesn't know what to say to that.

Maybe I need to clarify. 'I don't like showers, or baths, or whatever. But I'll go for a swim once a day, or more, sometimes.'

'Right…'

'And after a run, I'll rinse off in the shower, for sure. 'Cos I go for a run every day. Have to, or I've just got too much energy.'

'Okay, wow, that's a bit intense.'

The next woman is all about the flirt, telling me all the things she'd like to do to me if she gets me alone. I mean, at least it's not like with Addie, where all the unresolved sexual tension was unspoken, and what she actually said out loud is that she *didn't* want to be with me…

The woman says something about making a hickey, and I say, 'Oh, so you like being bitten?'

She pretends to fan herself. 'Um, wow! In bed? Definitely. Out of the bedroom, not really!'

'What about leash play?' I'm just teasing her, but I don't think she gets that it's a joke.

She leans forward, but she doesn't blush. Addie has such a beautiful blush, so quick, and it covers so much of her pale skin when she lights up. She's an open book when she's embarrassed … or aroused.

The woman answers, 'I'm up for whatever you are... Sir.'

Huh? I'm not a "sir". Oh, she means like a Dom/sub dynamic. Nah, no thanks. I try to keep my mouth shut until we move on to the next person.

The waiters bring out some dessert at some point, part of the drinks and nibbles package for this event. They hand me a lemon tart and delivers a slice of chocolate cake to the woman across from me.

'Do you want to go half-and-half?' the woman asks me.

'Oh, no, I never share food. If it's in my bowl, it's mine.' Best to establish those boundaries early, right?

She pulls back and looks really put off.

'I mean, I'm not against sharing,' I add. 'If you let me, I'll definitely beg food off your plate.' I wink.

'Sounds a bit unfair,' she whines.

Ugh. I hate a whiner. I think about how even when terrible stuff was happening to or around Addie, she wouldn't whinge about it. She'd always tell me how she was feeling ... sometimes loudly. But she didn't whinge. I chuckle to myself, remembering all the times she told me off.

The next woman asks me, 'So you're a cop? Wow, that's hot.'

I nod. 'Yep. Canine squad.'

'Do you like your job?'

'Yeah, normally it's good. There are some cases where you find yourself chasing your tail, you know.'

'Oh, I know!'

'Then you just have to shake it off. Life's too short to spend all day working, you know? Gotta make time to play, hey.'

'Yeah, right. What do you do?'

'Hiking, running, swimming... HIIT, obstacle courses, squash...'

'Wow, really active.'

'Oh yeah, but don't worry, I'm totally house trained. My girl, not so much. I mean, she knows she's supposed to ask for permission first, but almost every night, she ends up sleeping in my bed.'

The woman's face gets all screwed up, and I can smell her confusion and anger. 'What?'

I realise my mistake. 'She's a dog! Gal is my dog!'

'Okay, sure.'

Well, fuck. That could have gone better. Addie didn't seem to mind when Gal joined us in bed.

27

Addie

In the carpark, I spot a motorbike I recognise – a Yamaha Ninja. The same as Lee drives. Surely he can't be here, too...

Scott sees me looking. 'Huh, looks like Lee's hiking today, too.'

I only nod, wondering what to think about that. I'm a bit disappointed, I guess, but I'm not going to argue about it. I agreed to this hike because I'm spending time with Scott – as Friends with a capital F. So it's not a waste.

But I don't know if I'm ready to see Lee again. He always used to push my buttons, put me on edge. I don't want to find out if seeing me around Lee is still enough to make Scott jealous again. I want everything to stay calm and happy this time around.

I don't want to waste time feeling guilty because I'm attracted to both of them. Been there, done that. Nothing's changed except that I don't blame myself for having those perfectly natural feelings. They're both hot.

Lee gives off chaotic Golden Retriever energy, but that energy can turn into a raging cyclone if you don't take care of him

– or force him to take care of himself. And Scott is more like a German Shepherd, razor sharp and clever, and a devil in the sack, but he takes care of the ones he loves. And I think if I have to choose, I prefer being taken care of.

I don't say any of that to Scott. I don't want to know if he's still worried about it.

Once we're in the woods, Scott leads us off the track.

Lee's waiting for us there, in wolf form. I remind myself to give Lee the benefit of the doubt. Act like Lee didn't intentionally break up me and Scott, and kill the feral. I give him a little wave, and his tail wags, just a little bit, as if against his will. Scott glances over at me, then shifts.

Now it's just me and two wolves. *Freaky.* If I didn't know them, it would have been terrifying. Instead, it's just like being out for a walk with my dogs. I smile, relaxing a bit in spite of myself. Both of them start wagging their tails properly, happy because I'm happy.

Gosh, I love them.

Ohmigod, give it a rest, O'Connor. Turn up the brain, turn down the heart.

Scott nudges my hand as if to say 'let's go'.

'All right, but you're going to have to lead,' I say. 'I don't know where we're going.'

He pads off into the forest.

While we're walking, I ask, mostly sarcastic, 'Do you want me to make this look like I'm just walking my dogs? I could throw a stick for you to fetch or something…'

Both of them give the wolfy version of a laugh, panting and

whuffing the air.

I shrug. *Okay, I guess we're really going to hang out. So weird.*

As we walk, I think, *Of course, if they were actually my dogs, I would keep them on a short leash.* The wildlife here doesn't deserve to be hassled by off-leash dogs – and neither do any people we might come across. I remember all too well the fear and frustration I've felt in the past while walking towards some dickhead who won't keep their big dog on a leash.

We walk for a while, enjoying the scenery. Lee prances along a fallen tree and poses at the end, and I laugh. For a moment, it feels like nothing bad has ever happened between us all.

When we stop at bottom of the waterfall, tucked away behind the trees in the gully, Scott lies down next to me and rests his furry head on my leg. It's heavier than I remembered, his fur dark and silky.

Lee gives us space at first, padding over the rocks and sniffing at things. I smile and lean back against the rock, closing my eyes. The sun filters through the leafy canopy over us, lighting up my eyelids occasionally.

Eventually, Lee pads up to us, practically silent. I only notice because Scott exhales in greeting, a puff of air against my skin. Out of nowhere, Lee licks the side of my face.

I yelp in surprise and scramble to my feet. Lee dances back out of reach, then peeks a tooth at me in a wolfy version of a wink.

I laugh and run after him.

It's just like old times again. Chasing him around the beach. Being chased. We had such fun together, before everything went south.

Maybe it's time to let go of my bitterness about all of that. I definitely played my part, not being willing to acknowledge what kind of relationship Lee was looking for. Doesn't change the fact that I still don't know exactly what he was looking for then – or what he wants now.

I stop running when I can't see him anymore. From the big rock next to me, Lee pounces, being careful to keep his paws soft, claws out of the way. He hits me at the waist and knocks me to my knees, licking and tickling me until I'm laughing so hard I can't breathe.

'Mercy! Uncle!' I cry, tears of laughter leaking out.

Scott pads up, looking pleased.

Yeah, all right. I guess we can all try *and be friends again. Nothing to lose, lots to gain.*

When Lee is human again, he tells us, 'I went speed dating last night.' He watches me closely for a reaction.

'Oh!' My eyebrows shoot up towards my hairline. *Not what I was expecting. He's trying to replace me? Oh ick, Adrienne, not everything is about you. And it's been three years! Geez.* 'Oh, well, great.'

'Meet anyone you'd like to spend more time with?' Scott asks lightly. He's always so smooth, so composed.

Lee shrugs. 'Not really.'

I laugh and pretend to roll my eyes. 'Picky, picky.'

Scott and Lee pass a look between them, and then they're

both laughing at me.

'What?' I frown.

'It's just the dating scene at this age is an interesting challenge,' says Scott. 'That's why I avoid it.'

Lee explains, 'Half the women there just want to get married tomorrow. Doesn't matter who the groom is. The other half just want to dick-and-dash.'

I can't help laughing at that. 'Dick and dash?'

'Like DoorDash, but more fun.'

I silently wonder which one Lee was looking for.

In the car on the way home, with Scott driving – of course – he says, 'That was fun, all three of us hanging out. I liked seeing how you were with Lee today.'

'Yeah?'

'Yeah. I'd forgotten how different he is when he's around you.'

'How so?'

He opens his mouth to answer, then makes a face. He drives silently for a moment more, then says, 'When you're around, he's focussed. He doesn't act up as much. It's like he cares enough about you to *try* to be "good", and that's all you.'

'No, no.' I don't want us heading into dangerous territory again, with Scott saying Lee and I are a thing and then breaking up with me again. I can't take that kind of heartbreak again.

'No, I'm serious. Friend to friend. He knows that you accept him – and that's all he needs from anyone to make it worth it for him to try. He doesn't try for most people, because he knows most people don't give a shit about anyone but themselves. That's the truth.'

I nod slowly, frowning. 'I know. I'm not trying to do any of that, though. I've been avoiding him since I got back here. What you're saying sounds like I want to change him, and I don't. I don't think I can; I don't think anyone can.'

'Right, and he doesn't try to change you, either. And you're actually...'

'What? Am *I* different around Lee?'

'You're more relaxed. You laugh more.'

I laugh just hearing Scott say that. 'No, I don't. Really? Huh.'

He takes one hand off the wheel and rubs my leg. 'It's not a bad thing. It's half the reason I told Lee we'd be here today. He's my closest friend, Adrienne. And I care about you. I need us all to be friends again.'

I've been thinking for a while about showing up solo to Jazz's birthday party at Elle's place. But I want to have Scott there with me, as a 'friend'. So I invite him. It's a group thing, so there's no chance he'll mistake it for a date, and it's a low-pressure way to catch up, since all the attention will be on the kids. Nothing to lose, really.

His hand rests on mine whenever the car stops at a red light. Real friendly. I'm following my instincts here, and just hoping I'm doing the right thing, not leading myself on. I'm 99% sure I'm fooling myself.

As Scott parks the car, there's the big roar of a motorbike and sidecar riding up behind us. They stop, and I see Lee take off his helmet.

My stomach instantly ties itself up in knots.

'Hey guys.' Lee smiles, his face like sunshine, as always. He bends to let Gal out of the sidecar, and she skips between his legs, nudging him out of the way so she can greet me.

While I let Gal give wet kisses all over my hands, Scott pulls Lee into a hug.

'Hey man. Didn't know you were coming, too.'

Lee shrugs. 'Jazz met Gal once and got obsessed. I mean, who wouldn't?' Gal hears her name and returns to him, and he roughs up her neck and ears lovingly. 'We got an invite. So here we are!'

I don't really know why I'm nervous about both of them being here at once. *Because I'm hot for both of them, because I want to hang out with both of them, because I don't want to lose either of them...*

Okay fine, so I guess I do know why I'm nervous.

But that just makes me wonder what it could mean for us. So yeah, I'm nervous, excited... And desperate to not fuck it all up again.

And I'm also a bit worried about getting involved in Scott and Lee's lives again, risking contact with lykos again, for the sake of Elle and her kids. Jazz was only about a year old when Scott and I broke up and I left town.

But when we get there, that fear immediately dissolves because there's something far more worrying going on. I do a double take, but there's no mistake – that's Harry Sampson, Elle's ex.

'What is *he* doing here?' I ask Dad, practically hissing it.

'He's the kids' father, Adrienne,' he says drily. 'Heaven knows why, but Eloise wanted him here, and he actually showed up, more's the pity.'

I can't understand why Elle would invite that douche. This is the guy who abused her physically and mentally for years before she worked up the courage to leave, taking her babies with her. And I've spent too many nights holding her while she cried, listening to her heart breaking over the latest thing he's done, to stand here now and accept that apparently, he's still a part of their life.

I don't know what to do. I don't know if there's anything I can do, at this point. I just want him gone. My fists are clenched so tight that my forearms start to cramp.

Scott cups my elbow in one hand. 'I can keep him away from her, if you want.'

Lee waves his can of soft drink. 'Or I could just kill him.'

I laugh in spite of myself. I'm still not all that comfortable around Lee, but I know if I want to be with Scott – and I definitely do – then I need to find a way to be friends with Lee. Or at least tolerate him.

Just then, Elle wanders over, smiling at everyone. 'Thanks so much for coming! Jazz has been so excited, he's running around telling everyone there's some real, live police officers at his party.' She moves a bit closer to us. 'I also found some information I think you'll find interesting, if you have a minute. All of you.'

I raise my eyebrows; I've got no idea where this is going. 'Sure, of course.'

She waves us through the screen door into the kitchen, and pulls her laptop down from on top of the fridge. 'You lads know I'm part-time at the lab? Well, I saw some very weird evidence came in last week. Hang on, I just need to log in so I can show you.'

'What kind of evidence?' Scott asks, leaning on the bench.

'Wolfy evidence,' she says, and turns the screen to show us. 'Look at the slashes on this poor bugger's legs, and tell me these aren't exactly like pack claw marks.'

I would laugh – Elle is always saying stuff that would make other people cringe, like 'this poor bugger' about a deceased person – but she's right. They look just like the slashes I had when I got scratched by the feral werewolf in the valley, three years ago.

'Ah, shit.' Lee scowls.

'That's definitely a lyko's claws,' says Scott, 'but not from our pack.'

'How do you know?' I ask.

'I would know. I'm connected to all of them through the alpha bond.'

'More ferals, then, maybe.' Elle switches to the next image. 'Here's the bit I really need you to see.'

Lee whistles. 'Hooooly—'

'Nothing holy about that,' Scott says.

Claws have carved a message into the guy's back.

SURRENDER OR PAY

'That's dark.' I shudder, and rub my arms nervously. I need to look away, out the kitchen window, where the sun is shining and the kids are playing happily. One of the dads is dressed up like Batman, and some of the kids are piling on him, trying to wrestle him into submission.

'The last bit is less compelling, from the precinct's point of view, anyway,' said Elle, pointing to a photo of wolf footprints near the body. 'Without the carved message, this would've been written off as an animal attack. Instead, the team is assuming the killer brought a dog with him, and used a knife on the back.'

'Who's on the case?' Scott asked.

But we don't hear the answer, because there's a thump outside, then the sound of things clattering. Someone's knocked over the barbecue. People start shouting at each other, and all the kids start crying.

'Where is she?' we hear a woman's voice yell.

Scott stiffens. 'That's Mara. Lee, hold her off while we get the kids to safety.'

'Who's Mara?' Elle demands. 'What's going on?'

'Oh God, no!' I gasp. *Not here. Not with the kids here.*

I'm ashamed to find myself frozen. I'm stuck, feeling like I'm in a kind of trance, like this is a nightmare. I'm swamped by panic, because I remember what Grendel could do. I know how bad this might be. It's like years ago, when I would have flashbacks to his attacks, followed by panic attacks.

Elle doesn't hesitate; she runs for her kids. 'Jazz! Penny! Get inside right now!'

Lee charges out there, and I race after him, but Scott physically grabs me around the waist at the door and turns me back into the room. 'Stay hidden.'

'That's my family out there!' I cry, and barge past him.

Scott takes a deep breath, assessing the situation. He nods at Elle. 'Eloise, keep the kids inside. We'll remove the intruders.' Then he strides outside as well.

Mara's got some other guys with her, who muscle their way through the party while she keeps yelling, 'Bring out the lawyer! I know you're here somewhere. Come out, come out, wherever you are.'

Lee confronts Mara and shouts, 'Keep it down! This is a kid's birthday party, lady.'

I grab my Dad's arm and tell him a version of the truth. 'This is about one of the ones I put away. Can you get everyone inside?'

Dad doesn't ask any stupid questions; he just turns and shouts in a voice loud enough for everyone to hear, 'A'ight, it's time for cake, everyone inside! Last one in's a rotten egg!'

Everyone is confused by all the commotion, but together, Elle and Dad manage to hurry everyone inside, all the kids and parents tripping over each other.

Once they're inside, I step outside and block the doorway, and I look around the crowd of randoms until a woman in a suit meets my eye. I'm un-frozen at last, and panic is warring with a blood rage within me. As much as I'm terrified someone will get hurt, I'm equally furious these unwanted guests are here at all.

'What are you doing!' I yell. 'You come threaten my *family?*'

Lee glances back at me for a microsecond, and gives me a *look*. It's such a quick look, but it's very clear he's saying, *It's hot when you shout at bad guys.*

That gives me a bit of a thrill, I admit, even though I'm currently trying not to pee my pants with fear.

'Well you see, I still just need two tiny things,' the woman, Mara, says. She runs a dark-painted nail over her collarbone, and it lengthens, growing into a long, thick claw. 'You, and that dumbass over there. He killed my father. And *you*. You put him in jail. Made him lose his business, his income, everything.'

My knees tremble. Because I know she can kill me, if she wants to. I'm a puny human, and I felt how strong Grendel was, even without shifting forms. Add teeth and claws to the mix, and I'd be dead. Easy.

She points that long claw at me. 'You're human. And yet somehow you've ended up in a lyko pack. Interesting. You know, humans who love werewolves usually end up furry … or stone cold dead.'

Then I gasp, because my Dad has come outside again and has his service pistol trained on Mara. His eyes dart around the yard, and his brows furrow. It's gotta be clear to him that this situation is different from a normal police-and-felons situation, because nobody else has their gun out, just him.

'She got a knife?' Dad asks.

Scott nods.

Lee rolls his eyes and mutters, 'Sure, a knife.'

One of Mara's lykos growls at Dad.

Dad keeps his tone even, deliberately not escalating the situation, as he asks the growling guy, 'Okay, then, what's going on here?'

The guy just growls again, and fur began sprouting along his arms and neck.

Dad takes a step back. 'Ah, right. Feckin' lykos, it is.'

My brain doesn't have time to register that my dad knows about werewolves, because everything after that moves so quickly.

One of Mara's pack launches itself at Dad, turning into a wolf mid-air.

I throw myself towards the lyko, even though I know I can't do anything.

The lyko hits Dad in the shoulders and slams him to the ground.

Dad's gun goes off, but doesn't appear to hit anything vital on the wolf.

I get there the next moment, and try to push the lyko off my Dad, but nothing happens. It's a massive fucking *wolf*. Distracted, it swivels its head and snaps its teeth at me.

I know I *have* to avoid its bite, so I throw myself back. I fall on my butt, undignified but alive.

The next thing I know, Scott appears and with his superhuman strength, he rips the wolf off my dad. He throws the lyko at a wall, and the wolf turns back into a human, groaning on the ground. Scott immediately pins him and cuffs his arms behind his back.

I get to my knees and scramble back over to Dad. He's gasping, and his chest is covered in blood, torn into deep furrows. It looks like the wolf tried to dig its way into his heart. I rip open Dad's shredded shirt, and take off my jacket so I can use it to apply pressure to the wounds.

I'm trying so hard not to think about all the murder cases I've seen, and all the evidence that says my Dad needs a miracle right now. If his lungs aren't compromised, and none of his arteries have been hit, there's a chance he can pull through this. There's a drip of blood running down the left lens of my glasses, and I don't know if it's his or not.

Lee has gone furry and is dismembering one of the other lykos. When he's done, he looks over and gives a *yip* of concern towards me.

Scott faces Mara, still human but growling. His growl is so loud that it ripples through me until I'm shaking.

She doesn't argue with him this time, not now that two of her lykos are down. It's all happening so quickly. The rest of her pack mates are already fleeing.

Her eyes go wide. She pulls a gun with a silver barrel out of her suit jacket.

'Scott!' I scream.

My noise distracts her, which gives Scott the second he needs. He leaps forward, smacks the gun out of her hands, and goes to sweep her legs out from under her.

She springs backwards and drops to all fours, her suit blurring into fur. Then she's gone, running out into the street after her pack.

Lee howls after her, but Scott shakes his head.

'I don't think you should follow without back-up. We need to stay away from those fucking silver bullets. Get an ambulance and another blue-and-white over here from the station. I need to get inside and do some damage control with the humans.'

Lee bares his teeth in a submissive, wolfy smile, and shifts back to human form. He stays beside me and calls in a string of incident numbers into his police comms, mustering all the right emergency services.

I ignore everyone and focus all my attention on keeping my dad alive until the ambulance gets here. 'Stay with me, Da. I'm here.'

He doesn't say anything, but his eyes meet mine. I've never seen him look so scared, except the day we found out my mam – the love of his life – had died.

Oh God, am I going to lose him, too?

Time slows down, until every second takes an eternity. I've seen my father in bandages after an incident or two in his line of work, but I've never seen him actively bleeding in front of me. It's unnatural. Dad has always been so strong, so alive.

Once the ambulance is here, and Dad is inside, they turn the sirens on. That's when I start shaking. In my head, I repeat the name of the hospital they're taking him to, so I don't forget it.

As if from far away, Scott asks me, 'Are you okay?'

I'm numb, like a mountain, but beneath those walls of rock, there's an underground cavern where a wave of sheer terror is riding back and forth. Sweat is pouring down every inch of my body. My reply is quiet. 'I should help Elle wash the blood off the tiles before it sets. Then I need to get to the hospital.' I say the name aloud.

He puts his hands on my arms, so I have to stop and look up at him. 'No, Adrienne. Are you okay?'

I shake my head, feeling panic well up inside me. I'm going to either cry or throw up, or both. 'No. No, I'm not.' My voice gives out. 'Did I do this? Elle and Da and the kids, everyone's in danger because of me. Everything's going wrong. This is horrible. I should never have come back here.'

Lee pushes off from where he's leaning against the wall. 'It's not your fault, Addie.' His face is twisted with grief and guilt. 'They hurt your family because of me. But I'm going to fix it.'

I nod, hoping he understands that I'm agreeing with the need to drive off Mara's pack, not agreeing with him saying it's his fault. I sink to my feet, looking at the red staining my hands, and the dark pools marking the tiles and grass.

'Can someone watch over Elle and her kids?' I ask. 'I need to go to the hospital with him. But I can't stand the thought of leaving them alone.'

She's my baby sister, and I brought this horror into her life. I used to take care of her and the kids. Now it's all my fault.

'I'll come with you to the hospital,' Scott says. 'You've had a big shock. I don't want you driving right now.'

'I can keep an eye on them,' says Lee. 'If it's what you want.'

I nod. 'Yes. It's what I want. Just don't tell them what really happened, it'll freak them out.'

He strides inside without a word. I don't know what he

does or says to take care of them, but I'm grateful for it.

28

Scott

In the hospital, holding her dad's hand while he sleeps, Adrienne glances over at me just long enough to ask, 'Did I do this?' Then her eyes go straight back to her dad.

The question breaks my heart a little bit. I take her free hand in mine. 'Adrienne, no. No, you didn't. This person's dad was feral, and now she's decided she needs to get revenge for his death. None of that is your fault.'

She trains her gaze on her dad's feet, sticking up through the hospital blanket. 'My family would never have known werewolves existed, but I went and got myself involved in the pack. *Again.*'

I can see she's trying not to start crying again. 'Maybe. Although it sounded like your dad might already have known about lykos.'

'But he was getting out,' she says. 'He was retiring. And I knew it was dangerous to be involved in the pack, but I stayed. Am I a bad person?'

'No, you're not.' *How do I get her to see that?* She's in shock, but I know her concern is entirely rational. I feel terrible about it, because it might be true. If she and I never got together, and she hadn't gone to Kenny's bar, would Grendel ever have found her? I don't know. And that one decision has led to all the terrible things that have happened since then.

It might all be my fault.

But let's say Grendel *had* found her anyway, and Lee and I hadn't been there to protect her… I shudder just thinking about it.

And anything could happen next. Mara seems just as mad with anger as her father, but she's not feral or insane. She's calculating. She could have anything planned.

With Grendel, we just had to take out the leader and most of his pack fled the city. Some of them crawled back into line, and we absorbed those ones into our various packs around the city. Taught them the error they'd made by following a feral. But Mara's followers have ideas of justice on their side; from their point of view, she's right to seek vengeance for her father.

With the numbers she has behind her, she could kill off my pack one by one – or worse, steal them over to her own pack. There's probably already a few people in my pack who are more scared of Mara than they are loyal to me.

She could kill Adrienne any moment we're not watching her closely.

She could maim Lee, which I know he thinks is a fate worse than death.

And I don't know what's best to do. If I take out Mara, I still have to worry about her pack. If we try to persuade her pack over to our side, Mara will know we're not confident in our numbers.

I don't say any of that. Instead, I move over to stand next to Adrienne's chair and wrap my arms around her shoulders. She leans into me, grabbing my forearm and pressing her face into my jacket.

For now, the best I can do is to stay with her, reassuring her with my words and my presence.

I also send a text to my boss to let them know I won't be in tomorrow.

When her dad wakes up, I know I need to say something to explain the attack. I mean, he was torn to pieces by a man who literally turned into a wolf and ripped into his torso. 'Inspector, I know you must have questions about what happened.'

But O'Connor shakes his head. 'I'm not blind, lad. I know there's packs of lykos running around. Just always stayed well clear of them.'

I'm a little stunned, but relieved. One less hard conversation to have. One less problem I need to solve. 'In that case, I'll leave you two to talk.' I kiss Adrienne's forehead. 'I'll be right outside.'

After a few minutes, she calls me back in.

'He wants to talk to you,' she says, her lovely hand on my forearm.

'Okay.' I kiss her forehead, and we trade places. *This can't be good.* Maybe he wants to berate me for sending him – a decorated, retired officer – to hospital. Or worse, he wants to berate me for endangering her. I steel myself to face him.

'Sir,' I say.

'At ease, sergeant,' he tells me. 'My neck hurts looking up at ya.'

I sit on the chair next to his hospital bed.

'My girls are all I have left,' he says. 'It kills me that I couldn't keep either of them safe today. But Adrienne tells me you're as strong as ye look. So I'm holding you to account. Take care of them. If either of them get hurt on your watch, you *know* I know how to make it look like an accident.'

The corner of my mouth quirks in a half-smile.

'Don't get cocky, kid. I saw her when you two broke up.'

That sobers me up immediately. 'I'm very sorry, sir. That was a disappointing time for both of us.'

'Aye, well. We need you two working together, taking care of each other, not fighting. Because you may have to work this out without me. That goes for Lee, too.'

'You met Lee?' *News to me.*

'Of course,' he grunts. 'He's part of her life, the young hellion.' He waves a finger at me. 'Are ye sure you can trust him?'

I nod, no hesitation at all. 'Yes.'

'Why?'

The answer was already clear in my mind, and had been since the first time I saw them together, arguing in the precinct pit. 'Because I think he loves her as much as I do.'

29

Lee

Scott and Addie are already on the couch by the time Gal and I get there. He's got his arm around her shoulders, and I can see dry tears over her cheeks, puffy eyes behind her glasses, like she's been crying.

Seeing them sitting there, cuddled up together, hurts deep in my chest. I love them both, in different ways. I'm hot for them both. And it *sucks*.

I mean, I'm glad the two people I love have each other. They look so right together. But I'm not really part of it. And trying to stay out of it is like stepping on a rusty nail, heart-first, over and over.

I thought it was simple attraction, but that wouldn't hurt so much.

It's so intensely painful, remembering those three years without her. Three years of getting my friendship with Scott back to normal. I hate to think that any minute now, I could lose one or both of them all over again.

If they stay together, I'll still have to work with Scott, so I'll still have to be friends with him, unless Gal and I can transfer. It's fine. I'll just love him silently and forever. That's my current normal.

But will I ever be able to speak to Addie again without it hurting me? I don't know.

Inside the foyer, I let Gal off her leash. She's been here enough times, she knows the drill. 'Go on, girl.'

She pads off to find her water bowl in Scott's kitchen, tail wagging contentedly. She's happy to have done a solid afternoon's work, even if we didn't find everything we were looking for.

Scott sees me standing in the entryway. 'Lee, get in here and grab yourself a beer.'

Addie meets my eye for the first time all day, and gives me a crooked smile.

'Hey, Adam Ant,' I say, ruffling her hair.

The nickname makes Scott chuckle. What does he think about that, the fact that I've found a million and one names for his girl over the years? Does he think it's what a friend does? Or is he mad at me for still flirting with her?

'How you doin'?' I ask her.

'Been better.'

'Anybody want anything, while I get myself a beer?' My voice sounds strained, even to me.

'I'm good, mate,' says Scott.

'Another hot chocolate would be nice,' Addie admits. 'With a little something in it. Oh wait. No, actually, just the hot chocolate.'

I nod, and stride into the kitchen, away from the pounding of my awkward heart. Gal's had a good drink and is now sniffing around to see if she can find the dog treats that Scott keeps in a drawer.

A good, cold beer. That'll help me think straight. I pop on the kettle and rustle up some hot chocolate. I'm glad Addie changed her mind about adding anything to it. I'm not having another repeat of the bridge race. Addie can resent me for that incident all she wants, but I'm just glad she's taking care of herself these days.

I sit next to her on her free side, our shoulders brushing, and she tucks her feet up against my leg. I love that she knows she's safe getting all up in my space.

I pick up her feet and plonk them in my lap, just like I used to. It wakes up certain other parts of me, but I take a deep sip of my beer and think un-sexy thoughts. She needs me as her friend right now.

She gives a weepy smile. 'Ohhh, my guys. Both my guys. Thank you for being here. Thank you for everything today.'

'Of course,' says Scott. He kisses her, and something about it warms me, even though it's like a stab between the ribs. It hurts so much that I shift my weight, about to get up off the couch.

Then she turns to me, and searches my eyes. I don't know what she's looking for, but I hope she sees how much I love her and I'm here for her. She must be reassured by what she sees in my gaze, because she leans over and kisses my cheek. It's a tiny brush of lips against skin that rocks me to my core.

I stare at her, then down at my bottle. I stay on the couch after all.

Fuck. One little kiss on the cheek, and I'm right back where I started. Head over heels for some red-head legal hotshot. *I guess it was never really over, not for me, anyway.*

Gal comes out of the kitchen, looking disgusted that she couldn't find any dog treats within reach. She snorts at us and curls up on the rug, sprawling over our feet and then stretching away. It's been a huge day for all of us.

Over the rim of her hot chocolate, Addie says, 'Scott was telling me the plans for searching out this new pack's den, maybe taking out their leader. This Mara person.'

I relax back on the couch, stroking Addie's shapely calves. 'You're okay, you're safe.'

'Hmm, I know.' Addie puts down her hot chocolate and steals my beer.

'Hey!' I protest. 'Safe from them, not me! That's mine.'

She winks at me, and takes a big swig.

Scott raises an eyebrow. 'Meant to be sober, aren't you, love?'

She groans. 'After the day I've had…' But she meets his eyes. His gaze is kind but firm. She shrugs. 'Yeah, yeah, okay.' She passes him the bottle.

Then he grins and takes a swig from my beer as well.

'Fuck's sake,' I grumble, but I can't help but laugh. 'Mine!' I swipe my beer from his hand and pretend to punch him on the arm.

Finally, I start to feel the tension melt out of me. With all of us sitting together like this, being playful, nobody mad at anybody... It's the first time I think maybe this thing could work. The three of us.

My best friend and his Addie.

My Scott.

My Addie.

Our Addie?

I look up to find Scott watching me. He doesn't look mad. He's just watching. I wonder what he's thinking. I wonder whether I'll ever find the right words to tell him what's on my mind, what I want.

I feel like I've been locked in a prison for a long time, backed into a corner I can't get out of. I can't help flirting with Addie, but she belongs to Scott. I can't help loving her, but she loves him. I can't help loving him, but he loves her. And she's always thought loving him first means she *can't* love me. Even though I'm pretty sure she loves me, too.

It's mind-bending.

I'm starting to think the traditional relationship set-up isn't for me. I've seen enough families in my line of work to know the happiest families do things on their own terms. Sure, it's probably easier to take a census if a household is two adults, and two kids or pets or whatever. But it's also easier to hide unhealthy power dynamics in that kind of family. It's easier to let unfair labour fall on one person.

And all of that means I'm not interested in fighting it out *mano-a-mano* with Scott so that one of us could end up with Addie.

If the three of us could be happy, together…

I imagine coming home at the end of a shift with Gal, to find Addie at the kitchen table with her notes spread out before her, doing "just one more hour" of court prep. I'd get her to stop work to kiss me hello, and we'd go for a walk with Gal, shaking off the day. Later, Scott would wander in with a frown, his brows with that sergeant's permanent worry crease – he has that kind of job. But his face would ease into a smile at the sight of us.

Yeah, we could be happy.

Scott and I pass the bottle back and forth over Addie's head, not letting her have any more, joking about nothing, until the beer is gone and we move on to water. I love this moment. I want to live in this moment forever.

Addie starts snuggling up tighter against both of us, getting progressively more and more horizontal, her legs over mine and her head on Scott's chest. Finally, she takes her glasses off and I pop them carefully on the bookshelf next to me.

Addie turns a little and nuzzles up against Scott, and they start making out. But at the same time, she's grinding her butt backwards into my lap. I shift, suddenly achingly aware of how rock hard I am and how she can definitely feel that. I wonder if I'm about to be kicked out of the room.

She feels me hesitate, and she abruptly pulls up towards me, still enthroned in Scott's arms. I meet her eyes; they're half-closed, heavy-lidded with hunger. The sight of her makes me pant. She grabs my face in both hands and kisses me hard on the mouth.

She always tastes so good. The rose scent of her favourite shampoo wafts into me.

Scott growls, a low, impatient sound, and tweaks one of her nipples. Addie cries out in pleasure and turns back to him.

I stroke my hands down her amazing, thick thighs, and imagine peeling her jeans off. My dick has woken up in a big way now.

I make eye contact again with Scott, and his eyes are dark and hungry. Through the pack bond, I can feel not just his intense desire for Addie, which is almost overwhelming, but also a strong sense of approval. He approves how I'm touching her now.

He isn't making any move to push me away, so I'm just going to enjoy this and see what happens. If they do get really into it and send me away, at least I got to be with both of them for some of the fun. I run my hands over as much of her thighs and ass as I can reach.

Scott delves into Addie's mouth with his tongue, and pushes her shirt down, exposing her lacy bra.

Fuck. Me.

Her breasts are every bit as incredible as I've been imagining – full and heavy and the perfect size for a big hand like mine or Scott's. He leans down over her and slides her bra down over her breast. Then he takes a breast in one hand and sucks her nipple into his mouth.

She arches her back, wriggling her plump backside right up against my hard cock. My breath catches. It feels amazing.

I move slowly, giving both Addie and Scott time to say something if they want to change what's happening. My fingers trail up the inside of her thighs.

She moans.

Okay, I'm gonna go for it. I unbuckle her jeans.

She smiles at me, then at Scott.

I run my fingers along the edges of the red, cotton panties I've uncovered. I look up at Scott, checking he's still okay with this.

His voice is gravelly as he tells me, 'Touch her until she comes.'

Fuck yeah.

Addie looks down at me, breathing hard.

With both hands, I lift up her ass and rip those jeans down to her knees. I palm her v through her panties, and she gasps, her eyes closing again with pleasure.

Her cotton panties are already damp. The scent of her arousal floods the air.

Both Scott and I growl with pleasure.

'You're so fucking hot,' I murmur. 'So gorgeous.'

She whines, clearly desperate to be touched directly.

I push her panties to the side and slide a finger up and down her centre. Her whole body tenses, focussed on that touch. I start small, never-ending circles around her clit.

Scott drags her attention back to him by sucking on her nipples again, switching from one breast to the other, then back again.

I pull her panties down, and she wriggles, her butt driving against my cock even harder, as Scott fists a handful of her hair. I slide one finger inside her, and it's so easy. She's so wet and ready for me. Her core clenches around my finger as I add pressure to her inner walls.

I add another finger and begin moving it in and out slowly. My thumb and the heel of my palm rub over her clit with every movement.

'Holy shit,' she gasps, grabbing my arm, then Scott's, then mine again.

Scott laughs and lifts her arms, pinning them above her head. 'Something unholy, maybe.' With her arms pinned in one hand, he claims her mouth again, and palms a breast with his other hand.

I explore her some more with my hand, revelling in her bushy hair, lightly trimmed but otherwise natural and free. One of my fingers drifts over her arsehole while another finger rubs her clit, and she bucks against my hand.

'Ooh, she likes me touching her ass,' I told Scott.

'She does, does she?'

I draw some of her wetness down to her arsehole, and caress it with one finger. My other fingers continue to fuck her pussy, ignoring her clit for a moment.

With my other hand, I massage ever-so-lightly on her lower stomach, adding pressure so my fingers can find her most sensitive inner spots. She bucks against my hands, crying out with pleasure.

'Lee, oh God, oh fuck!'

Her voice cuts out as I find her clit again. I rub circles over it, never-ending circles that match her rhythm, until she's writhing over us both.

'You're being so good.' Then Scott covers her eyes with one hand and says, more commanding, 'Now, come for Lee, there's a girl.'

I rub faster, and her whole body tenses, her legs shaking. Her thighs grip my arms like iron, and I grin as she shatters against me. She screams out her orgasm like she doesn't care if the whole street hears it.

In the aftermath, her body sinks down against us, loose and trembling. Murmuring praise, I trail my slippery fingers up and down her luscious curves. *God, I could stare at those tits forever.* She smiles slowly, then breathes out a laugh.

'How you doing there?' Scott asks.

'Wow.'

We all chuckle at that. She's still breathing hard, so I pick up a blanket from beside the couch and drape it over her half-naked body. She's rubbing her eyes now, clearly exhausted.

'So satisfied,' Scott murmurs.

If she wasn't so tired, *fuck*, the things we could do. But I meet Scott's eyes, and I can tell he's thinking the same thing. *Not tonight.* And that sucks, because not tonight might mean never, if Scott either of them regret what's just happened.

'Let's get you to the bathroom,' Scott says. 'Clean you up and tuck you into bed.'

'Yeah, don't want a UTI,' Addie sighs, and kisses him. As she sits up and wriggles off of my lap so she can stand, I help her pull her jeans back up. She waggles her butt in my face, and I smack it.

'Shameless!' I say. I watch them walk to the bathroom. Then I just stare at the ceiling while they're gone, tugging on my pants and trying to decide if I want to rub one out or not.

When she gets back from the bathroom, Addie puts her head down on Scott's cushion and throws her legs over me again. She meets my eyes with quiet curiosity, and she's blushing.

I wink. 'That was fun.'

She smiles slowly, and nods. 'Thank you.'

'Thank *you.*'

She buries her face in the cushion and shuts her eyes. I can feel her fall asleep almost immediately; she turns into a warm weight that keeps me on the couch.

When Scott finally comes back into the room, I say quietly, 'She's out like a light. You need a hand getting her upstairs to bed?'

He shakes his head and pulls a blanket out of the drawer under the coffee table. 'I think I'll let her keep sleeping now that she's out. I'll check on her later.'

'Right. Yeah, I'll leave you to it.' I carefully manoeuvre myself out from under Addie's feet.

She makes a sleepy noise of complaint, but doesn't open her eyes.

When I pick up Gal's lead from the coffee table, Scott moves around the table. He doesn't need to do anything else to catch my attention. There's a change in the air, in the energy between us.

'Lee, listen.' He shifts his weight on his feet, his face grim. 'You're my best mate, you know?'

I nod.

'I know we've had our disagreements in the past,' he continues, 'but I'm hoping that's behind us now. For her sake, and for ours. When we focus on her, like tonight, it's so good. When we're competing, it's not.'

I don't answer right away. I can't tell if he's saying there's a chance for all of us to be together, or if he's saying I need to stay on the sidelines. I know I'm losing the moment, but I guess I'm not brave enough right now to ask for what I really want. Not yet.

So for now, I tilt my head, eyes down, neck bared to him – wolf submission. 'I need you in my life, Scott. You're one of the good ones. And I know she needs you, too.'

He nods. 'She needs both of us around.'

But I don't know if he means it the way I do.

I say, 'Come on, Gal.' We drive away as efficiently as I can with a partial hard-on, and I spend the whole drive wishing I knew what to say. Why can I never find the right thing to say?

30

Addie

I wake in the dark, disoriented. I'm not in my bed. I'm on a couch, in a strange house.

Oh, right, Scott's place. The pieces click together: the party, Dad in hospital, Elle and the kids in danger in their own home.

I can feel tears welling up again, so I deliberately push my mind to happier thoughts. I put my fingertips to my lips, remembering how Scott and Lee touched me on the couch until I came so hard I saw stars.

What do they think about it? I wonder. *Was that as hot for them as it was for me? Did they talk about it, after I fell asleep?*

I get up to get myself a glass of water and stretch my neck, and I hear footsteps on the stairs behind me. My heart picks up an anxious beat before I remember it's probably just Scott. I drink my water, then turn to face him.

He leans against the kitchen wall; he's quiet, curious. 'You're up.'

I smile. 'So are you.'

'Let's get you to a proper bed now; it'll be much more comfortable for sleeping.'

I'm a tangle of thorny memories right now. I don't want to sleep in his guest room, alone, remembering the scared look on my Da's face. So I say, 'Only if you come with me. I don't want to try to fall asleep again. I want comfort, and I want to make you as happy as you and Lee made me.'

'I'm glad you liked that.' He touches my face, just lightly.

I lean into the warmth of his hand against my cheek. 'I really, really did. Did you?'

'It was amazing. You were incredible. A goddess.'

His fingers wander down to trace my lower lip, and I inhale with a bolt of desire, hot and sudden. I don't want to think, since all my thoughts are so sad right now – so I just act. I grab his T-shirt and yank him against me, and our mouths come together hard and fast.

His hands slide down my curves and softness, and I'm lost in it, pressing all of me against his strong body. Our mouths are hot against each other's in the cool air, and his fingertips blaze little trails of fire along my skin everywhere he touches.

I bring one hand to the back of his neck, holding him there as we kiss. My other hand grabs onto his arm, holding on for dear life. I catch his lip in my teeth, and he makes a low groan, sending a thrill all the way to my toes.

His hand gently cups my throat, and having his hand there doesn't feel bad, like it did when the feral Grendel had their ragged claws around my neck. This is so different. It feels good. Safe and dangerous at once.

He lets go and lifts me – so easily, as if I weigh nothing. He seats me on the kitchen bench and I draw him in close against me with my legs. As his lips drag down my jaw, then my throat, I arch my back. My breasts press against him.

I can't help myself; my body is running on pure instinct in this moment.

His tongue dips in the hollow of my neck, and then he bites down, holding me still but not breaking the skin. I gasp. My legs wrap around his hips; my heels drag up his thighs.

His nose trails down my chest and traces the low neckline of my shirt, and it shouldn't be sexy – I don't normally think noses are sexy – but somehow it is. My breasts feel so heavy, so lit up.

I want this. I want this so bad.

But suddenly, I hear Mara's words at the party again.

Humans who love wolves end up furry or stone cold dead.

A chill runs down my spine.

Scott's big hands stop on my thighs, and he tilts his head, peering at me. 'You good?'

I shake my head, and he pulls me closer, his arms wrapping around me. I rest my forehead on his shoulder for a moment, breathing. I don't want to think about what that bitch said. She put my Dad in the hospital. She doesn't know anything about what could be good for us.

This time, falling in love, if that's what this is with Scott and Lee, feels less like falling and more like slipping on a rock I already know is wet. I tried to watch out for it, avoid it, but I just have to take that step. And this time, it's my choice.

I run my hands up and down Scott's biceps for a minute, gathering my focus back into my body. *Damn, he's sexy.* 'I've missed this,' I sigh.

'Yeah.' He helps me down off the counter and moves to the stairs.

I follow him, up the stairs to his room. I don't touch him; I just let the air charge up between us.

His eyes are dark with hunger again by the time I climb into his bed and lie down. He runs his hands up my side. 'What do you want, beautiful? We can just sleep, if you want. Or I can get back between your legs and help you forget the day.'

I gasp and kiss him, turned on even more by the thought of him tasting me. 'Do you have condoms?' I ask. 'Because I'm still on birth control, but you know. You can never be too careful.'

His mouth tilts up in a smile, and he points at the bedside drawer. 'Yeah. But I meant what I said. I can't wait to eat you out.'

He pulls me down the bed and tugs my panties off easily, then slides my legs over his shoulders. I grab his hair and moan as he takes charge of me in the sexiest way possible.

Later, he holds my hands above my head as he slides on a condom and fucks me hard, and I cry out his name as I come again on his cock.

I just can't help thinking, as we make our own version of paradise in the dark, that the only thing that could make it even better is if Lee was still here, too.

31

Scott

I wake up in my own bed, totally refreshed – so I must have gotten some deep sleep, even if it was only a few hours – and I'm alone. Which would normally be perfectly normal, except that last night, Adrienne was with me. Now, there's an empty space in my arms.

I stretch, wondering why it hurts so damn much to wake up alone today. It shouldn't really be enough to make me miserable first thing in the morning. But it wasn't our first time together, and last time we were together, she was a snuggler in the mornings.

Her father is in the hospital, though. I could excuse just about any kind of reactions from her right now.

But when I come downstairs, she's there, brewing coffee. In one of my button-up shirts, and nothing else. Okay, so it's long enough to cover most of the parts Lee and I explored last night, but there's still nothing hotter.

She looks up and smiles. 'Hey.'

I'm so relieved to see her there that I wrap my arms

around her waist, bring her ass back against me, and plant a kiss just behind her ear. She makes a happy sound and leans her head back onto my shoulder, and I can't help myself. I kiss the side of her neck, then her collarbone.

'Mmm, love that,' she says. 'I'm having coffee, you want some?'

'Yeah, good idea.' I let her go and get another mug down from the cupboard. I try tell my cock to calm down from where it's already at half-mast again, and try *not* to remember how she bit my earlobe last night while I was inside her... How she sounded when I made her come that fourth time...

At the coffee maker, she glides her hands around my chest and glows up at me. 'Last night was ... amazing.'

So she's thinking the same thing I am, after all. I smile slowly, closing the gap between us, until all her soft bits are rubbing against me. I'm both filled with gratitude and an urgent desire to protect her, and wanting to pin her against a wall again. It's crazy-making.

'Glad to hear it,' I say. I tilt her head back and kiss her thoroughly, taking her pretty little mouth and making it mine.

The coffee maker beeps, letting us know the coffee is ready.

She looks down and clears her throat. 'Yeah, for a moment there, I almost forgot everything that happened yesterday. Thanks for that.'

I know that's not all it was for her – or for me, either. But I don't have time to get into that with her, because the back door swings open.

I take two quick steps over to it, hands in fists, instantly in defensive mode after Mara's attack yesterday.

Lee looks up at me in surprise, and Gal brushes between us both, panting happily. 'Hey, man.'

I unclench my fists and exhale. 'Hey.'

Addie comes over and hugs him. It's the warmest I've seen her act towards him in weeks, apart from last night on the couch.

'Hey, how you doing?' he checks. 'Gal and I just dropped by to check you guys were okay before we head to work.'

She shrugs. 'Thank you for last night.' She meets my eyes again. 'Both of you.' She waves her coffee mug at him, and narrowly avoids spilling it. 'You want some?'

He steals her cup and gulps. He coughs and hands it back. 'Shit, that's strong.'

I laugh, amused. *But is it good that he's here again?* The situation from last night plays again in my mind like a movie, and I can't think for a second. Addie's stopped being mad at Lee, and now they're flirting a little with each other, carefully, playfully... *Why did I enjoy it so much last night, if I'm already feeling jealous again this morning? Is it harmless?* I honestly can't tell.

'Gal and I already checked on the others, too, this morning,' Lee says. 'So you don't need to worry. Your dad, Eloise and the kids, Charlie – everyone's safe.'

She leans into him again and lets out a big sigh. I can tell she's holding in tears. 'Thank you both.'

'No sweat, Anteater. You know, even when we weren't... I mean, ah...' He glances over at me, clearly unsure if he should say what he's about to.

I shrug, not sure what he's thinking.

He says, 'We both looked out for your friends, your family. I want you to know that.'

'You guys. You're my heroes, both of you. Thank you.' She takes a big sip of coffee, clearly embarrassed. She clears her throat, then asks Lee, 'So, have you eaten?'

'Nah, I was just going to head to work.'

She smacks him on the shoulder. 'You need to eat! What are you doing!'

I laugh at them and pull out a frypan. 'Bacon and eggs?'

While I crack some eggs, Lee puts on some Taylor Swift album and these two start dancing around in the kitchen. Gal runs in as soon as the smell of frying bacon fills the air. Adrienne laughs over something Lee says, and smacks him with a teatowel.

Seeing them together... I shouldn't be jealous, but I'm seeing green. There's practically a forest full of envy clouding my vision.

I've got to set that feeling aside, though. It's not helping anyone. And I wasn't that jealous last night, when Lee was touching her... *You were right there, too, encouraging them*, I remind myself. *She wasn't cheating on you.*

When it's ready, Addie dances over first and rubs up against me, and I put some bacon on her plate, but hold onto the plate when she moves to take it away. 'Pay the toll,' I joke.

She chuckles, then kisses me until I almost drop the plate. She grins as she walks over to the kitchen bar stools.

Lee looks away.

For a moment, I regret kissing her in front of him. It's enough to make me think I need to talk to them again, both of them. Lee's my friend, but I can't be getting jealous as hell any time he has her full attention, and I hate that he's feeling awkward around me.

While Addie, Lee, and Gal chow down, I put some bacon and eggs in a wrap for myself so I can take it to the station with me.

After Lee and Gal have left, I cup her elbow and say quietly, 'Adrienne. Can I talk to you for a moment?'

Her smile fades. 'Of course?' She says it like she's asking me what's wrong.

I bring her to the couch, where we all hung out together last night, so intimate, so free with each other.

'Scott, what's up?' Her eyes are wide open.

I don't want to hurt you, and I don't want my jealousy to hurt me. 'Clearly you have something with Lee, and he's my friend, so I'm trying to be okay with it.'

'We're just friends.'

I shake my head. 'No, you're not. And I know *he's* not. And I can't be casual about you, Adrienne. I love you.' That's a lot easier to say than I thought it would be. It feels so natural to love her, and to tell her that out loud.

'I love you, too!' she gasps, and hugs me.

I hug her back. Then comes the hard bit. 'But if you want to be with him, you should be with him. Not me.'

'I'm with *you*. I want to be with you.'

'Okay. Okay. I'm trying here.'

'So am I. I mean, look, yeah I love you both, but in different ways.' She puts her hands on my biceps, like she did last night, her hands light but her grip fierce. 'You have nothing to worry about. And I figure, if I want you in my life, that means I need to include Lee in my life, too. So I did include him.'

Can't argue with that. I'm the one who told him he needs to be friends with her, so we can all work together. I've put my heart on the line and said everything I can. Now I guess I need to figure out a way to fake that I'm okay with this, at the very least.

I say, 'I need to go check in at the station, catch up on some work. Can you please snib the latch to lock the door behind you if you head out later?' I grab my jacket, and I feel the weight of her staring at me as I leave.

Why is this so hard? I just want to ask her to choose me. Pick me. Put my name at the top of her list. I don't want to ask her why again. *Why did you kiss Lee, back when we broke up? Why does he make you laugh more than I can? Why can't you just be friends?*

It's been so good, being together again. I've let her in again. But now, even after last night, after being as close as you can get to another person with her, I feel like I'm just hanging on, waiting for her to disappear with him.

Is she going to break my heart all over again?

32

Lee

So it looks like I've been friend-zoned again. Can't believe we were all over each other last night, and now this morning she's only making out with Scott again. And it's pretty clear they did more than that while she was sleeping over last night.

But in spite of how much that sucks for me, I know there's something between the three of us. I know Addie would do anything for me and Scott. So I want to do anything for her.

Yeah. I want to make sure she's never in danger again.

So I send her a text message.

hey adam ant. don't worry about these fuckers. take care of your dad and gal and i'll come see you later, after we've taken care of the feral's baby.

I think about adding something like "you know i love you right" but then I don't. *Getting soft, princess?* I smack my own head. *Christ. Nearly caught ya talking feelings again.*

And then I whistle for Gal, and we hop on the bike. She can tell we're on an important mission, and she's excited.

It takes two days, two days of Gal and I eating not quite enough and wandering the industrial outskirts of the city, sniffing out trail after trail. But we find them. They meet in the boiler room of the chicken nugget factory, where they can hide their wolfy scent under the stench of boiling and frying poultry.

They can't hide from Gal and I, though. She's my silent companion, padding as quietly as we've practised a hundred times, over grates and up metal stairs that an untrained dog would make a racket on.

It's late, well after 10pm. Mara and her pack have gathered and are starting to talk, most of them snacking on chicken off-cuts from the bins while they argue.

I line up a shot, with Mara's head and shoulders right in the crosshairs. My hand doesn't even shake on the leather grip of the pistol.

Gal suddenly sniffs, and gets to her feet, growling quietly.

Ah, shit. My body stiffens, and I jump up, but not fast enough.

As I'm still orienting myself, a silver bullet catches me in the shoulder. It stings worse than any pain I've ever felt.

I reel back, knock over a barrel, and I know I only have a second to get out of there, or both Gal and I are dead meat.

I shoot back, and the lyko who crept up on us ducks.

As soon as they're out of the way, I fire a full round at the window next to us, shooting out the glass. Gal skips ahead of me, out onto the little metal balcony. We're only up two flights of stairs, and there's a skip just below us that we can land on.

It'll be fine.

Probably.

'Jump, girl!' I yell to Gal, giving her the matching signal. She leaps down onto the skip with a thud.

I follow her, clambering over the railing a bit less gracefully. I definitely bugger my knee on the landing, and I know that's going to hurt like a mother. But I barely feel it; for now, it's just a shock, and then we're sprinting for the bike.

I don't quite make it to the bike when I feel another hundred little stings in my back. Another bullet? Shrapnel? I have no idea.

I grunt and we make it onto the bike, which is behind a wall, thank fuck.

I rev the engine, and we get the fuck outta there.

Unfortunately, my body starts shaking with the shock of the injuries after just a few minutes of driving at high speed, so I have to pull off the highway into the forest. Gal licks my wounds, and I try to stay conscious. Whatever happened where that silver bullet got me, I know it must be bad, because I start chucking up from the pain.

I check my phone. It's only got 5% battery, since I haven't charged it in the days while Gal and I were hunting, but it's enough. I click on Scott's name.

33

Addie

I call Scott as soon as I read the text. My hands aren't shaking yet, because adrenaline is helping me stay focused, but my gut hurts so bad with worry for Lee that I almost double over while I'm talking to Scott.

I know Lee can handle himself. I know how strong he is, and crafty. And I know he's taken Gal with him as back-up.

Scott shows up at my door ready for a long search. He takes one look at me and gathers me into his arms. I exhale against his chest, all my stress coming out in a big, hard breath.

'Hey,' he says against my hair, and kisses my forehead. 'Don't worry about it. He's a big boy, he can take care of himself. And if he's in trouble, we'll find him.'

'Okay. Okay.'

Just then, my phone starts ringing. It's Eloise, so I pick up straight away.

'Hi, Elle.'

'Hey, Addie. How's Dad doing?'

'Okay, I think. I haven't been back to the hospital yet today, but a friend checked on him for me this morning, and he was stable.'

Elle's voice turns indignant. 'Why aren't you there now, at the hospital? I've got the kids, and I was there yesterday, too. I can't be there every day.'

'I'm not asking you to. I'll be back there again this afternoon. I'm just … I'm out at the moment, with Scott, looking for Lee, he's run off.'

'You're out with some guy, looking for another guy who's run off? Addie, do you even hear yourself? Come on. Da is family. Who are these feckin' guys?' Her accent is getting stronger again; she's angry at me. 'The ones who brought feckin' werewolves to Jazz's birthday party? You would put all of us in danger *again*, wouldn't you!'

'I'm sorry.' My voice shakes. I hate anyone being upset at me, but especially Dad or Elle. They are the closest people to me in the entire world – or at least, they have been, until I met Scott and Lee. Maybe they still are. Maybe Elle's right, and I shouldn't be out here, wasting my time on these two man-wolves.

She hangs up, and I swallow hard, trying not to cry.

My sister's the closest relationship I've had, for most of my life at least. This is – apart from me ripping the head off her Barbie when we were kids – the biggest disagreement we've ever had.

Reaching over to squeeze my hand on my knee, Scott asks, with sincere concern in his eyes, 'You okay?'

I stare out the window, wishing I could feel safe again. 'Nope. Just drive.'

Scott and I drive around the valley every dawn and dusk for two days, looking for Lee. I can see him getting frustrated, running his hands through his hair more often. Stress lines around his eyes for his friend. Sneaking looks at me because I'm talking less than usual, because I'm completely stress out, too.

Finally, I pull him aside. 'Hey, listen. I know that we just spent all week looking for Lee. But that doesn't mean anything about how I feel about you. I still love you.'

'I know,' he says, but I can tell he doesn't believe it. 'Adrienne, I can't help wondering...'

We're interrupted by a ringtone. It's Scott's phone.

'It's Lee!' he says, his face showing relief for one second before he picks up and immediately switches to sergeant mode again. 'Where are you?'

When we find him, he looks like shit. He's so bloodied up I'm amazed he's still alive. Gal looks pretty rough too, and she's whining with stress and hunger.

Scott puts an arm under Lee's shoulder and lifts him up with an easy grunt, then packs him into the car.

'Don't be too mad, bro,' Lee says. 'I've got so much fucking intel for you. We're gonna bring 'em down eeeeasy.'

'Right, or you just scared them away from their hiding place for good,' Scott snaps.

Scott drives us all back to his place, where there's room for

Ray to do her healer thing and patch him up properly.

Scott stays downstairs to call Ray to come over. I can also hear him calling some others from the pack, so they can come too and hear the information Lee has for us all.

Lee and I head for the main bathroom, where Scott keeps his first aid kit.

I spin to face Lee, frustrated by Scott leaving, by him wanting to draw lines in the sand between him-and-me and Lee-and-me. It feels so unfair to me, and I end up taking that frustration out on Lee, which is unfair to him. 'What is wrong with you? You can't keep doing this crazy shit. Going after Mara alone, without back-up? Are you insane?'

Without warning, he throws a punch straight into the mirror. It smashes with a loud crunch.

I flinch back.

He pulls his hand back. It was already bruised and dirty, but now his fist has bleeding cuts in a few more places. 'I'm a *werewolf*, Addie!'

'Doesn't mean you have to act like one!' Clearly, he's already written himself off, but *someone* has to call him on his crap. I'm not naive enough to think anyone can save him from his dark side except for him – so it's not gonna be me – but I can't help myself. It's in my DNA to try to make people see reason.

'Addie, this is what we do. We defend what's ours, we have a crazy temper, we go a bit crazy sometimes, and we *break shit.*'

'Scott says you can keep it under control.'

'I'm not Scott. Stop trying to turn me into him.'

I blush, hot and immediate. 'I'm not.'

'Of course you are. Everyone can see you've still got the hots for him.'

'Not the point! The Lee who once brought me lemon squares? That's the Lee who's my friend.'

'*That* Lee only did it to get on your good side. *This* is who I really am.' Then he winces.

I soften immediately. 'You're wounded. Turn on the light, we'll need more light to patch you up.'

He glowers.

I smile angelically, and step outside to flick the light switch myself.

He mutters, 'I can do it,' and shuts the door on me.

I just wait patiently outside the door, knowing he'll need my help eventually. After a while, I hear some swearing, so I say, 'I'm coming in, stand back.'

I open the door to see him struggling to reach behind his back with a pair of tweezers. Even I know we've got to get those bullets out – the silver isn't good for him.

His eyes show he's in physical agony, and he doesn't bother to hide it. 'I can't reach, Addie Bear, I just need you to dig them out for me.'

'Oh, geez. Yep, I'll try. I'm not a doctor, though.'

'That's okay. Ray's coming. Can't go see a doctor anyway.'

'Why? What would they be able to tell?'

'Temperature, blood pressure – you name it, most of it is different.'

'Well, okay.' I slid the tweezers in as gently as I could, and grasped hold of a silver nub that was slick with blood. 'Oh noooo, I don't like doing this. Sweet Mary, mother of God... You okay there?'

'Shit. Balls. I'm going to *kill* Mara.'

'Lee, you can't do that.'

'Watch me.' He turned his head, panting in pain, and winked. 'I took these bullets for you, pretty lady, but when you've got them all out, I'm gonna go kill someone *for me.*'

'How could you put yourself in such a dangerous position? Wasn't today reckless enough?'

'For you,' he says firmly. 'If it comes down to it, I will jump over *any* obstacle to put myself between you and danger.'

I shake my head. 'You need to protect yourself as well! You can't just throw your life away to save mine.'

'Why not?'

'Because I care about you, you big idiot.'

He smiles at me over his shoulder, then winces again. 'Yeah?'

I focus on pulling out the next sliver of bullet casing. 'Fine,' I say. 'You want to talk about ... you and me? Let's talk.'

Lee's voice turns to gravel. 'That's the thing, I don't know what to say. 'Cos right now, I want to tear your clothes off and take you on the bathroom floor, and just lick every inch of your body while everyone downstairs wishes they were us. But that's probably a bad idea, right?'

I meet his eyes in the bathroom mirror.

His gaze is so sharp it could cut glass right now.

I clear my throat. 'Umm, right. Yeah, no. Bad idea.'

'It's just... You have a thing for me.'

I can't help the smile that flashes across my face.

He grins. 'I know it, you know it. I think you could be with me, and you could be with Scott, and we could all have something amazing. But watching you eye-fuck both of us makes me hot. I'm not trying to get you to choose either of us. I'm just trying to get you to choose something outside the box. I'm not apologising for that. Not this time.'

I stare at him in the mirror, blown away by his attitude and his words and this brutal honesty. It's too much. I'm not used to this level of being unnerved and vulnerable, and I want to run away, and I want to get closer, and I want him to keep talking about what we three could have. And I feel so, so guilty for wanting that.

I can't say anything. I can barely think. I give myself a moment, and pull out the last few fragments of bullet. I'm faster now that I know how to lift them out.

When the last piece of silver pops out of his back, his whole frame shudders for a moment, and then relaxes. He turns around and takes my hand, smiling.

'I need to clean up the blood,' I stammer.

'It can wait.' He tugs me in, until I'm standing between his legs. He takes my hand and strokes my wrist, igniting something.

My core reacts, and I lick my lips, unbearably turned on by his hard thighs on either side of mine. My heart is racing; I'm barely breathing. I try to pull my mind out of the gutter.

He studies me for a long moment as my blush grows.

'Haven't you thought about it?'

'About … being with you? Or both of you?' I'm startled into honesty. 'Yeah, of course I've thought about it! Are you kidding? After that night on the couch? I've thought about it a *lot.*'

He smiles, a hunter who sees their prey has frozen, ready to be caught. 'Then what's the problem, Alley Cat?'

'It's Scott,' I stutter.

'I know.' His eyes are warm. 'That's why I left, to find Mara and her cronies. So you and Scott wouldn't have to break up again.'

'You — what?' That definitely wasn't what I was expecting. I'm flabbergasted.

'You were so worried that you'd caused it, when your dad got hurt. I thought maybe you and Scott would break up, and you might move away again, to try and draw Mara away, keep your family safe.'

'You went after her … for me?' I shake my head. 'You're amazing. But you didn't need to do that. I mean, it's great that you found them! Now everything can be over soon. But you put yourself at risk…'

'I wanna make sure you stick around. I care about you, too, Addie.'

It doesn't escape me that he's using my real name, no nicknames right now.

He touches the side of my neck lightly, and his fingertips trace a line down my shoulder, then my arm, to rest on my hip. His fingertips leave a trail of fire in their wake, and I shiver with anticipation.

I try to remind myself we need to talk to Scott before we do anything, but I can barely form a coherent thought. I look down at where he's pressing up against my body.

But his hand leaves mine; he puts his finger under my chin so I have to lift my gaze.

My eyes lock with his, and I want him so bad that I'm aching. I feel it in my belly, in my core; even my nipples are getting hard already. Heat is rushing through me.

He takes my glasses off without asking, sets them on the shelf. He cups my face with one hand. He's moving slowly, giving me time to say no.

Maybe I should say no.

Instead, I stare at his lips until that wicked mouth of his curves into a smile.

I lean in and kiss him, hard. He tastes like salt, like sweat, and I can't get enough.

Now the hand that was holding my hip moves, and he slides it between my legs. I gasp, and he captures the sound with another deep kiss.

I'm tempted to move my own hand farther south, to rub his cock through his pants. He's growing so hard, pressed up against me, and I want to move so that I'm not between his legs anymore; I want him between *my* legs, pressing into me.

My voice is quiet as I start, 'Lee, I want...'

Footsteps sound behind us, and I jump backwards, out of Lee's touch. He smirks at my reaction, then winces when he sees who it is.

Scott looks us both up and down, and sniffs, just once. He

knows. There's no doubt in my mind he can smell what we were just doing. Even if he couldn't smell it, he can see I'm flushed; he can see I've taken my glasses off. His eyes get that guarded look again.

'Pack healer's here,' he says tersely, and walks out again.

My heart breaks. *Noooo, no no no. Fuck! Did I just fuck it up again? Why couldn't I just stick with Scott? Why am I hurting all of us like this? And why the fuck does Lee keep turning me on when he knows Scott doesn't like it?*

I wash my hands, straighten my clothing, and then follow him. I don't say another word to Lee. He just watches me wordlessly, his eyes pained.

In the hallway, we pass Ray, who's dressed in scrubs and carrying a heavy-looking esky marked FIRST AID. Scott nods his head towards the bathroom, and she nods in acknowledgement.

She sniffs in my direction, scenting God knows what – arousal? fear? confusion? soap? But she just smiles at me, then enters the bathroom to see Lee.

As Ray works on Lee, Scott goes to the kitchen and pours a cold glass of water for each of us. I'm glad for the cool sensation, waking me up from the fever dream that is the tension between the three of us – me, Scott, Lee. Even when Lee is upstairs, he's somehow here with us.

After we drink, Scott rubs his hands up my arms. I turn wordlessly and sink into his arms.

He kisses the top of my head, and says slowly, 'It's hard when someone gets hurt … when you love them.'

I sob, even though I'm trying to hold it together. 'Yeah. I do,

I love Lee, and I don't like seeing him hurt. I don't want him getting hurt again.'

'I don't, either.'

I look up at him, and he looks so sad.

'Listen,' he says. 'When I first saw you had feelings for Lee, I kept waiting for him to do something so terrible that you would hate him. So I waited. But each time he annoyed you or scared you or pissed you off – you kept him around. And I like who he is around you. And I don't want to lose that person – the Lee who's with you. So if I have to let you go, to make sure that person stays…'

'No, I don't want to lose you, either, though. You're both my guys. My men. Maybe I don't have an "other half"; maybe I'm cut into thirds, and both of you each have a piece.'

Scott shakes his head. 'Adrienne. I'm a jealous person. I don't think living in thirds could work. So I guess…' His thumb rubs my arm, and my stomach sinks into my boots. 'I have to let you go, don't I? We've done what we said we would; we found the bad guys and we're gonna lock them up. So we have to be done now.'

I'm crying outright now, my breath coming in little sobs. 'No, I can't be done with you. I can't.'

Ray picks that moment to come downstairs, which is probably just as well. She says, 'He'll probably need to rest today, if not tomorrow as well. Sit on him if you have to; whatever it takes to keep him in bed or on the couch.'

Scott nods to me, saying, 'I'll have to leave you to it, Adrienne. I have to go do some … clean-up.'

I try not to cry, and he must see it in my eyes, because he looks sad for a moment.

'I'll be back later, when the pack gets here,' he says, and leaves.

I go back upstairs, to find Lee bandaged and swearing softly. That's enough to tell me he's in pain; normally, he'd be shouting the house down with jokes and complaints by now.

Just then, my phone rings. I flinch, and look at the screen.

Charlie. Oh, shit, whoops. I'm late for brunch with my best friend. I think she'll understand why I'm late, but there are no guarantees she'll be patient about it. I pick up and start apologising immediately.

'Girl, it's fine, at least you ditched me for one of those hot dudes this time, instead of just boring work. Shall I come pick you up? Where you at?'

I give her Scott's address. 'See you soon. Thanks so much!'

Lee watches me, dark and curious, in a way that makes me want to cancel brunch and get back to what we were doing before. He could take me right here on the bathroom sink.

God, this flip-flopping is starting to drive me crazy.

I make a vague gesture in his direction. 'Um … I have to go meet Charlie, and you're supposed to spend the day resting.'

He's silent for a long moment, his eyes showing a myriad of emotions – hunger, sadness, confusion, hope, fear.

On impulse, I ask, 'Do you want me to bring you back a coffee?'

34

Scott

I book an emergency appointment with my psychologist. I consider therapy an essential part of being a cop. Having a professional to unload with means I don't accidentally take it out on the people I care about. Like my pack, and Lee, and anyone I'm dating.

They're surprised to get my call, but not hugely. They work with cops a lot.

But for once, I'm not sure where to start. I say, 'It's not about work. Nothing terrible happened. I'm just in a bit of a personal situation, and I don't know what to do. And I don't want to hurt the people I care about by doing the wrong thing.'

'Doing the wrong thing is a big fear of yours, isn't it?' It's not really a question.

I bristle. 'It's not a *fear*; it's important to get things right. Especially with this.'

'Okay, so it's about getting it right for the people you care about. What's the situation?'

I groan. 'Some kind of … throuple … triad … situation.'

They don't hesitate at all, thank goodness. 'Do you mean a polyamorous type of situation? You and two others are together? Or do you mean a love triangle, where you and someone else are both hoping this person will choose you?'

'I was thinking it was a love triangle, at first. But now, well, maybe it's a poly thing, I don't know… I feel like I *should* know what this relationship is. It's ridiculous that I don't.'

'No, it's not ridiculous. Relationships can be complex, and you can have lots of complicated feelings about a relationship, even if you do think you understand what's happening. So, tell me about this poly relationship.'

I spill my guts as fast as I can, eager to get past this awkward moment to the part where they give me advice. 'You know my friend, Lee.'

'Yeah, of course. You've been a good friend to Lee. You've always been there for him, since before he became a cop. Took him under your wing.'

'Right, and then we became real friends, not just this mentor-mentee thing. Anyway, Lee and I both like this woman. Adrienne.'

'You've spoken about her before. Is she the same one…?'

'We dated three years ago, yeah.'

'Why did you break up? Back then?'

'Ah, because of Lee. Or because of me, I guess.' I scrub a hand over my face. 'I got jealous. Lee and Adrienne kissed once, and they said it wouldn't happen again, but I couldn't handle it.'

'How did you two end up back together again, then?'

'I couldn't help myself. I still love her. As soon as I saw she was back in town, I started working towards asking her out again. That's how I've ended up in this situation.'

'So what is the situation?'

'Well, Adrienne and I have been spending time together, as friends, since she got back into town. And I thought I'd done a good thing by persuading her and Lee to try to be friends again, as well. But the other night, we were all hanging out together ... and Adrienne had a hard day, and we were comforting her.' I slow down, caught up in the memory, so vivid it's like reliving it. 'And we were drinking, and we started fooling around ... and we ... I let her and Lee...' *God, why is this so difficult to say? I'm not embarrassed, am I?* 'I let him touch her, kiss her.'

I love that my therapist doesn't bat an eyelash. There's absolutely no hint of judgement. 'How was that?' they ask.

'Incredible. Amazing. I want to do it again. But now it's so awkward between the three of us. Because it's like I've given us all permission to hook up together, but I still can't *stand* to see him flirting with her.'

'Do you see him flirting with her often?'

'Well, yeah, all the time. We're spending a lot of time together at the moment.'

'And does Adrienne take that well? Does she flirt back?'

'Yeah. Sometimes it seems like she's trying to just treat him like a friend, but there's so much tension between them...'

'So you're worried Lee and Adrienne still have something going on?'

'It's not that I'm worried about it; I *know* they've got a thing for each other. Whether they mean to be or not, they're connected. As much as I know she loves me, she's also into Lee. It's like they can't help it.'

'And so if you feel like you've given the three of you permission to hook up together the other night, then why does it bother you if Lee and Addie have feelings for each other?'

'She's my girlfriend.'

'Is she? Have you talked about it?'

Shit. 'I guess not.'

'Okay, so it sounds like that would be a good conversation to have.'

I sigh. 'Yeah, and I will. Soon.'

'Great, so since we know that conversation will happen, we can set that aside for now. You were saying that regardless of how you all hooked up or what's happened recently, it bothers you that Adrienne is also attracted to someone else. Even if she doesn't act on those feelings?'

'Hmm. Yes.'

'How does that sit with you?'

'Not good. Sounds possessive. And I don't own her. But she knows that her actions are hurting my feelings. She should care about that, as well.'

'Do you get the sense that she does? Care about that?'

I groan. 'Yes. Very clearly.'

'Okay, so you both care about each other. And you both care about Lee. I wonder, Scott, if you weren't dating Adrienne, would you still be annoyed if you saw her flirting with Lee? Or if she started dating Lee?'

'No, obviously not. I'd be happy for the two of them. They're both amazing people.'

'Interesting, because people who are monogamous would say it's not obvious. Most monogamous people say they'd feel jealous if the person they had feelings for started dating someone else, even if *they* couldn't date the person themselves. Compare that to people who believe in polyamory. They say they feel compersion when two people they like are happy together. Do you know that term?'

'Umm, no, I'm not exactly a scholar, doc.'

We share a laugh.

'That's okay,' says the therapist. 'Compersion is when you feel happy for someone unconditionally. So you can be happy about things that don't necessarily benefit you, or things that would otherwise cause you to feel jealous or possessive. Things like your girlfriend being with someone else as well as being with you.'

I'm silent for a long while, taking deep breaths and thinking it over. I've never heard of compersion before, and my head is starting to hurt from all the talking. 'I always want her to be happy.'

'Do you lose anything if she's happy with both Lee and you?'

I shake my head vehemently. 'No. Well, maybe. I guess I lose the security of knowing that she'll stay with me.'

'But we never really know that someone will stay with us, do we?'

I growl under my breath. I'm not enjoying one second of this. *But...* 'You're making sense, doc.'

'Let's take a step back from you being in this situation for a moment, and examine some of the backdrop. The social, cultural values that you're bringing to this with. When you're jealous that Lee and Adrienne are happy around each other, what are the cultural values or expectations that underpin that?'

'I guess that whole thing about looking for "The One". The idea that true love is just two people ... and they love each other so much, and their love is so unique, so special, that it doesn't include anyone else. Like if they wanted to include someone else, it would be cheating. And if one of them wanted to cheat on the other one, that would mean they didn't really love them. Like, that's the whole premise of monogamy, right?'

'Absolutely, that's what monogamy says. And right now, we live in a society where that's a big part of our dominant culture, and it supports most of the patriarchal systems we live in. So that's the background. It's important that we can take that step back and recognise the context, because you can get some distance from your thoughts that way.'

'Yeah, that sounds good.'

'Like we always talk about, you want to be able to say hi to your thoughts, like "hi brain!" and just wave hello at those thoughts. So that instead of just thinking whatever you're thinking about Lee and Adrienne and just assuming that's the truth, you can examine those thoughts. Are they true? Remembering that they're based on a social construct, on a culture. Can you *guarantee* that they're a hundred per cent true, no doubt whatsoever?'

'No, that's impossible.' This is familiar ground. Many cops struggle with black and white thinking, and I'm no exception. Thanks to years of therapy, I can now recognise when it's happening, and look for the grey.

'So now, if there was a couple where both of the people wanted to include someone else, would we still say that was cheating?'

'Well, no, that's swinging. Or poly, or whatever.'

'And is that not as good as them being a closed couple?'

I shift uncomfortably in my seat. 'Well, for people who want to be poly together, that's fine for them.'

'But not for you?'

'No. Maybe. I don't know.'

'Where's the limit for you? Would you be okay with having a threesome with Lee and Adrienne?'

I splutter, 'Geez, doc! Fuck.' Then I laugh at myself and think about the other night. *No denying it, that was fun.* I shake my head. 'I don't know. Maybe that would be okay.'

'Would you be okay with the three of you all going on a date together?'

'Yeah, that would be weird … but it might be fun, too.'

'How about if it was on a night when you couldn't be there as well, and just Lee and Adrienne went on a date together?'

'I don't know. This is all just a lot.'

'That's all right. We'll make that your homework for the week, to sit down and consider every aspect of polyamory. Maybe watch some videos about the different types and ways that people can have polyamorous relationships. Think about what actions you would be fine with, and what you wouldn't, and what might be okay but only under certain circumstances. Then have a little think about why each of those soft and hard limits is or isn't important to you. This might just be the start of many important conversations you're going to have to have with Adrienne and Lee. If you want to keep them in your life.'

'I do.' I exhale hard. 'But if I'm honest, it's fucking terrifying.'

'Well, let's look at that. You're feeling some fear. Practise some self-compassion; you're allowed to be afraid; after all, it's a change you're not totally in control of. Then figure out what exactly you're afraid of in the situation. And then in our next session, maybe we can look at whether those are fears that you can be okay with.'

'What do you mean?'

'I mean, can you be okay with *not* feeling okay about every aspect of this situation? Does it need to be an all-or-nothing relationship? Could you be polyamorous and have some hard feelings that you learn to manage? Or if you can't manage being polyamorous with them, could you still have *some* kind of relationship with Adrienne, and keep your friendship with Lee? You don't have to lose both of them at once.'

'Yeah, I don't want that. I want to keep both of them.'

'So, we've got a little bit of time left. Let's dig in for a moment. Do you feel like it's fine for other people to be polyamorous, but not okay for you?'

I shrug. 'I already got my heart broken once by Lee and Adrienne kissing. I mean, at least they told me about it, but still. If they wanted to be together, they should have just done that, instead of going behind my back. Except they both said it was an accident. Sort of. Ugh, it was just a mess.'

'And more recently, do you feel like they've been open and honest with you about what they want?'

'Well…' I stop, thinking of the conversations we've been having lately.

He bared his neck to me in wolfy submission. 'I need you in my life, Scott. You're one of the good ones. And I know she needs you, too.'

And I remember her saying, *'I love you both, but in different ways. If I want you in my life, that means I need to include Lee in my life, too.'*

'I don't know that either of them has said it in plain English,' I say slowly, 'but they've made it clear with what they're saying and doing. They want all three of us to be together, somehow.'

Which will be impossible if we can't stop Mara from carrying out her revenge on Adrienne. I have to make sure she'll be safe.

'And anyway,' I continue. 'I do have something to lose now. I've come so far. Built my life, my career, from next to nothing. And yes I had white male privilege, but it still wasn't easy. Now I'm finally a sergeant, a leader.' Let the therapist think that means whatever they want it to; I know my role as pack alpha is equally important. 'If people knew we were a throuple, they would talk – they always do – and my reputation is important. Maybe it's not worth disrupting the status quo, just for some … fucked-up sense of love or loyalty or whatever I feel for Lee, and for Adrienne.'

That makes me stop and think. *A fucked-up sense of love or loyalty*…

I'm still convinced Mara killed the person who turned her, but she said they were dead now, and I couldn't find any murders in the right timeframe. What if the person who turned her was her father, and he was doing it out of a fucked-up sense of love? And what if her response, going all out to avenge him, is because of a fucked-up sense of loyalty to her dad, even though he turned her? That would explain why I can't find any evidence of a murder to pin on her.

Yes. His bite wouldn't have made her feral herself, but it would have turned her. And the trauma of being turned by your own dad was definitely enough to mess with most people's heads.

'Where did you go just now?' asks the therapist.

'Just thinking about the case I'm working at the moment,' I say slowly. 'Trying to find a way to stop a killer, but we don't have enough evidence at the moment.'

'Well, that's good!' they say encouragingly. 'Sounds like it's time for us to wrap up for the day. Just before you go, remember to look for evidence behind the thoughts about Lee and Adrienne. Not just evidence that reinforces a fear of being left alone. Evidence that your friend, and your lover, want to be in your life for the long term.'

I smile. 'Okay, doc, will do.'

35

Lee

Charlie is short but spunky, and I'm impressed that she keeps her cool. She makes zero fuss about having to come pick up Addie for their brunch date from Scott's place. That is, right up until Addie leaves us alone for a minute.

'I'll just go get my phone, I think I left it in the kitchen,' says Addie. As she passes me, she ducks down to where I'm stretched out on the couch and whispers in my ear, 'Be good. Don't do anything stupid.'

I laugh, surprised. I drawl up at her, 'But angel, stupid is so much more fun.'

As soon as Addie disappears, Charlie leans over the back of the couch and peers at me intently. 'So what's up with you two?'

Well, no use hiding things, I guess. I aim for a smooth, easy tone. 'We kissed three years ago. And then again today. Now it's weird.'

'Because you want what Scott and Addie have?' She narrows her eyes at me.

Oh yeah, she knows exactly what she's asking. I hate the power dynamic here, the fact that I'm stuck on the couch, too tired and sore to stand up. So I answer honestly, to get her off my back: 'Because I want Addie.'

'Ohhhh.' Her eyebrows rise up towards her hairline. 'You know she's sleeping with Scott? *Again.*' She rolls her eyes.

'Ah, well, what can I do? I'm in love with a woman I can never have.'

'Why can't you? Isn't poly supposed to be less taboo now? And you already know she's into you.'

I inhale sharply, and it makes a stab in between my ribs that makes me cough. So Addie must have said something about me to her friend! But it's not her I'm worried about convincing. I explain, 'I'm not sure the other person involved would agree.'

'Oh, it's easy! You just tell your best friend that the one woman you can't live without...'

'Is the same woman he can't live without?' I scoff. 'Charlotte Rose, now is not the time!'

'Now is the only time! And how do you know my middle name?'

I wink. 'I know everything.'

'Whatever, wolfy boy. Look, if you don't do something now, you're going to end up alone.'

'The worst thing in the world, I'm sure.' After she's silent for a moment, I say quietly, 'Hey. For what it's worth, I'm sorry for getting you mixed up in this.'

She play-smacks my arm. 'In your love life? Darling, this is the kind of drama I *live* for.'

'No, I mean all the wolfy drama. If I hadn't become friends with Addie, you never would've been attacked.'

'Why is it your fault? Did you ask to become a werewolf?'

'No, of course not.'

'Then as much as it pains me to admit, you're innocent. Just like the rest of us. We do the best we can with the hand we're dealt.' She sighed heavily. 'That's life. We're all just a bunch of suckers.'

I sit back, stunned. I've never heard someone say exactly what I think – that some people get dealt a shitty hand, and you just have to deal with it – and then turn that into a reason to go *easy* on myself. I've always figured the exact opposite: life sucks, so you have to suck it up. Because even though my life has been a fuck-up almost from start to finish, everyone still expects me to try to be perfect.

Could I really view myself, after everything I've done, as innocent?

When Addie gets back from brunch with Charlie, I can tell she's thinking hard. I have to say, 'Hey, Advil. Stop chewing on that gorgeous lip already.'

She smiles, but it's strained.

'What's up?'

She gathers herself together and says firmly, 'Enough is enough. My loved ones have all suffered enough because I'm being hunted. And so have your pack. So I have an idea.'

'I hate it already,' I say, but I smile so she knows I'm not serious.

'Use me as bait, so you can catch these creeps and put them away for good.'

Scott chooses that moment to walk in, already shaking his head. 'No. Immediately no.'

They argue for a while. He's saying she just wants to sacrifice herself. She's saying he doesn't believe she's as strong as she really is. *She might have him there.*

Eventually, I judge the argument has gone on long enough, and Addie is starting to sound tired. So I throw a couch cushion at Scott. 'Truce? I need a beer!'

Addie laughs, and Scott makes a disgruntled noise, but he goes and gets us all some cans of lemonade.

We've all just cracked open our drinks when Kenny arrives. Then Vicki and Ray show up. Before we know it, a *lot* of our pack are here, and they all want to talk with Scott.

Vicki speaks first. 'A lot of the pack have been coming to Radhika injured. I think some of us are beginning to resent having to keep defending themselves against Mara's pack when … again, *some* of us, not all of us, feel there's no good reason for us to be fighting.'

She doesn't glance at Addie, and I'm glad. I know Addie already feels awkward for being the reason the two packs are fighting. And I can see she feels awkward being here while they talk about it. She's hunching her shoulders and curling in on herself, trying to make herself smaller.

But really, she shouldn't worry about it. I'm the one who killed Grendel. Mara's anger is my fault. I'm the elephant in the room, taking up too much space.

I can feel my pulse racing as I start spiralling, trying to think of a way to fix this. I have to do something. But what?

'Well, we looked into her,' says Scott. 'We don't have anything we can pin on her, either here or where she used to live. And the lyko we took in isn't squealing.'

It's not just me who's fidgeting now, getting more agitated. Everyone in the room is either pacing or scowling.

Eventually, I snap, 'Enough already! We've all been hurt by this. We get it. I'm sick of her hiding in *our* city and doing these cowardly hit-and-runs on our people. We know where they are. I'm going back there!'

'Not without back-up,' Scott says.

'Stay safe,' Addie murmurs, her eyes flicking between us both.

Scott shakes his head. 'We can't promise that, darling.'

She looks surprised, but she shouldn't. This is the man she fell for, the man who's my best friend: a leader who would do anything for his team; a strong man who works hard to stay in control; an alpha whose pack has been threatened.

'Let me help, then,' she says. 'I can draw her out for you.'

I chuckle under my breath. Bold, for her to tell us to stay safe when she wants us to let her play bait. But I say, 'She's got a point, boss.'

Scott glares at me.

I shrug, palms up. 'Lady wants to end these battles by bringing the enemy out of hiding? I say we let her, and we just make sure we have enough of us there—' I gesture around at us pack members. '—to get the jump on the enemy before they can hurt her.'

'As long as you have an actual plan for what to do about those silver bullets,' says Kenny. 'No offence, but I don't want to die today.'

I nod. 'Yep, agree.'

'If we had a way to get wolfsbane into them,' says Ray, 'then it wouldn't matter that they have silver bullets; they would be in too much pain to be thinking about firing a gun.'

'I could try to slip something in their drink?' Addie says.

I laugh. 'Kid, they would see you coming a mile off.'

She pokes out her tongue at me.

I grin.

'Can we lace our bullets with wolfsbane?' Vicki asks.

Scott grimaces. 'We'd risk getting it on ourselves…'

'But it's not poisonous to humans, right?' Addie waits until everyone's looking at her. 'So I have an idea.'

Once she's outlined her plan, everyone just stares at her in awe for a minute.

I nod. 'I'll be right behind you.'

Scott throws up his hands. 'I'd rather anything else, but since I can't think of anything better, or safer, this'll have to do.' He waves to Vicki. 'We'll need you as well, and anyone else from the precinct who knows how to deal with lykos.'

36

Addie

I go to the chicken factory, sweating my ass off. Lee told me how to get in, and I do it carefully, knowing he's watching, following silently. I'm so glad he's there.

Inside, it's not lit at all, since it's after-hours. I wish I could see in the dark, or hear every pin drop, like the guys can. So I could see the enemy coming.

I wish I hadn't been in so many murder and assault trials, because I have a pretty good idea what Mara and her pack could do to me, even if they weren't superhuman. One thing I'm very certain about is that they won't take it easy on me, after everything they blame me for: Grendel going to prison, then dying; the death of some of Grendel's pack; putting some of Mara's pack in prison. These are all people who think they can trace everything bad that's happened in their lives back to me.

When Mara appears, I'm so terrified that I feel actual, physical pain in my stomach. My hands are trembling as I try to hand her the papers.

Mara just stares at the papers, then at me. 'What is this, little human?'

I say, 'I'm suing you for assault.'

She sneers. 'You're what?'

I clear my throat and shake the papers at her. 'You have been served notice. You will need to come to court with your defence prepared on the date it says in those documents, or face criminal charges and civil penalties for failure to appear.' My voice shakes.

She snarls, a wicked sound that literally makes my bladder squeeze. She snatches the papers out of my hand.

I pull my hand back and cross my arms so she can't see how badly I'm shaking with fear.

She glances at the papers in her hand, and flicks through them quickly. 'What bullshit have you drummed up now, little lawyer?' Then she gasps in pain. 'Ow, what the fuck?' She drops the papers. Her hands are already breaking out in blisters. 'What is this? What did you do?'

I step back, hoping the guys are close. 'I'm just taking you to court so we can do this legally. Properly.'

'*Wolfsbane*,' she hisses. Her eyes darken, and suddenly I know I'm dead.

This was a big mistake.

My back hits the wall, and I look around, but I can't see a way out unless I run right past Mara. Or maybe I could jump out the window behind me? Lee said that's how he and Gal got out when they came here.

I take a quick glance and gulp. Two storeys down onto hard cement. Yeah, not a great idea – for a human like me, anyway.

She advances on me slowly, her nostrils flaring. Her fingers spread and her nails lengthen into foot-long claws, but she doesn't go full wolf. 'Thought you could take me down with some silly papers? Bitch!'

One of her claws slices down my face, and I scream. She's close enough now that I could push her away if I land a front kick. I lift my knee, but not fast enough – she slashes claws down my leg and I fall to the ground.

Then out of the darkness, I hear Scott yell, 'Police! Stand down!'

He and Vicki are approaching, dressed in full police gear. Their guns are drawn. They're walking slowly towards the base of the stairs, herding three of Mara's pack in front of them.

Thank goodness. I put a hand over the cut in my cheek and scurry backwards until my back is against the wall.

Jumping through the window onto the floor beside me, Lee says, 'Left it a bit close, did we? You all good, A-Team?'

I start laughing hysterically. 'A-Team! Ha!'

He growls at Mara. 'Come near her again, and I'll rip you to bits. You know I can do it.'

She snarls, barely human, 'You don't know anything.'

Lee circles her, drawing her away from me. He grins as he says, 'You wanna know something crazy? It was me. I did it.'

Her face lengthens, as if she's changing form without conscious thought. Her voice when she speaks again is almost unrecognisable. 'You killed my father?'

Lee nods. 'Yup, sure did. He was fucking feral.' He's led her almost to the stairs now as he says, 'I was just taking out the trash.'

She leaps on him, done with human words.

Lee uses her force to pull her down and over the stairs, wrestling to keep them both in human form as they slam down a flight of stairs.

When they land at the bottom, Scott runs up with a pair of cuffs. He gets them on her blistered wrists and hauls her to her feet. He says, 'Mara Grendel, you're under arrest for assault and intent to murder. Anything you say or do may be used against you as evidence in a court of law.'

Ray rushes over with a huge syringe filled with a green liquid, and injects it quickly into Mara's thigh. Wolfsbane or some other kind of sedative, I assume.

Lee groans on the floor next to them.

As the drug takes hold, Mara snaps at him, 'You'll pay, boy. One way or another.'

Scott turns to the other three pack members. 'She's gone, fellas. Anyone who wants to join her in jail right now, offer's open.'

They all shake their heads vehemently. One of them says, 'She was getting a bit crazy. Like, unhinged.'

'All right, then.' He wears his authority like a jacket, muscles bulging as he manoeuvres Mara's limp body towards the exit. 'Spread the word. If there's any lykos left in my city by the end of the week who haven't joined my pack or a pack I know, I *will* be having a little chat with them.'

Once Mara is unconscious in the patrol car, Scott turns wolf and tackles me to my knees. He plops his 70-kilogram frame on top of me, sniffing all over me, licking all the bleeding bits.

'Ew, gross, Scott!' But strangely, the wounds on my face and leg do sting a little less after he's licked them. I remember him saying once that wolf saliva had healing properties. 'Thanks babe.' I hug him as hard as I can, suddenly desperately grateful that it's over and we're all safe.

He responds by trying to get closer, putting his paws over my shoulders, which knocks me to the ground.

I laugh, pushing futilely at his rock-like muscles. 'Babe. Get off, I can't breathe.'

Lee walks up and nudges Scott aside. 'Hey, turn human, dude. We gotta wrap this up properly.' He shakes his head. 'Can't believe *I'm* the one saying that.'

Scott turns human again. Before he gets up, he whispers in my ear, 'I'd like to bend you over and spank you for putting yourself in danger, and then fuck you until you promise you're okay.'

I blush, hot and immediate. 'Yes, please.'

Scott tells Lee, 'Get her back to my place, and Vicki and I will take Mara in.'

37

Lee

I walk into the spare room at Scott's, and hold up a first aid kit from the saddlebags on my bike. Addie's lying down on the bed, looking exhausted.

'I can clean myself up, you know,' she says.

'I know.' I walk up to her. 'But you don't have to. You helped me when I got a back full of shrapnel, and then tonight you nearly got shish-kebabbed on some crazy wolf's claws… Lemme do the first aid this time.'

She nods quietly and I start dabbing iodine over the slices in her face and neck. It hurts me to see that pretty face marred, but my blood goes cold when I see the blood on her neck. I wish I could've hurt Mara more before they took her to the station.

Addie is brave about it, barely whimpering as I clean the wound and apply a couple of butterfly clips to staple it shut. Then a waterproof sticking plaster.

'My poor face,' she whispers. 'I must look terrible.'

'Not with how carefully I've cleaned and closed it. And I

saw Scott lick it, so it probably won't even scar.' But I can see the pain in her eyes, so I add, 'Still gorgeous, don't worry.'

She stands and starts taking off her jeans, and even though she's groaning with pain, my mouth goes totally dry with desire. I help her ease the denim down over the wounds on her leg – they're deeper cuts than the ones on her face – and then get her back on the bed.

As I clean each of these wounds, she holds her breath. I wrap her leg from calf to thigh, covering each of the slices carefully.

As I tie off the last bandage around her upper thigh, she touches my hand.

She says quietly, 'Thank you.'

'For what?'

'For being there with me today. For getting her away from me.'

'Of course.' She won't meet my eyes, so I slide a finger under her chin and tilt it up. *God, those eyes are going to kill me.* 'You sound shocked. What, did you really think we wouldn't show up in time?'

Her lips part. 'I hoped you would.' She licks her lips, and I can't help but notice that with my heightened scent tracking, her scent has changed. The air is filling with strong notes of arousal.

She's into this. She's into me. I know I'm not thinking clearly, but I can't get enough of her. I have to be closer. I let go of her chin and move myself closer, so I'm standing between her legs.

She just looks up at me, eyes wide. I ask her with my eyes,

with my posture, with the tilt of my head towards hers: *Do you want this? Because I want to kiss you.*

Her pulse picks up in her throat, and she starts breathing harder.

I lean into her until my mouth is a centimetre from hers, and we're sharing hot, hard breaths. I grin.

She tilts up that last centimetre.

As soon as the gap is closed, I take her mouth in mine. Her body sways into me, all soft curves pressing up against me. Those thick thighs squeeze against mine, and I'm wild for it. She's completely up in my space, completely into this moment with me, I can feel it.

We make out for a few moments that feel like a year. But eventually, reluctantly, she pulls away. She stays close, resting her forehead on mine. She's panting, her hair like a red curtain blocking off the two of us from the rest of the world. 'We can't... Not again.'

I shake my head. *Not this again.* 'I don't let anyone tell me what to do. And I certainly don't plan on letting anyone tell me who to love – or who not to love.' I have to force the next words out: 'But if you don't love me, I'll back off.'

She grabs my forearm. 'Of course I love you.'

Those words fill me up until I feel about 10 feet tall. This amazing, intelligent, beautiful, funny woman loves me!

I pull her up against me and breathe her in deeply.

Then she adds, 'And Scott. I never stopped loving him. But I never stopped loving you, either.'

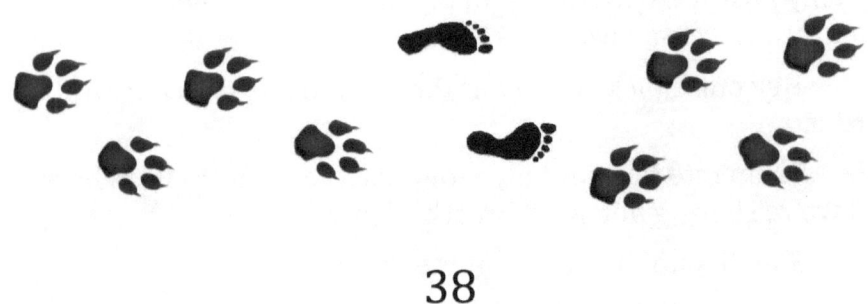

38

Addie

He pulls back when I say that, but I hold him still. He has to have heard that last bit – because it's true. I love Scott. But I love Lee, too.

In Lee's eyes, I see his hunger matching my own. It's a yearning for more, to be closer, and it's even more than just the physical, chemical reactions we set off in each other.

I lean in, and our mouths meet in one satisfying, shared breath. Then Lee jerks back, making a sound in the back of his throat. 'Umm, hey, Scott.'

I let my hands fall, and glance over.

Scott is standing in the doorway, gazing at both of us. He doesn't *look* mad, so I think I've got a chance to try and plead our case, once and for all. It shouldn't have to be one or the other – Scott or Lee, Lee or Scott. We shouldn't all have to keep breaking each other's hearts.

I take a deep breath and look into Scott's eyes as I say, 'I'm hoping you can see that I love both of you. That I need both of you. I've tried enough times to tell you.'

Scott raises an eyebrow and says, 'It's true, you have told me. And I don't want to interrupt.'

Oh God, is this it? Is this the moment I lose them both all over again? I can't help myself; tears well up and my throat tightens, and a little hiccup of a sob escapes me. That breaks me, and tears just start streaming down my face, blurring my vision of both of them. 'I love you both.' I wipe the tears away, desperate to make them understand. 'I love you *both*. Don't make me choose. I need you, both of you.'

Lee looks down, clearly uncomfortable, but he nods.

Scott sighs. 'It's just not really a wolf thing, you know. It's not even very common for humans… But the thing is, I can't walk away from you again. Either of you.'

Lee rubs his nose. 'I love you, mate.'

Scott laughs. 'Same, bro. No, look, I see how happy you two are together.' He waves a hand in Lee's direction. 'And I did my best to stop this happening, but I don't want to anymore. I'd rather try being the three of us. Together.'

I'm so relieved that my whole frame is vibrating. 'Yes! As long as we're all together, we'll be okay.'

'Babe.' Lee opens his arms.

I step into his arms, carefully, trying not to bump any of my painful spots.

He says, 'You know we're here for you. Well, as long as it's not a full moon, anyway.'

Scott nods, ignoring Lee's silliness but responding to his sentiment. 'We'll both be here for you.'

Tears spring to my eyes, and my voice starts shaking.

'Good. Because I meant it, I need you both.' I lift my chin to kiss Scott, long and slow and thorough. The combination of his hard body against mine and the warmth of his lips makes me hot and light-headed.

Then I slide back just a little, moving slowly, giving Scott time to accept it, and turn to Lee.

Lee grins that wicked grin of his, then grips my jaw and draws me down to him. As he kisses me, he smiles against my mouth. His thumb caresses the dip of my throat, and he groans my name.

I lean into his chest and reach out with my free hand, catching Scott's.

I'm neatly nestled between them, Scott hard against my back. Scott's hand wanders up my hip to my breast, and I know he can feel my heart beating overtime. He presses a kiss to the back of my neck, and I shiver with desire. I drop my head back against his shoulder so I can kiss him back.

Lee's eyes meet mine, and he's practically radiating desire for me, for us, for the three of us together. I put my hand behind his shaved head and pull his mouth to me, and we tangle together.

I'm a sunflower blooming against Lee's battle-scarred grin. I'm the sun beaming, reflecting off the rock-hard moon. Scott's arms widen to hold both of us, his strength washing over us like a wave.

This is what I was missing. I knew it and I didn't think I could have it. And it's worth all the confusion and years of heartache it took to get us here.

Totally worth it.

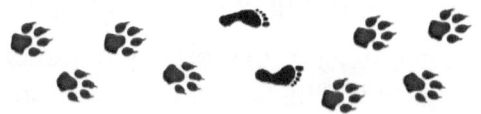

A month later, we've settled into an almost-routine. I sleep most nights at Scott's place, because it's big, and comfortable, and I have nightmares after the things those ferals have put me through. It's nice to wake up from a bad dream in someone's arms. Instead of waking up alone in the middle of the night, I'm always being cuddled by someone strong and warm.

Scott's rostered hours are fairly regular, so we're both usually home about the same time to cook dinner or decide what to order on UberEats. Then Lee and Gal join us most days whenever their shift finishes.

I can't physically spend equal time with both of them, because all of us work different hours and long days. So instead, I just try my best to give both of them enough of my attention that they both feel loved and appreciated. And between the two of them, I feel completely overflowing with joy at how loved I feel. They're devoted to me, and to each other, and it's heaven.

And on weekends, we spend as much time together as we can, all three of us in the same place at the same time. I still sometimes have to work weekends, but it's much more enjoyable than it used to be, with someone always around. I definitely don't mind my work being interrupted by kisses, teasing, walks with Gal, and other, much more pleasurable activities.

When I'm exhausted at the end of a big work day, we have a quiet dinner filled with laughter and taking care of each other, and then we go snuggle in bed. When Scott and Lee and I all snuggle together in the afterglow, in one big pile of warm limbs and lazy kisses, there's nothing that could bring me down.

I can't believe how comfortable my two men have gotten with us all being together. The fact that a few months ago, we weren't able to share each other at all, and now, their favourite thing is fucking me together… It's bliss.

I'm also not sad about the fact that I now spend almost no time in my own crappy apartment. I'll renew the lease when it comes up in a few months' time, because I'm still a lawyer, so I know you can never be too careful.

But I don't think I'll be using it much. I don't want – or need, it seems – much alone time away from these two amazing humans. Sometimes when I need a break, I'll go read an ebook on my phone, and Gal sits on my feet. Scott just catches up on extra work while Lee does push-ups in the living room.

When I tell Charlie, she's happy for me.

'Just remember the usual safety precautions,' she says. 'Don't give them a key. Don't forget protection, unless you want to give birth to a *litter* of puppies. And don't tell them your deepest, darkest secrets. Save those for me.' She winks.

I laugh. 'God, you're the best. Thank you.'

'Darling, I'm just glad you finally told the guys you wanted two-for-one. Now you all get to enjoy it!'

All three of us and Gal often go for a Saturday afternoon walk that takes us past Elle's street. We've been a throuple for a few weeks

now, but I don't think the three of us have been at Elle's place since the birthday party. Gal's tail is wagging; she knows we're here to play with the little ones. I walk up to her door, meaning for us to go in and catch up, or watch the kids so she can have a nap or something.

But Lee clears his throat, and I turn. 'Do you want me to go?' he asks.

'No!' I reach out, grab his hand. 'I want you with us – all of us.'

He smiles, but he's shifting his weight on his feet. Not our devil-may-care werewolf feeling nervous, surely?

'What are you going to say to Eloise?' Scott asks.

'Umm, well…' I don't know how it hasn't come up, but we haven't actually decided together how we're going to try to present in front of others. 'I guess I just thought we … wouldn't? Can't we just be ourselves?'

Lee laughs.

'She's going to make some assumptions anyway,' Scott rumbles. 'She seems fairly intuitive.'

I touch his cheek, still holding Lee's hand. 'I know, and seriously. I'm not worried.'

Let people assume what they want, that we're a triad or a throuple, or kinky swingers, or that we're all cheating on each other. We know what we are – three people who are meant to be together.

Elle opens the door and smiles at all of us, and it's a genuine smile. 'Come in, good to see you.'

In the living room, Dad is playing some video game with

the kids. Elle's controller is on the floor; she must have been playing, too, before we arrived.

'Hey everyone!' I call. 'Sorry we interrupted your game!'

Dad just laughs. 'The more, the merrier.'

We connect some more controllers and play games together. When the kids get hungry, we stop to eat and laugh and catch up. It's a fun time, and nobody seems angry at anybody else.

As we're leaving, Elle pulls the three of us aside.

'I was wrong,' she says. 'About you two being bad for her. You kept her alive. My baby sister. Thank you.'

I pull her into my arms, and we both start crying happy tears.

At last, I feel safe, and whole, and free to love the people I love.

Acknowledgements

Thank you, dear reader, for reading this book – hope you liked it! (If you did, please leave a review on Goodreads or Amazon, and tell everyone you think might like it.)

Thank you to my friend Séan Fagan (musical director), for teaching me some of the Irish Gaelic phrases in this story. I picked the surname O'Connor for our hero because it's an Irish surname that comes from the Gaelic *Ó Conchobhair*, which comes from *Conchobar* or 'lover of hounds'.

Grendel's name comes from the monster in the Old English poem *Beowulf*, written 700 to 750 AD/CE. In the poem, Grendel is a descendant of Cain and represents all that is inhuman. So when Beowulf kills him, he has to use his bare, human hands to do it. I found that story intriguing.

Thank you to Regina Collins for being my beta reader on this project! I needed someone I could trust with the unhinged parts of this story, and you gave such valuable feedback, and did it kindly.

Thank you to the wonderful humans who helped me navigate the poly world for the first time. You've been such fun to play with! If any readers interested in trying polyamory or ethical non-monogamy, I recommend the book *The Ethical Slut*, but there are also countless YouTube channels with advice.

I acknowledge the traditional owners of the country on which I currently write, the Turrbal and Yuggera peoples. I thank the elders past, present, and emerging, for your life's work of caring for the land, sea, animals, and people. Sovereignty was never ceded.

Other books by TJ Withers

Fire Dancers series:

Fire Dancers in the Sand (2021)

Fire Warriors on the Mountain (2022)

Fire Gods in the Ice (scheduled 2024)

Other novels:

The Tavern (scheduled 2024)

About the author

TJ Withers (she/they) is the author of the YA fantasy series *Fire Dancers in the Sand* and *Fire Warriors on the Mountain*, and a mental health advocate.

She spent years in the publishing industry as an editor and marketing officer, bringing other people's books to life. Now she enjoys writing and publishing her own stories in rare moments of free time.

You can find TJ on social media, working as a copywriter, and generally trying to survive single mum life. She also loves painting and running.

For more by TJ Withers...

follow me on TikTok (@tjwauthor), Instagram,

or subscribe at tjwithers.com

www.ingramcontent.com/pod-product-compliance
Lightning Source LLC
Chambersburg PA
CBHW030420180626
46812CB00005B/2099